B(

by

Ted Lewis

(Author of Get Carter)

Ted Lewis
Group

First Published by Michael Joseph Limited in 1976

Boldt© The Estate of Ted Lewis

ISBN 978-1-9161028-5-9

Set and Design by Reflex Graphic Design Limited, 17 Hansford Square, Bath, BA2 5LH, 01225 832551

Artwork by James Usher of Barton upon Humber

Published on licence by Muse Publishing for the Ted Lewis Centre
www.thetedlewiscentre.org

Preface

Ted Lewis, who is credited with being the 'Father of British Noir', wrote nine novels. *Boldt* was his sixth. Two of Ted Lewis's works were semi-autobiographical and the others followed the springboard of *Jack's Return Home/ Get Carter*, for which the novelist is best known. These six, including *Boldt*, were unquestionably hard-boiled stories set in the darker side of humanity.

In *Get Carter*, the central character of Jack Carter made Lewis's reputation and enhanced the already creative talents of film director, Mike Hodges, and actor, now Sir, Michael Caine. However, the novelist's literary and other artistic work disabuses any suggestion Lewis was a one trick literary pony. Indeed, as an artistic polymath, his additional capacity as a graphic artist and jazz musician enabled him to wear his skills with unassuming confidence during his short life.

There is no doubt that from an early age, Edward Alfred (Ted) Lewis, appreciated violent adventure, probably unwittingly engendered by a frequent diet of 'horror comics' on which he fed as a child when confined to bed, suffering with rheumatic fever. This predilection was enhanced in his local cinema as he enjoyed cowboy westerns in which nonchalant death and violence from fist and boot were an essential part. His Grammar School English teacher and later mentor, the author Henry Treece, habitually read out aloud the hard-boiled novels of Raymond Chandler. It is unsurprising, therefore, that in 1955 aged 15, young Lewis contributed the seriously frightening and haunting short story, *The Legend*, to his school magazine. Courageously, it left readers hanging on a violent end which might, today, be the result of concerned parental objection. The 1955 noir crime film, *Shack Out on 101*, was Ted's adolescent favourite but he also continued to be an addict of the genre well into later life.

But Lewis was not, himself, a violent man, although flawed, as many an artist often is: a hard drinker with a cavalier attitude to the opposite sex, relishing the atmosphere when amongst a periphery of the gangster world in Soho. He also understood and accepted, not uncritically, the obvious endemic of police corruption. His capacity to immerse the reader in the credible exploits of gangsters and thugs, identifying their motivation, remained during the short seventeen years he developed the noir genre. This skill climbed to an incomparable height in his ultimate final masterpiece, *GBH*. In *Boldt*, however, he introduces characters with casual racial bias and rooted xenophobia. Lewis, himself, never gave any suggestion of such prejudice.

Boldt was written by Lewis in 1975, first published in 1976. His eight-year-old marriage had broken up the year before with its attendant difficulties involving the children and he was also an embryo TV crime series writer with deadlines. His literary agent, Toby Eady was enjoying several years in the USA. American gangsters, bent cops, ruthless private eyes and the law of the gun were in the author's blood so, needing money following bankruptcy, Lewis set the location of that novel in largely unfamiliar territory in which the principal character is a maverick US detective. Boldt's honesty bends with necessity and he exhibits contempt for and abuse of women as well as casual demeaning of African Americans which would probably be unacceptable to publishing houses today.

The plot involves a race against time in the urban jungle to find an assassin, hired to kill Boldt's brother who is an up-and-coming ambitious politician. Ted Lewis wrote quickly, distractedly and without polish but an urgency, laying down a fast-moving patois style narrative which propels the writer into the depths of squalor. The presentation of dialogue does not accord with traditional publishing style but this has been retained in original form. The first sentence in *Jack's Return Home (Get Carter)*, designed appropriately to captivate the interest of readers, was the spare 'The rain it rained'. In *Boldt*, the reader is catapulted into Detective Boldt's world by a one-line casual racial pejorative. The language becomes progressively unacceptable but arguably forms part of the essential picture of characters that were typical in the nineteen seventies and even much later. The other side of the racial coin can be found in Angie Thomas's *The Hate U Give.*

Today we are in a decade of MeToo, Domestic Violence disgust, and a clutch of disclosures of police power over reluctant women who fail to submit. Detective Boldt would not have been any kind of public opinion survivor.

He smashes, rapes, and neglects his women or those he has peripheral contact with and looks down on racial stereotypes. Hero or zero?

Is it a mistake to condemn or reject as it is to adulate or admire the artistic presentation of characters who emerge in literature? Turn to Charles Dickens and you have one answer. To the depths of Noir, you have another. It is unacceptable for a publisher to hide behind the art of the narrative although it is necessary to identify the pro or ante. The pros have it for Detective Boldt. He is credible in his cravenness and so absorbed have readers been that they legitimately urge him on to his self-appointed crusade in the fleshpots of his understood urban gangster dominated underbelly of society. The con is being a prisoner of propriety and rectitude. As he did as a schoolboy, Lewis totally succeeds in bringing us credibly within the world of his characters. His style of writing even mimics those of the Bronx style patois, a technique clearly the despair of a conventional editor. Lewis's text in *Boldt* lays the ground for the masterpiece of *GBH* and nods to the iconic success of *Get Carter*.

Monty Martin

Acknowledgements

This edition is published by Muse Publishing a
and we would like to thank all those associated with its
printing and production.

The late Frederick James Challinor
made the publication possible.

Special thanks go to Carol Thornton for retyping the
manuscript and Moira Trafford for proof reading what
was a slightly esoteric format and grammar.

Trustees and members of The Ted Lewis Centre
have been continually supportive of this publication
and work tirelessly to have the work of Ted Lewis
recognised and promoted.

James Usher is an artist of distinction and painted
the creative cover.

Richard Ireland designed the manuscript
with skill and insight and kept calm in the face of
queries and alterations.

Finally, last but not least, The Estate of Ted Lewis
for licensing the publication of this edition and those at
David Higham Associates who courteously handle
their literary and business affairs.

Part One

The spade is five ten tall and as shiny as a black silk stocking and her writhing body shines out from the satin sheets like heat in negative, a hot contrast to the pot-pale sandyness of the blonde girl who is at present chewing on the spade's left ear-lobe and fingering one of the spade's nipples with all the loving attention a child gives to a new toy. And while this is happening, I'm on the brink of sinking myself into the spade's oily warmth, my tip tickling on the black curls of her pubic hair. Her legs are doubled up and her knees slide upwards, rubbing against my shoulders as I prepare for re- entry.

Then the phone rings.

I close my eyes with a different intensity and say the word instead of acting it out. I pull back and get off the bed, walk over to the bedroom door and lift my shoulder-holster off the hook. Then I open the door and go through into the hall and pick up the pay-phone receiver.

It is Murdock.

'This is Murdock,' he says.

I nod although there is no one to see.

'Draper's on your ass,' Murdock says.

'And that is the end of the news?' I say.

'It's worse than usual. He's on to the car three times since you went up there. If you don't stop fucking, he's going to fuck you when we go in.'

'It'll make a change from his licking assholes.'

'I've got no more change. I'm in Muriel's. The car's outside.'

'Mind you don't cop a ticket,' I say, put the phone back and walk into the bedroom.

It would be nice to feel I'd been missed but the plain fact is that they're doing just fine without me.

The fair girl has just finished going down on the spade and the spade is heaving both her pelvis and a great sigh that ends in a shuddering groan that complements the shuddering of her body. I stand in the doorway and wait for the heat to disperse. The blonde sits up and runs her tongue across her teeth and the spade stays where she is, legs splayed, eyes closed, clenched fists gripping the damp sheets. I begin to pick up my clothes from the chair by the bed and as I lean forward the holster slips from my shoulder and falls to the carpet, its heavy sound smothered by the thick pile.

'You should have hung it in a better place,' the blonde girl says. 'Five minutes ago, I could have.'

The spade comes back from wherever the blonde had sent her and props herself up on her elbows.

'Where'd you go, baby?' she says.

'The way of all flesh,' I say, pulling on my shorts. 'But don't worry about it too much.'

The spade falls back again.

'I won't, honey,' she says. 'Not while Jo-Ann's around.'

Jo-Ann grins at me and I button my shirt and strap on the holster, tuck my shirt into the waistband of my pants and then I sit down on the chair next to the bed and slip on my shoes. Jo-Ann asks if I've got a cigarette so I feel in my coat which is draped on the back of the chair. I take out my pack of cigarettes and lean over the spade and Jo-Ann fishes one out of the pack. The spade leans up and takes one too except that as she tries to shake the cigarette loose all the others fall out, decorating her tits and her stomach. I begin to pick them off her and Jo-Ann says, 'It could catch on.'

'Yeah,' says the spade, 'this is one I've not seen.'

'If I leave you a couple to smoke later do I get a discount?' I ask. 'Plus the fact that the auditorium had to be evacuated because of fire.'

The spade smiles. 'You're a cop,' she says. 'You should know this case you ain't never going to prove. No way. Besides, you're on reduced rates already. The house takes cents, not dollars, when you call.'

I stand up and take out my wallet, lay some bills on the bed and say, 'Here, buy a pack of cigarettes between you.'

'Or maybe a book of matches,' the spade says.

I put my coat on and go out of the room. I leave a bill with Muriel then go down the stairs and out into the early May sunlight. The dust from the traffic hangs like unwashed lace in the sun's rays.

I begin to walk the block and a half to where Murdock told me he'd be, but I don't go direct. Instead, I drop in the Q. E. Tavern and sit at the bar and order a lager from the tap. While I'm waiting for the man to fill the pot a kid slides on to the next stool, hair a burst of tight curls, gold-rimmed glasses, tan jacket, polo shirt, flares, stacks. He puts a white bag full of groceries on the counter in front of him and waits, as if he's waiting for the barman to fill my pot and give it to me then he can place his own order. While he's waiting, although he tries not to, he looks round the bar a couple of times and adjusts his glasses once. The froth pushes up over the rim of my pot and the barman slides the pot in my direction. I lean forward as if I'm going to pick it up but I speed up the action and grab the grocery bag, taking a grip on the kid's left wrist so's there's no way he can leave without cutting his hand off, although he jerks this way and that like a rabbit on the hump. The barman comes up with his insurance and now he's taken us in instead of us being just assholes on stools, he knows which way to point it which makes the kid freeze his wriggling. I push over the grocery bag and it isn't a tin of Campbells that clacks down on to the bar. I pick the Colt up and put the barrel against the kid's wet top lip and say to him, 'Now all I can take you for is the permit, and you're only going to get small time, whatever, but just how did you intend to do it? Did you intend waving it like a daisy, and then when the man here comes up with his, then what? You going to pull the trigger, after you found it, by which time your eyeballs would have been shot out and finding the trigger would've been even harder? Is that what you intended to do? Or did you imagine the man here was going to give you all his money just at the sight of you handling that fucking thing? You were going to scare him to death just by taking that thing out of your groceries? You don't think this man knows a stick- up artist from a fuck in glasses? You don't think he's also got a guy over there in back who jumps when a little foot button's pressed and comes up from right behind you and takes you out from there? No, you don't, do you? You don't think any of that.'

The kid's mouth is working like a goldfish and his face is the colour of ice cream. Finally he manages to speak. 'I got a sick wife,' he says. 'She's sick.'

'Yeah, and she's got a sick husband,' I tell him. 'I watch the Late Show too.'

'She's got to go in hospital. Have this operation.' The barman puts his pistol back and says, 'I can't move. You'll have to come back after five. That's when I get off.'

'Sure,' I say, putting a cuff on the kid's wrist. 'I'll be back.'

'It's true what I say,' the kid says. 'I needed the dough to see they do right by her. I never done anything before. I got no record.'

'You have now,' I tell him. 'Pick up your groceries.' I finish my beer and then we move off the stools and across the bar, out into the street and, as we go through the door, I tap the heel of one of his boots.

'You were going to run for it in these?' I ask him. He doesn't answer.

'Why didn't you pick something really fast, like stilts?' When we get to where Murdock's parked the car, he's already in it, smoking, arm sticking out of the open window. I get in the back with the kid.

'What's this?' Murdock says. 'An asshole,' I tell him.

Murdock moves the car away from the kerb and crosses over the street and stops at a red light. I tell Murdock about the kid and he says,

'Draper's going to look a prick now.'

'That's right,' I say. 'I mean if we hadn't seen this suspicious character outside the bar, and stopped the car for me to follow him, somebody might've got shot, maybe more than one.'

'Right,' Murdock says.

The red light changes and Murdock slides the car forward. Ten minutes later we're in front of the bright glass walls of the new department building, shaped like a detergent box against the dusty duck-egg blue sky. The letter 'O' from POLICE has fallen away from the brickwork where it was fixed.

We park the car and hustle the kid inside the building, hand everything over to Garson, then take the lift and press for Draper's floor. The lift stops twice on the way up. The first time Fuller gets in, carrying a file as neatly as he shoots his cuffs and knots his tie and combs his hair. The only thing sloppy about him, the only thing he lets go of, is his mouth when he smiles at seeing me and Murdock. A minute goes by and then he says,

'Going to collect your medals?' 'What for?' says Murdock.

'Remembering where the building is,' Fuller says, and nearly pisses his pants at his great awesome wit.

'What building?' I say. 'This building?'

'Yeah, this is a building,' Murdock says. 'This is a building, isn't it, Fuller?' 'Oh, this building,' I say. 'I get it. He means this building.'

Fuller colours up and says 'Yeah, okay.'

'This is the building you mean, Fuller?' Murdock says. 'Forget it,' Fuller says.

The lift stops and the door slides open. We watch Fuller get out and the door closes behind him. The lift takes off again and Murdock shakes his head. Then three stops later we're at Draper's floor and we get out, walk down the corridor and go into the office next to Draper's office, where Ruth Higgins is typing something on her I.B.M.

'Good morning boys,' she says, not looking up from her typing. 'Right,' Murdock says.

'You're right,' I say.

'It's that kind of morning, then,' Ruth says, zipping the papers out of the machine. 'You tell us,' Murdock says.

Ruth puts the papers in the tray and takes some clean sheets from another tray.

'There's nothing I know,' she says, rolling the sheets into the machine. 'You know I never know anything.'

I lean over her desk.

'I would like,' I say, 'to take one night out, to find out what you don't know. That would give me great pleasure. What you don't know would be wonderful to discover. Because there isn't nothing, nothing in this world, you don't know.'

'Go tell my old man,' she says, starting on the machine. 'I don't even know the time of day as far as he's concerned.'

'Then neither does he,' Murdock says.

'Oh, he knows,' Ruth says. 'Trouble is we're in different zones.

Draper's square figure shows behind the frosted glass and then the connecting door opens and he stands looking at us.

'Detectives Boldt and Murdock to see you, sir,' Ruth says, her face as straight as ever.

Murdock grins.

'So it is,' Draper says. 'Thanks for the introduction.'

Draper turns away and walks back into his office. Ruth carries on with her typing. Murdock and I walk through the open door.

Draper's office looks and smells like Draper. The impression is of aftershave and leather and veneer and light alloy. The window behind Draper's desk gives a panorama of the city, a view extending beyond the suburbs. Draper walks behind the desk but instead of sitting down he leans against the window frame.

'So?' he says.

'So you wanted to see us, sir,' I reply.

'I wanted to see you,' he says. 'It's you I wanted to see. I wanted to see you an hour ago. Where the hell have you been?'

'Apprehending an armed criminal, sir.'

Draper gives me his long flat stare and decides to take a dive in this one, as there's no way he's going to win.

'Doubtless I'll be reading about it in your report? 'Yes, sir.

'And the report won't be written on the back of a bill from the Giaconda or on a satin sheet from Muriel's?'

'I don't know. I haven't written it yet, sir.

Draper carries on with his staring for a while and

then he moves to the leather chair behind his desk and does some more staring from there. Then he says, 'Your brother.'

I don't say anything.

'He's coming to town soon,' Draper says, 'and he's bringing the flag with him.' 'I know. I watch T.V.'

Draper takes a cigarette from a box on his desk.

'It'll be really interesting, don't you think,' he says, picking up the dome-shaped lighter off his desk. 'I mean if he gets the nomination. And after that, the rest. Interesting for you and me and the department and every other cop in the whole fucking country, don't you think?'

I shrug.

'Or will it be particularly interesting for you? Like the job opportunities your brother'd have in handfuls. I mean, he'd sure be some brother if he didn't bounce one off you.'

'He sure would,' I say, smiling at Draper and pursing my lips slightly, as though I'm about to blow him a kiss. Draper lights his cigarette and blows out smoke and hangs onto the lighter rolling it around in his hand.

'The only thing that surprises me,' Draper says, 'is that he didn't come round before, or that you never went after him. Is it that the Department is such a meaningful part of your life that to leave would make you feel cold and empty deep inside?'

'Yes sir,' I tell him. 'That's right, sir.'

Draper puts the lighter down and stares at that for a while as a change from staring at me.

Then he says,

'For a man of the people, your brother is a very unpopular guy.'

There was no way I'm going to comment on that, even though I agree with what Draper's saying.

'I mean he's certainly unpopular with me, and from what I gather mingling at the golf club, he's not exactly got one hundred percent of the ticket. Still, I expect you meet one or two of his supporters. The occasional one. Tell me, do his supporters always carry guns with their school books, or does it just seem that way?'

'I guess they have to carry them with something.'

Draper opens a drawer in his desk, takes out a file and flips it open to reveal that the file contains a single sheet of lined note paper.

'What I really can't stand, though' Draper says, 'is the uselessness of it all. Your brother won't get the nomination, everybody knows it; he knows it. He's building, that's all he's doing. He's selling himself for the future, he's getting his face known. Sooner or later, he'll do a deal and Tibbetts will carry the party and your brother's support will not go unrewarded. And if Tibbetts gets the Presidency and the state of the nation deteriorates, as it will, then when the term is up your brother is better placed next time to carry the nomination. So for now he's happy for people to ask who's the handsome guy carrying the big bass-drum. Except that some people are going to be asking for reasons your brother won't appreciate. Reasons that are going to cause us a lot of useless extra work.'

Draper pushes the file across the desk and spins it round so that the paper is the right way up, and I don't have to lean forward to read what's on the paper because the message is made up with the familiar cut-up newsprint of various types and sizes. The message says, When you come to this city, take time out to say goodbye to all your old friends.

I look at Draper. Draper smiles a small smile.

'A valentine for your brother. Left in the mailbox at party headquarters last night. Dropped there by hand.'

I shrug. 'Every politician gets one of those one time or another.'

'That's right,' Draper says. 'That's very true. But sometimes they're more than just one of those. Sometimes there's a final message that just happens to come out of the barrel of a gun.'

'Sometimes.'

'Yeah,' says Draper, getting up. 'And that sometimes isn't going to be in this city, not while I'm in this job. Because I like this job, and the reason I like it is because it's smooth. I know the state of play between us and the rest, and all we have to do is a nice, clearly defined job.' He picks up the paper. 'But this, this is messy. A worry I don't need to worry about. If this kook delivers then we're all in for a rousting, and I'm at the top of the heap.'

He walks round the desk and stands in front of me. 'And, of course, I'm also concerned that a lunatic with a gun should not interfere with our democratic process, a process that sums up everything that made this country great.'

He delivers this line with an expression on his face which is totally at odds with the words he is saying. Which is Draper all over.

He leans back and props himself up on the edge of his desk. Murdock shakes a cigarette out and lights up. 'You don't seem particularly concerned that some nut with a gun might be waiting in your brother's closet when he gets to town.'

'Maybe I don't think the nut means to deliver.' 'You're psychic, too.'

I shrug.

'Or maybe your brother's where he is and you're where you are and that kind of gets under your skin. Maybe it's something like that.'

Now Draper likes this kind of conversation, not just with me, with anyone. This is one of the reasons he likes his job, because it means he's in a position to talk like this and not get whacked in the mouth.

'It could be, sir,' I tell him. 'But I wouldn't want a full scale investigation on it.'

'I always wondered how it came out the way it did. In your family, I mean. The fact that he's there and you're here. How does it come out that way? Was he born with more of his fair share of endowments, and you were born with what you have? Or did the folks give him preferential treatment. I mean, I can see how they would, as you came first.'

'Whenever I'm asked,' I tell Draper, 'about my brother, I say, "well, there's always a black sheep in every family," and then I leave it for them to figure out which one.'

'That's funny,' Draper says, 'that's a funny joke. If Cavett should ever have you on his show, remember that one, hey?'

'I'll write it down, to make sure.'

Draper turns away and goes back behind his desk.

'Bolan has been given this one. Bolan is in charge of all security arrangements. What he says goes and it goes with my full backing. He can tie this town up any way he likes while your brother's circus is performing.'

I light a cigarette and wait for Draper to get to whatever point he's making for. He could reach it any time within the next sentence or the next thirty-six hours. 'Now there'll be your brother's regular guys but what do they know? They don't know the town and they don't know the people in it. All they know is how to jump on a truck after a sniper's a million maybe two million miles away. And then what happens is it's our guys who pick up the guy anyway. Listen, I hate what your fuck of a brother stands for, he's out to fuck this country, but I don't want him taken out in my town. Now Bolan is the guy who could give Fort Knox some hints, but he's like a map of the city, all straight lines. That's why I'm talking to you two. I want you to make silver snail tracks across Bolan's intersections and stay on the level of the snail's belly and sniff out anything Bolan might miss. I want you to crawl the whole square footage of this city and pick up anything Bolan might miss from his gun turret. Bolan rousts the city, you roust its foundations because that's your level. Nobody crawls in or out you don't know the colour of his jockeys. Anybody gets a hard-on you come and tell me how big it is. Somebody planning to vacation in South America, you read his mind. All other activities, you forget about them. If the Mayor runs over thirty-five school kids and you're driving by at the time, keep on driving. Don't even report it, it might stop you figuring three moves ahead of this nut who sent your brother his valentine.' 'Do we check out the letter?'

'That's being done. Don't worry about it. Any information comes up, you'll have it passed on to you. All that kind of work stays with the regular guys and if you come up with anything that needs a routine follow-up just pass it on and keep moving.'

I light a cigarette, lean forward and drop the match in Draper's ashtray. 'So at long last our methods have been recognised at a high departmental level,' I say.

'No crap,' Draper says, 'no jokes. Just get out and make sure nobody's staring down a telescopic sight a week tomorrow.'

'It's as close as that?' Murdock says.

'Yeah,' I say, buttoning my coat. 'I've been counting the hours.'

Going down in the lift Murdock tries to get me to talk about what's just been said in Draper's office but after a couple of openers he gets the message. When the lift door stops, he just follows me as I walk out of the building and over to the car and I get in and he gets in and the doors slam and the dull faraway morning city roar is cut in half. Murdock sits there, lights a cigarette and waits patiently, a state of affairs he's got used to since he and I were teamed together nearly three years ago. Not only is he good at waiting patiently for me to let go with what's happening inside my head, he's also good at waiting patiently for his promotion, an event which no way will occur while he's working alongside me, a non-event he could do something about if he wanted to, but he seems to like the arrangement the way it is. Christ knows why. So there we sit in the half-quiet of the car, two middle-aged cops, defenders of mid-America and its middle-aged ways, in the middle of our declining careers, listening to the hum of the city as it travels through time towards the day's end.

I take my pack of cigarettes from my coat pocket but the pack is empty so I crumple it up and jam it back in my pocket. Murdock reaches for his own pack and shakes one out for me, and to save an echo of the performance he flips a book of matches into my lap. I light the cigarette and bend the match, rolling it between my thumb and forefinger, then I say, 'I lied up in Draper's office.'

'Oh?'

'About the note. About not taking it seriously. Ever since the first, when I got the first breath of wind of my brother making it from State capitol back to home town to raise some nostalgic dust, I had this feeling. Nothing rational. Just uneasy, nervous. Even before Draper opened the file, I knew what was laying in there. Apart from anything else, it was typical, typical of my fucking brother that he should be the one that sets something off that somebody else has to take care of, on his fucking behalf.'

'You make it sound like it's his fault.'

'Yeah, I know. It's not his fault. But nothing ever was, and that knowledge makes me see things the way I do, in respect of him.'

Murdock shrugs. 'Well,' he says, 'we get it, whichever way you look at it. We got the deal and all we can do is what Draper asked. Am I right?' 'Yeah, you're right.'

'So have you any ideas where we go from here? Because I'm as sure as the Devil's in hell I haven't.'

I pull a face and roll the window down, looking across the city at the thickening mid-day haze.

'The letter is from a political nut or just a plain nut. Now the guys we usually deal with aren't political and not many of them are nuts. They're too interested in their ways of turning a buck to have time for either of those luxuries. We could try a few people, in particular places, but later, because only luck would give us anything from them.'

'You mean everything else is sheer deduction?'

For the first time since leaving Draper's office I grin. 'No, but we can start at the beginning. If somebody's going to try and whack him out then he's got to find himself a place to do it from. Now my brother is arriving in the afternoon and leaving the next morning. He arrives by train and leaves from Blyth Field. He appears on Travers's early show and again on Beth Cusack's breakfast hour. The night he's guest of honour at a funding dinner at the Norton and oh yeah, the afternoon, before Travers's show, he's talking at the University; in fact he goes there before he goes to his hotel. So we have routes, and the big one is from the railroad station to the campus because that'll have the placards and the motorcade and all the other crap. So first off we go along the route and we check it out and if nothing shows we pass on all the likely vantage points to Bolan.'

'Surely Bolan will check that route himself?'

'He will. All the hotels, all the frontages, he won't leave anything out. But you're forgetting Draper. We'll be on our bellies. The guy we're after might trip over us.'

'Yeah, we might get trampled on too; which end of the route do we start?' 'The end he does. The railroad station.'

Murdock switches on the ignition and backs off, sliding out of the department lot.

The railroad station is out of keeping with the rest of the area of the city where it lies, it's nice and neat and clean. But apart from the stockyards, the station is ringed by an industrial complex taking in everything from the manufacture of toilet bowls to the destruction of old automobiles. The only commercial area, apart from the station itself, is a block exactly opposite the station, built in exactly the same style and at exactly the same time, presumably intended to balance the crisp oasis the station makes in the middle of the sunlit sprawl, but instead underlining the incongruity of planning against a tide of runaway development.

'Station Whiz,' Murdock remarks as he pulls into the station car park. 'What?'

'Always reminds me of Station Whiz,' he says. 'Remember in Captain Marvel? Billy Batson?

The radio station he peddled his papers outside of? Station Whiz.' 'Oh, yeah,' I say. 'Station Whiz.'

We get out of the car and walk round to the main entrance, through the automatic glass doors and into the cool church-like atmosphere of the lobby where the floor is conveniently swept by a four-wheeled vacuum tractor driven by a miserable-looking spade, defiantly whistling different tunes in a different key to the ones on the background tapes. We cross the wide-open spaces until we're beyond the ticket windows and then we flash our badges at the barrier and start to walk along the platform immediately in front of us.

As we wander along Murdock asks, 'what happens when the train draws in? The usual Panavision smiling?'

'Yeah, the arrival'll be well covered. But Bolan will have taken care of that. Nobody'll be on the platform he won't know about. Nor in the station building. And there's no way from beyond the other side of the train a man could get a clear target. I guess it would have to be pretty stupid for the guy to figure this was the best place in the world for what he plans to do.'

'If he was a bomber, it wouldn't be so difficult.' 'Yeah, but he'd never get out again.'

Murdock shrugged. 'Some of them don't want to.'

'He'd still have to get in with whatever he planned to use, past Bolan's security.' 'Well,' says Murdock, 'that's true, but I wouldn't write off this place yet.'

'The only time I write anything off is when my brother leaves Blyth Field for Washington. I don't want his boyish charm telling me I told you so in front of the T.V. cameras.

We walk around the station platforms for a quarter of an hour or so, then we go back through the main hall and cross the road and approach the station's twin block. In the centre of the development is the Chandler Hotel, flanked on the left by a would-be high class apartment building called the Chandler Arms. At floor level, on either side of the two buildings, are the shops with four storeys of apartments, going right and left to each end of the block. And beyond each end of this desirable lump of real estate are the humming clanking fringes of the industrial area.

We walk into the lobby of the Chandler Hotel and it's not exactly as if they've got three conventions going on at the same time. A couple of old birds are sitting together on a long low divan, suitcases stacked in front of them, staring straight ahead, straight-backed, as though somehow it wouldn't have been seemly for them to relax and enjoy the plush comfort of the divan. Over at the reception desk a tall guy in a flecked suit and dove grey shoes is trying to talk his wife out of making the most of a dispute with the clerk over some details on the bill and the clerk is getting to the point where he's pissed off enough to hand it over to the manager. So I say to Murdock, 'the bar. We got to check it out. Maybe even a sniper's got to drink.'

'The bar,' Murdock agrees, and we go to the bar.

The bar is not quite as lively as the lobby. The air conditioning is pretty rowdy and the noise we make on the thick piled carpet as we cross to the bar is quite spectacular. The barman shifts from one elbow to the other as we approach. The bar is all dark stained panelling and green leather, so that if the guys who drop into the bar want to, they can pretend for an hour or two that they're the Lord of the Manor with a couple of lurchers stretched out in front of the log gas fire. Even at this hour of the day the bar has an after-dinner atmosphere, with its dimmed candelabras and mounted tartan cloths centred on the wood panelling. We slide on to the stools and the bartender strolls towards us at just the right pace to allow us to make our minds up about what we're going to have.

Murdock decides on Scotch whisky – which isn't much of a decision because he never drinks anything else. I ask for a vodka with lemon and ice and the barman, even though he knows we're cops, is polite and good and quick with the drinks. He's in his mid-forties, tall, a little overweight, but he moves like a dancer, well-groomed, the kind of guy who always looks as though he's only recently stepped out of the bathtub. When he's set the drinks down in front of us, he wanders away to leave us private without looking as though that's what he's doing.

'You know,' I say to Murdock, 'this place wasn't even built last time I saw my brother.' 'It had Florian behind it.'

'Yeah, and look at it now. A beautifully designed tax loss. As if he needs one, legitimate, I mean. His mattresses are stuffed with thousand-dollar bills.'

Murdock calls the bartender again and orders the same. The bartender gives it to us and Murdock takes his in one go.

'How's your brother-in-law?' I ask him.

Murdock puts his glass down on the counter.

'My brother-in-law's fine,' Murdock says. 'He's great, as always. He uses me as practice for the Elks. He makes one of his speeches last night. He says, "look, do you realise what a strain your presence is putting on our marriage?" Christ, Jean hates his fucking guts, she likes having me around so he can make his speeches at me instead of her for a change. So he goes on, he says, "You realise Jean is likely to break down if you're here much longer?" So I say, "fine, I'll get out now. If you loan me the kind of money they're asking for apartments these days, then I'll walk straight out of the door." So then he says, "why not move back in with Joyce, on a business basis? You're both adults. Until you're settled," he says. I'm about to tell him that Joyce has got tanks in the drive-in case of any such eventuality when Jean comes out of the bathroom where she must have been listening and she lays into the prick and reminds him of where the money came from for the down payment on their place. He says, well that's not exactly the point, he didn't expect me as part of the interest, and she says, "the man I married, Mr Wonderful." He asks her to cut out the crap but before he's half-way through telling her, she hauls him one off and he goes like stone, you know, like Buster Keaton? He holds the pose for a minute or two, then swings round and goes out of the door and out of the house and Jean looks at me and I look at her and she bursts out laughing and so do I. Then she says, "I hope the bum never comes back. But he'll be back," she says, and of course he is, about one a.m., just in nice time to wake the whole fucking household. Of course he's tanked, and him and Jean slug it out on the landing. The kids wake up and start crying, so I go on to the landing and drag him off Jean and give him a couple of neat ones that send him straight to dreamland. Then Jean tries to pacify the kids who've seen the whole fucking affair and then after that she, of course, rounds on me, because I'm standing there, and says why did I do a thing like that, laying out her old man with the kids looking on? So I go into the bedroom and pick up my stuff and bye-bye.'

'Where'd you go?'

'Yeats. I got a room in Yeats.'

'Yeats? Jesus, why'd you go to Yeats?'

'It's not so bad. I get the room free. I don't even have to tell him I'm getting the room free, he's so fucking scared when I show up.'

'It's a wonder you didn't empty the place. I mean, just by showing up.'

'I told him; I wasn't interested in the other patrons. Just a room, I tell him, and coffee in the morning, then I'll go away.'

'Why didn't you call me? You could have come over to my place.'

'It was only for one night. It was two a.m. by the time I left Jean's.'

'You could still have phoned.'

'I see you the rest of the time.'

'What about tonight?'

'I may go back. My stuff's still there.'

'Move in with me.'

Murdock shakes his head.

'No, I may go to the Westerby for a few days. The manager thinks I know something about him. I would have gone there last night if it'd been earlier. I'll go there tonight.'

Murdock taps the counter with his glass and the bartender makes up two more. While he's doing that there is the sound of voices behind us, and as I look into the mirror beyond the bar I'm faced with a typically charming piece of Americana, the double date. It's perfection, straight out of a Coke ad. The girls first, they're marvellous. Fashion marches on, but after all, fashion only reflects life and in the case of these two girls, life 1966 style is as far as they want to go. Now today, if they were dressing like everyone else their age, they'd be in long skirts and the charcoal tops and the crinkle-cut hair and they wouldn't be laughing – not in the way they're laughing, anyway. With these two there's no smell of musk, no feeling that they change their underwear maybe once a week, no feeling that make-up has been put on top of make-up. Sure, they're in a certain kind of fashion, a fashion acceptable to whoever might be employing them; they've got leather and they've got cheesecloth but it's conservative and even the one with the bubble-cut wouldn't look out of place in a Disneyland outfit. And they look clean, you can almost smell the talcum, and they're not anonymous broads from the campus, they're like daughters, like you imagine daughters ought to be like. Through them you can almost visualise the kind of parents they might have, the kind of love, rightly or wrongly guided, those parents might have given these girls.

And the guys, the two guys, one of them could play the lead in The Tab Hunter Story, and the other one could be his faithful friend who gets the hand of Tab's girl's confidante. They're even wearing ties.

The four of them spill into the silence of the bar, full of life, apparently only conscious of their own immediate situation. The girls allow the guys to shepherd them to a booth and there's a lot of stuff about deciding what they're all going to have, then the one who looks like Tab Hunter detaches himself from the group and comes over to the bar to order. But, of course, his name isn't Tab Hunter; for all his blondness he's called Harold Schwarz, and I know him very well. And he knows me and Murdock, but he's not aware of either of us until he's two-thirds of the way to the bar and then, when he realizes that Murdock and Boldt are sitting where they're sitting, it's too late for him to do anything else but complete his approach. The bartender glides into a serving position and Schwarz orders four draught lagers. The bartender goes to work and Schwarz begins to go back to the booth but as he turns from the bar Murdock says to him, 'Hello, Harold.'

Schwarz pretends he hasn't heard and keeps on going but Murdock says, 'talk to me Harold, will you?'

I look towards the booth. None of the others is taking any notice of what's going on at the bar and Harold takes this in too, so it's easier for him to turn round and look at me and Murdock.

'Never knew you worked this ground, Harold,' Murdock says. 'There's nowhere he doesn't work, is there, Harold?' I say.

'Join us,' Murdock says, sliding off his seat and leaving room for Schwarz to get between the two of us. 'Have a drink.'

'I just ordered one,' Schwarz says.

'Have a drink,' I tell him, so he climbs on to the stool and sits between us, glancing over his shoulder at the booth. I say to him, 'don't worry, Harold. Your partner won't be leaving without you.'

'What would you like, Harold?' Murdock asks. 'Not lager, hey? Something a little stronger?' 'A Bacardi with Coke,' Harold says. 'Some ice.' Murdock passes his order.

'So,' I say to him, 'it's looking good today, hey? Nice merchandise. Should work out good, something classy. A collector's piece for buffs. Only make sure the dog isn't a little mutt, huh? You need at least let's say, a Borzoi; I mean, it'd be a real shame to penny pinch on production costs, you agree?'

Schwarz shrugs and gives a faint smile. The bartender sets the drink down in front of him but Schwarz makes no move to touch it.

'What I can never figure,' I say, 'is not the pick-up, not the act, because I can see how that would work, you looking the way you do and all. No, what I can never figure is the transition, the pitch; where you go from this to getting them to do what you always manage to get them to do.'

'That's right,' Murdock says, 'how's it done, Harold? Paint the picture for us.'

I look over my shoulder, towards the booth. The two girls can't see what's going on but Schwarz's partner has picked up the scene and he's trying to figure whether to sit tight or make for the exit. Schwarz picks up his glass and takes a sip.

'You guys sure never let a guy get bored,' he says. 'I mean, how can a guy get bored trying to figure out what the guys he's talking to are talking about?'

'You don't know what we're talking about?' Murdock says. 'That's right,' Schwarz replies.

Murdock leans away from the bar slightly, makes a right-angle of his arm and punches Schwarz hard in the kidneys. Schwarz arches his back and I grab his tie and pull hard so that Schwarz's face crashes against the counter, in the process overturning his glass so that a mixture of rum and coke seeps into the lapel of his white sports coat. I keep my grip on Schwarz so that he can't lift himself up from the counter. The bartender has already turned his back on the scene and is now bending down below the level of the counter to attend to some stock-taking he's overlooked. I look over my shoulder again and now the girls are into the scene but they don't know what the Christ to make of it. The guy with them doesn't want to have to think of how to express the essence of the situation to them so he gets up and begins to wander across in the direction of his partner.

'You don't know what we're talking about?' Murdock says.

Schwarz can't answer for the moment, so Murdock punches him in the kidneys one more time.

'Hey,' says Schwarz's partner, a little unsure, and who wouldn't be. I turn round on my stool and face Schwarz's partner.

'Yes?' I say to him.

Schwarz's partner is not as good-looking as Schwarz but he's in the same All-American mould and he even has creases in his pants.

'What goes on?'

'You want some of it?' I ask him.

He doesn't answer. Murdock says to Schwarz, 'You still don't know what we're talking about?'

Schwarz manages to nod his head.

'That's good,' Murdock says, 'because now I don't have to embarrass myself by going into details.'

'Like I always say,' I say to Schwarz, 'my partner's too sensitive for this job. That's why he gets angry with people like you. You bring him face to face with his problem.'

Schwarz breathes out and with the breath comes the word 'Florian'. I smile and close my fist over a piece of his hair, turning his head so that he's looking up at me.

'Florian,' I say to him, still smiling. 'Oh, yeah. He'll look after you. We wouldn't dare because Mr Florian would take care of it, and there'd be no point. But Harold, I've got to tell you, you're wrong. Because if you got trouble from us, we could make it stick, because basically Mr Florian wouldn't even get his secretary to get the number for him. It'd be too much trouble, because he doesn't care enough.

He'll just get somebody else, even double their pay and if that annoyed you, and you decided to talk to us about Mr Florian, you wouldn't be telling us something we didn't already know, and basically, we don't care about you, either. We could take you down now, but you don't interest us today. We don't care about you today. We just wanted to say hello. Another day, we'll want to talk to you, but not now. So why not live a little, Harold? Enjoy life. George, buy Harold another drink. His other drink got spilled.'

Murdock calls the bartender and I release my grip on Schwarz's hair and my grip on his tie. He straightens up as best he can and the bartender sets down three more drinks in front of us. Murdock and I lift our glasses but Schwarz slides off the stool, bumps into his partner and makes his way back over to the booth, his partner following after him. The two girls are open-mouthed. Schwarz says something to them and they get up very quickly, all four of them hustling out of the bar in a tight bunch, not one of them ever once looking back.

Murdock says, 'he's one I'll enjoy, one day.'

'Maybe,' I say, 'but Florian'd never let us make it stick.'

Murdock shrugs. 'It depends. Maybe one day it'll suit Florian to wave goodbye to Harold.'

'And you think he'll have us to hold the flags? You're crazy. Harold would be whacked out and even the Devil'd have a hard time finding the corpse.' The bartender drifts back up the bar towards us. 'Two more,' I tell him.

He gets us two more.

'You get busy here these days?' I ask him as he sets

them down.

'No,' he says, keeping a straight face,' but we get plenty of action.' Murdock grins. 'You know him?' he says. 'The Beautiful American?' 'Never seen him in my life before,' the bartender replies.

'Sure,' Murdock says. 'Have a drink?'

'In the mornings I drink gin and fresh orange juice.' 'And the rest of the day you drink anything,' I say. The bartender grins and goes to work on his drink.

'Santell around?' I ask him.

'Mr Santell?' he says, slicing the lemon peel. 'Sure, he'll be in his office, I guess.' I slide off my stool. 'We'll be back to pick up our tab,' I tell him.

Murdock follows suit and we walk out of the bar across the lobby to the reception desk. The desk clerk is alone now but the memory of the bitchy dame and her husband lingers on in his expression. I stand in front of him. 'I want to see Santell,' I tell him. The desk clerk looks at me. 'Mr Santell's very busy,' he says.

'Too busy to come and do your job for you, besides his own?'

The desk clerk practises his sneer but he picks up a phone. A second later he says, 'A couple of cops want to see Mr Santell.'

Somebody on the other end of the phone says something.

'Who?' the clerk asks, looking at us.

'Boldt and Murdock,' I tell him.

'Boldt and Murdock,' he says into the phone. There is a pause, then he puts the phone back on its cradle.

'He'll see you,' he says.

I smile at him and shake my head, then Murdock and I walk to the door that leads to the short corridor down to Santell's office. At the end of the corridor there is a small reception area and as soon as she sees us come through the door into the corridor, Santell's secretary gets us and opens the door into Santell's office, waiting by it, smiling, as if we're the best thing that's happened to her all day. We go into Santell's office.

If Santell ever went to college, he must have been voted the Guy Most Likely to Become a Hotel Manager. He must have looked like a hotel manager in his crib. He is the neatest man I ever saw. He's also the greyest man I ever saw. His white shirt looks a riot of colour against the rest of his outfit. Even his office must have been designed by a decorator who'd lost his coloured pencils. No wonder his secretary is pleased to see us.

Santell gets up and leans forward slightly over his desk and stretches out his hand in Murdock's direction. For a second Murdock is thrown but then he gets the idea and shakes hands with Santell, then Santell shakes hands with me and indicates the two chairs which have been neatly arranged on our side of the desk. We sit down, followed by Santell.

'What can I do for you, gentlemen?' he asks, and while he waits for an answer the secretary reappears with a tray and on the tray is a very nice coffee set. She puts the tray down and Santell reaches for the coffee pot and pours, leaving us to add our own cream and sugar. 'We have a scare,' I tell him. 'We need your co-operation. We have this note, one of those threatening notes.

Somebody says they're thinking of loosing off a few shots at a prominent person and of course as yet we've no way of knowing whether or not it's for real, but we have to check everything out. Now your hotel is well placed to cover the station frontage. Obviously, on the day in question we'll have this place staked out pretty well, have everything pretty well tied down, but we're not, of course, only interested in preventing anything happening, we'd like very much to get the guy who sent the note. And so what we'd like you to do is to let us look at your bookings for the past week and for next week and at the same time let us have any observations you may have on any of your present guests that you think might be interesting to us.'

Santell takes a sip of coffee and then shakes his head. 'There's nothing for you here,' he says, 'not now, at least. That I can tell you for certain. There's no one in this hotel at this time who you could possibly be interested in.'

'Well,' I say, 'you're very certain. That's good because it means you keep a sharp eye on your customers, but, well, maybe there's someone who you'd never think could interest us in a million years, and, maybe, they just might.'

Santell shakes his head again. 'To begin with,' he says, 'there are only three singles booked in the hotel at this moment. Now none of them has a room facing front, and if they had, none of them is staying beyond the week-end. So that rules those three out. Apart from a honeymooning foursome, I would hazard a pretty fair guess that none of our remaining guests are below the age of fifty, or are other than what they appear to be: good solid citizens who are too close to cashing in insurance policies to be over-concerned about firing off rifles at other people, political or otherwise.'

'Just the same,' I say to him, 'I'd like to see your register, and your advance booking list.' 'Of course,' he says, pressing a buzzer on his desk, 'anything you wish.'

'I mean, even you could overlook some things. Or did you know Harold Schwarz was operating in your bar these days?'

For the first time a trace of colour shows on Santell's face, but only very faintly. 'Harold Schwarz?' he says.

'Mr Santell doesn't know who Harold Schwarz is, George,' I say to Murdock. 'Oh really?' Murdock says. 'Well, well.'

Santell colours up a little bit more.

'Do you think we ought to tell him?' I say to Murdock.

'No, better not,' Murdock says. 'I'd hate to upset Mr Santell.'

Santell's secretary comes in and Santell snaps at her to get the stuff we're asking for and it's her turn to colour up. Murdock and me just sit there and wait for the girl to go out and come back again. She leaves the stuff on the desk and goes out. Santell makes no move to hand us the stuff so Murdock leans forward and begins to go through it. I take a cigarette from a box on Santell's desk and say to him, 'I'll be putting a couple of men in the hotel as of today and my partner here'll be taking a room for the duration. I want him to have a room overlooking the station and I want the rooms either side to be kept vacant. The rest of your guests I'm afraid will have to put up with a certain amount of inconvenience – spot checks, that kind of thing, but don't complain to me; Bolan's your man, or Draper, Draper's authorising everything. Or even Mr Florian, if you care to complain, but he won't thank you for it, because this is going to be one of those nice things, leading city businessmen co-operating with vigilant police department, and the papers will write it nice and big. So there you have it.'

Murdock says, 'I can't see anything in the book, but maybe we should have a couple of these advance bookings checked out.'

'We'll have someone come over and get some copies made and hand all that over to Bolan,' I tell him.

I light my cigarette and then I pick up my coffee cup. Santell watches me drink, then says,

'with or without a bath?' 'What?'

'The room for your partner. With or without a bath?'

'Oh, with,' I tell him. 'Us dirty pigs got to bath all the time. Like the niggers, we got to take care of our stink.'

Santell doesn't say anything else. Murdock puts the stuff back on the desk and the two of us stand up.

'Thanks for your time,' I say to Santell, but this time he doesn't get up and give us the treatment.

Murdock and I leave the office and go down the corridor back into the lobby. I start to make it back to the bar.

'Where you going?' Murdock says.

I turn round. Murdock has stopped by the reception desk.

'I'm going to pay the bar tabs,' I tell him. 'Why?'

'One more guy on our side.'

I turn and go back into the bar. The bartender takes up his position, I sit down on a stool and I say to him, 'You want to be of some assistance to the Police Department?' 'That depends,' he answers.

'On what?'

'On whether or not I have a choice.' 'Well, what do you think?'

'I think I'm going to be helping the Police Department.'

'That's right,' I tell him. 'Now, all I want you to do is, the next time I come in, to tell me about anybody who has come in here you think I'd be interested in. And I mean anybody. Particularly anybody staying in the hotel.'

'Well,' he says, 'that's fine. I can do that for you, but I'm not really sure of what you have in mind. It'd be easier if I knew what kind of person you were thinking of.'

'Yes, I know it would,' I tell him. 'But if I had an idea of who I was looking for then I wouldn't be asking bartenders to work on my behalf. Just anybody, when you look at them you get a kind of feeling … I don't know, they could be capable of anything. Loners, mostly, I guess.'

'Well maybe you could tell me what exactly they're most likely to be capable of.' 'Assassination.'

The barman strokes his throat with his forefinger.

'Yeah,' he says. 'Well, if anybody comes in with a hunting rifle, I'll let you know.'

'I'd appreciate it,' I tell him, and put some money on the bar. 'The change is yours. And also there'll be more for information leading to an arrest.'

'You know, I suppose, that I'm already being paid for information of a different kind?' 'Who by, Lambert?'

'That's right.' 'So?'

'So if you see him, tell him about your request, would you? Mr Lambert's a man who likes to know what's going on.'

'Yes, I know that,' I say. 'I'll pass on the news.'

I get off the stool and go out of the bar. Murdock is still waiting by the reception desk, only now he's looking at a girl who's impatient for the clerk to show up. I don't blame her, and I don't blame Murdock either, because the girl is without doubt the most beautiful girl in this part of the city at this time. She's probably around twenty-one or two and although her clothes are casual they've been bought at the most expensive stores. She's wearing a pink voile shirt with a long collar and puffed sleeves and over it a V-neck sleeveless pullover. She's also wearing white Oxford trousers with deep cuffs and two-tone round-toe shoes. Her hair is very, very black and it's long, falling right to the waist of her pullover. She jams her hand down on the buzzer and leaves it there for a minute or so but still nothing happens. 'The clerk's in a mood,' I tell her. 'He thinks the manager doesn't understand him.'

She turns her head slightly, and it seems that's all it takes for her to take stock of who's talking to her because immediately she turns back to her previous position, not saying anything.

'If you like I could get the manager,' I tell her.

This time she turns fully and although her eyes hardly move, I get the impression I'm being flipped over the way a good dealer flips over a playing card.

'I'm sure you could,' she says. 'But if I wanted him, I'd be quite capable of getting him myself.

Like I'm capable of making my own pick-ups. But if, on the other hand, you'd like to earn a dollar, you could always hang around and take my luggage up to my room.'

'Maybe I'll do that,' I tell her. 'But don't you think that might be a little risky?' She shakes her head. 'No,' she says, 'Not at all.'

I shrug. Murdock chips in, 'Come on, Roy. No risk, no excitement. Took me eight years of my old lady to find that out.'

'Oh, I don't know,' I say. 'The excitement might be in finding out if she means what she says.' 'And pigs always find out, don't they?' the girl says.

I smile at her. 'We have our ways, but obviously you already know that.'

'Everybody does,' she says, and just then the desk clerk appears and she turns away again.

Murdock and I walk across the lobby and out of the hotel. As we walk back to the car Murdock says, 'well it's a shame, but I have to say that was one you lost.'

'It's a shame all right,' I agree. 'You don't see many like that in this town.'

'Still,' Murdock says as we get in the car, 'you might bump into her again, when we come back.'

'Yeah, and next time I'll wear a mask.'

'On the other hand,' I say, 'I hope I don't.

'What?' Murdock says, starting up the engine. 'See her again. I like to sleep nights.'

'Yeah,' Murdock says. 'And by the way, thanks. That was a nice play about the room.' 'Draper's got to think everything's nice this week.'

Murdock takes a left down the side of the hotel complex and we drive slowly east through the factory area. The day is duller now and noon traffic reflects the neutral colour of the sky.

'No need to worry about this part of the route,' I say to Murdock. 'Bolan'll station observation points and he'll check out the area all through the day. There's nothing here for us.'

We're now nearing the end of the industrial complex and we're running into a small urban area with an edge of city intersection which forms the centre of this dead, characterless suburb. There are the usual blocks of stores and business premises and a couple of bars and garages and very little else. The area has a neutral feeling, as if the people around are only there briefly to make some kind of transaction, and the minute it's been made, they'll disappear back where they came from, quick. The place has only one establishment that makes the neighbourhood any different from a hundred others, and that is a place called Clark's. It's right at the intersection, down about fifty- sixty yards, where the stores begin to straggle out to nothing.

'Why don't we call in at Clark's?' I ask Murdock.

'Why don't we?' Murdock replies, slowing down for the red. 'There's always somebody willing to help us in Clark's.'

'Yeah,' I say. Murdock takes the right and a couple of seconds later pulls into the kerb outside Clark's.

The proprietor of Clark's is a traditionalist. He believes in keeping things the way they've always been. That is why the outside of Clark's hasn't been painted in the last twenty years; why the sidewalk in front is never swept; why the windows onto the street are never cleaned; why the missing 'K' in Clark's has never been replaced; why the cracked pane in the front door has never been attended to.

Murdock and me get out of the car, but before we even draw into the kerb we've been caught and boxed by a group of four niggers standing by Clark's entrance. Their broad-brimmed hats, their leather and suede coats and their coloured shirts make them look like cartoon characters on a live action background against the drabness of Clark's frontage. As we step on to the sidewalk Murdock and me automatically unbutton our coats so that the niggers are reminded of what we're carrying; not that they don't know, but any one of them could be high enough to forget in the event of being turned on to some action. They're all grinning that terrifically happy grin that reflects the amusing world around them, or at least, the way what they're on has refined it in their minds. One of them, one in a cream hat, blows us a kiss as we approach Clark's entrance, and the others almost fall over, it's so funny.

Then, because the laughs are coming, he says, 'they

been more fuzz round today than I got on my ass, fuzz.'

'I'll prove that statement one day, sugar,' I say as we walk by.

'Today, man,' he says. 'Do it today, sugar. I'm low on kicks right now.'

I stop and face him. 'Now that is a downright lie, honey,' I tell him. 'Now ain't it?'

The nigger pouts at me. 'I'm clean,' he says. 'So clean, you try and bust me. I ain't carrying nothing.'

Murdock pushes open the door.

'Yeah, yeah, yeah,' I tell the nigger. 'You're probably right, but maybe I'll just check your hat, because even you, sugar, you may get careless one day.'

Before the nigger can take in my words, I shoot out a hand and grab the brim of the cream- coloured hat and putting a whip on my arm I flick the hat high above the passing traffic. It lands somewhere on the far side of the road. The nigger's face slips somewhat and so do the faces of his friends, so it's up to them to find some way of getting those faces back in their original positions. But the nigger with the mouth can only say, 'you fuck, you cocksucker, look what you done.'

I smile at him. 'That's what I love to hear,' I tell him. 'I love to hear it. A smart mouth nigger blowing it. I mean, come on, can't you do better than that, shortenin' bread? Hey sugar chile?'

I smile at him again. Murdock leans on the door and I go into Clark's, Murdock following after me, and the door swings to behind us.

Now the first part of Clark's is pretty much in keeping with the outside. It's a small ante-room, as shabby as the front, and it smells of the three guys who are playing draw poker round a folding green baize table next to the entrance into the second part of Clark's. The three players all know Murdock and me and we all know them. The game doesn't pause just because we've come in, but one of the guys, a guy called Arthur Montgomery, says, 'hello, friends, how are things with you this afternoon?'

Murdock says to me, 'is it afternoon, Roy?'

'Shucks, I don't know, George,' I say to him. 'We been working so hard this morning I'm damned if I know what time it is.'

'Well,' Murdock says, 'you can rely on Arthur. Christ, if Arthur tells us it's afternoon, then Christ, it must be, because Arthur knows what time it is, don't you, Arthur?'

Arthur says, 'you two going in?'

'No, we're not going in, Arthur,' I say to him. 'We just dropped by to ask for the brand name of your deodorant.'

'I don't use one,' Arthur says.

'You don't say?' Murdock says. 'He doesn't use a deodorant. How about that, Roy?'

I shake my head in amazement and Arthur gets up, taking care to bring his cards with him. He goes over to the door and kicks it; the door opens slightly, not revealing anything or anybody behind it, and Arthur says, 'two guys coming in. Cops.'

The door doesn't move for about a minute and then it's pulled in a foot or so more, giving Murdock and me just enough room to go through one at a time. After the door's been closed behind us and the curtains beyond have been drawn and we're inside of Clark's and Clark's, you have to admit, it's quite something. Considering where it is, and considering everything else.

The whole point about Clark's, which in a sense is in keeping with the unreality of its situation, is that there's never been anybody called Clark that's had anything to do with the place. As long as I've known it, it's been run by a guy called Moses Shapiro and Moses in himself adds to the unreality of the place, not only because of his personality, but because he doesn't belong to anybody. Nobody owns him. Not one of the organizations has a piece of him, and that in itself makes Moses a pretty unusual character. But if it weren't for that, that apart, Moses doesn't need that kind of immunity to make him special. Moses is bigger than life in every way, apart from his size. He's the only queen I ever met who could take on anything that happened to be pushed his way. I know professionals who'd never say a wrong word or ever put a foot wrong inside of Clark's because of what Moses would be likely to do to them if their play didn't happen to suit him. Moses, with his bald head glowing above his kaftan, his silky trousers and his furry slippers is able to take any six or seven guys apart without breaking sweat. His fat ringed fingers and the gross muscles on his arms and legs go to work as if that's the only thing he was born to do, which of course it isn't: he was born to persecute everything that isn't gay. Moses is one of those guys who isn't satisfied with the guys who aren't gay, or at least don't think they are. He likes to use his muscle – in fact rape with a view to corruption is his bag, and as a rule, if Moses sets out to bear down, then whoever he's bearing down on don't stand a chance, no way. In fact some of the guys Moses has had, never walk back to the other side of the line. Of course, it's not all muscle with Moses; he uses softeners a lot of the time, and two of those softeners are two sisters, real sisters, real girls, called Agnes and Marcia Garner. The two girls appear to be waitresses inside of Clark's which of course, they're not: they're pulling for Moses and they do a beautiful act.

They're two girls like you've never seen, they both look as though they took Liberal Studies at college; as though they were voted the two most likely to marry the president of the local Chamber of Commerce; the two most likely to be Young Mothers of the Year; the two most likely to be chosen by *Seventeen* to model this year's fashions; they'd make Natalie Wood look like Yvonne De Carlo along side of them. But when they go to work, that's something else entirely. I'd like to see anybody try and stay away from the two of them and succeed. They operate like you've never seen. They can take the pants off you and have Moses take over at sucking your dick so that you'd never know it.

When you finally tumble it's too late because by that time there's Moses's two other little helpers,

Arnold and Chris, and there's no way you could lift yourself up off your back, or your face, whichever the case may be. After that, no use making any kind of complaint, because for that you need witnesses, and inside of Clark's witnesses you're just not going to get.

In spite of all this, Moses runs a flourishing business, mainly because he lays off his regulars, because his regulars are important to him, they come back and they come back, and mostly anybody who's anybody in this city is from time to time seen talking to Moses. Christ knows why, because for all his independence Moses can't do anything for them. He can't do anything for Florian, for example, and he can't do anything for Florian's wife, but they love to be there, they love to be sitting at the high stools with Moses, being insiders to his private scene, watching how it works out with whoever he's got his eye on. Sometimes, if they're inside enough, they can watch how it works out in the end. A lot of money comes down to Clark's, from time to time, and the rest of the time Moses relies on the steady custom of hustlers and grifters and entrepreneurs that make Clark's a full house from 11 a.m. to 11 a.m. day after day.

So Murdock and me go through the door and into the part of Clark's that counts. It's pretty much alive and our presence doesn't slow it down any. The hustlers don't stop hustling and the grifters don't stop grifting and the games keep going. Moses and his little gang are perched up on the two-foot-high area at the far end of the room. Murdock and me don't make for that area but instead we move towards the curved bar. There are no vacant stools but Murdock moves in front of me and stands behind two small-time fags, saying to them, 'those high stools, you know, they're not too good for your balls. Could easy get them busted on those narrow seats.'

They both turn and give Murdock the face but they're not going to be consistent and they slide off and slide away leaving Murdock and me to take their places. Murdock dusts his seat off before he sits down.

'I can't take talcum powder on a dark suit,' he says. 'It's hell to get off.' 'Yeah,' I say, 'especially talcum powder that's mobile.'

So we're sat down and it's the usual thing about us trying to get served, being cops, while all the free spenders are pushing it over the counter. There are three people behind the bar, all like Moses, one a nigger queen with silver hair and the other two young guys who look as though they'd sway from the smoke of your cigarette. But they're all very good at studiously ignoring a couple of pigs who only want a couple of small drinks to wash the company down with. So in the end Murdock demonstrates how pissed off we both are by picking up the glass jug that holds the water, swinging it away from the counter and dropping it on the floor. For that we get the nigger and we're about to get Moses as well. The nigger drifts down the counter in our direction and you've got to hand it to him, he does a very nice thing; he looks for all the world as though he's on his way to attend to us, but just before he gets there, he pretends that a different member of the clientele has caught his eye and he makes a big deal out of making the drink just right, with all the crap. That takes another three or four minutes, and then he fixes his divine presence in front of us, a nice, faint smile on his lips, just to underline the fact that we know that he knows what he's dealing with.

'Well,' he says, 'I guess it's about time you two made an appearance. We was all wondering if maybe you'd been taken out or something like that. You know, by enemies of society.'

By now Moses has shifted his great bulk over to where we are and he's making a big production out of not stepping his slippered feet in the pieces of glass.

'Hello Moses,' I say to him. 'I never knew you could dance.'

Moses is around six three and wider than me and Murdock put together, but the voice that issues from his lips is as thin as a confederate dollar.

'Yeah,' he says, 'and I can tromp, too. That I'm good at.' 'I've heard that,' I say.

The nigger queen says, 'Do I serve the gentlemen, Mr Moses?'

'Oh sure,' Moses says. 'Give them all they want. That way they leave me alone, because they frighten me, you know, they really do.'

'And what would you gentlemen like?' the nigger queen says.

'I thought you'd never ask,' Murdock says. 'A piece of your ass, with brown sugar if you've got it.

The nigger queen's eyes go slitty and he has to stand there while Murdock and me sit grinning at him. In the end Murdock says, 'give us some vodka and some scotch, in separate, clean glasses. And one for yourself and Mr Moses.'

'Moses,' I say, 'why don't you sit down. I got something to talk to you about.' 'I don't like sitting down with pigs,' Moses says.

'I know that,' I tell him. 'I know how you feel, but why not force yourself just this once. I really do have something to say.'

Moses shrugs and says, 'up there. There's more room.'

Moses turns away and makes for the raised area, Murdock and me following after him.

Sitting at the table are Agnes and Marcia, dressed like twins in white blouses and white slacks, half full glasses of Pernod in front of them, and when we get to the table the one called Agnes says, 'and I was wondering what I was going to have to do to get an introduction.'

'I know,' says Marcia. 'I know the feeling. You didn't know how you were going to live with yourself if you hadn't of.'

'Beat it,' Moses says to them. 'Save the jokes for when I tell you.'

The girls get up and leave the table and Murdock and me sit down in their places. Moses sits down too and the nigger queen brings the drinks, sets the tray down and goes back to tend to his bar and his customers.

'So what is it?' Moses says after he's drunk half of his iced coke. 'And why do you think I should be interested?'

'Well, I don't think you'll be interested Moses,' I tell him. 'But the main thing is it won't hurt you or anything around you, what I'm going to ask. My brother, the famous politician, is coming to town to show everybody he's still the nice guy he always used to be. Now, there's somebody who thinks that great event can be made even greater, kind of secure some place in history, if my brother doesn't make it out of town again. Just some guy with a gun or a bomb, Christ knows what, except that it's felt, we feel, the guy isn't just writing notes to us as therapy, we feel he's really going to try and deliver. Now, this city being the size it is, we need every piece of luck we can get – we can't just leave stopping this nut to the regular procedures. In your case, like in nearly every other case, the guy probably won't come within five miles of this place. But if he did, and supposing he spoke a word over a few drinks and it was heard, passed on to us, why then, that would be the break we needed, wouldn't it?'

Moses downs the rest of his coke. 'Why the fuck should I care if your brother gets whacked out or not?' he says. 'Maybe if I bumped into the guy I might ask him if he was O.K. for ammunition.' 'Maybe, but Moses, look at it this way. You don't care if he isn't whacked out. Politics don't interest you. The only thing that interests you is keeping this place going and that's all. So, just supposing you heard something, why not give us a break? We give you a break all the time, that's why this place never closes.'

'This place never closes because of the dollars that go into your department every week so don't give me any of that crap.'

'Sure, but if it closed, if we had to close you down,

there are other places with money going out of them, so we'd survive, we'd still make a living.'

Moses shrugs. 'The thing is,' he says, 'if this hypothetical guy should spill his guts in here, a highly unlikely event in itself, then you'd never know, not if I don't care to tell you.'

'You're right, Moses,' Murdock says, 'but we were just counting on your naturally friendly nature.'

Moses takes a cheroot from the top pocket of his kaftan, sticks it in his mouth and feels about for a light until Murdock flashes his lighter and lights him up.

'In my experience,' he says, 'no guy who's planning this kind of no-percentage deal is going to walk in and out of bars shouting his mouth off to the assembled throngs.'

'A point, Moses,' I agree. 'But then he sent a letter telling us about what he's got in mind, so maybe he's the kind of nut who wants to get caught. Before or after the event, I couldn't guess at, but it's a possibility.'

Moses gives a soft whistle. 'Wow,' he says. 'They giving you night classes in the psychology of the criminal mind, that's what they're giving you these days?'

'What do you say, Moses?' Murdock asks. 'You going to help us out, in the event, or not?'

Moses stares at the smoke curling from his cheroot and says, 'what's the hassle? It's a million to one, so I won't break any sweat. Sure, I'll play my part in keeping death off the streets of this city.'

'You'll pass the word around your staff?'

'Yeah, but keep your fingers crossed it ain't actually one of them.'

'None of your staff could keep their hands steady for the required length of time.'

Moses gets as close as he ever gets to a smile. Then he gets up and he says, 'I got to go now and sit in my office trying to figure out how much those bitches been cheating me out of lately. I don't have to tell you gentlemen that while you're here, there's a drink for you if you want it.'

'You're a real sweetheart, Moses,' I say to him.

'Don't let anybody tell you different,' he says, and goes out back.

Murdock and me sit there in silence for a few minutes. The room is getting a little more crowded and a little more gaudy as the afternoon crowd starts getting set for the rest of the day. We watch the scene from our elevated position and after a while Murdock comments, 'in this job, over the years, I've got used to all kinds of things, things that twenty years ago I would have thrown up over, but never, never, will I get used to being around Moses.' 'Yeah,' I tell him. 'I know what you mean.'

'It's not what I know about him that gives me the creeps,' Murdock goes on. 'I can live with that, although I make sure I don't think about those things too often. It's what I imagine about him, what I imagine he's capable of. That's what really gives me the fucking creeps about that guy.'

'Yeah. He makes me feel like going home and going to bed with a nice book, like *A History of Torture though the Ages.*'

'Hey,' Murdock says. 'You see who I see?'

I scan the crowd but I can't see anybody what might warrant Murdock's remark. 'There, look,' he says. 'The far side of the blonde fag, at the end of the bar.'

I look again and then I see who Murdock's talking about, a little guy called Pete Foley, trying to get the attention of somebody, anybody, behind the bar. With Pete that always takes time, and that's the kind of guy Pete is, right down the line. There are people who consider themselves failures in life, who are bitter about the breaks, but if you took them down to meet Pete Foley then within five minutes, they'd realise what roaring successes they'd actually been. If Pete ever did anything right or had anything good happen to him, then the event was so unusual that he wasn't used to the words that could express such an event to the rest of the world, and so nobody ever got to know about it. But what you could get from Pete, you could get all the news about everybody else's successes, because that's what Pete feeds on, the successes of other people, successes he'd like to achieve himself. He's a mine of information about who's done what, and what they made out of it, and consequently, he's sometimes a big help to Murdock and me. He loves to hang out with the guys who've made it, and he loves everybody to associate him with their achievements.

'Shall we have a word with Little Pete?' Murdock says. 'Why not? He goes everywhere there is to go.'

We wait and watch while Pete works at getting his drink, and about five minutes later he's got it, and he puts the glass to his lips and whips his eyes all around the place. They pop a little bit when he sees us and where we're sitting. Murdock crooks his finger and Pete looks this way and that, a parody of a guy who doesn't want to be watched, then he manoeuvres his way through the crowd, steps up to where we are and puts his glass to his lips again, looking at us over the top of it.

'Hello, Pete,' I say to him. 'How's your luck?'

Pete takes the glass away from his mouth and with his free hand he makes a shaky fluttery movement.

'Comme ci, comme ça.'

'Yeah,' Murdock says. 'As if you'd tell us. As if you'd tell us about your successful killings.' Pete shrugs and smirks, really pleased that we figure he may be knowing more than we do. 'You guys get me all wrong,' he says. 'You know me. Never was a guy to get involved in a wrong play.'

'Oh sure,' Murdock says. 'But one day, Pete, you're going to make a mistake, and me and Roy here are going to be around because that's a day we won't want to miss.'

Pete's growing by the minute. His smirk turns into a grin and he says, 'I ain't saying nothing. You guys heard what I said and I ain't saying any more. You figure what you will. I told you, I'm not into things'd be any interest to you guys.'

I shake my head.

'O.K. Pete,' I say. 'We won't push it. Wouldn't be no use anyhow.'

'Why don't you sit down and join us?' Murdock says. 'Things were getting a little slow around here, anyhow.'

'Well,' says Pete, 'I guess I might. Only I hope there

aren't too many people in this place right now to see me do that particular thing.'

So Pete sits down and looks round the room to see how many people are taking in the fact that Pete Foley is sitting down with Boldt and Murdock, and of course, hardly anybody is, but Pete is doubtless computing that number into a higher score.

'So,' he says, 'how's it with you? Still filling the penitentiary with the losers?'

'No, not really,' Murdock says. 'It's kind of slow right now. That's why we're down here, why we're touring round. Trying to drum up business. You know how it is, we get stamps for every conviction.'

Pete cackles his appreciation, and he's almost coming in his jockeys, cracking wise with a couple of cops.

'Listen,' he says. 'I could tell you, I could really give you goods on some of the characters in here.'

''Really?' I say to him.

'Oh, sure,' he says. 'You'd never believe it. But of course, you understand, I never would, not with me sitting up here. I mean, some of those guys, they could easy get the idea if you guys moved in on them, after me talking to you guys.'

'Yeah,' Murdock says. 'I guess you got a point there, Pete.'

'Better believe it,' Pete says. 'But there's one particular thing, something concerns a guy who ain't here right now, if you'd care to hear about it and provided it's worth talking to you about.'

'We're always in the market, Pete,' Murdock says. 'Tell us about it.'

'Well, it ain't anything, really. I mean, it ain't like a caper or anything like that. Nothing you can really move in on, but I heard, well, some day soon, a trio of guys is going to try and knock over the guys who bank the takings of one of Mr Florian's games, which one I'm not sure yet. The way I hear they're going to do it is to open up on the guys who are carrying it while they're between places, and naturally, so's Mr Florian doesn't know who to go after, they don't intend to leave anybody around who can tell. But I only know when it's going to be, not which one.'

'So why don't you go tell Florian?' I ask him.

'Yeah,' Pete says. 'But you pay, that's certain. And Mr Florian might think I know more than just about this particular job and he might decide to ask me.'

'Well,' Murdock says, 'we got better things to do than be security guards for Florian and his millions.'

'Yeah, but it's going to be out on the street,' Pete says. 'I mean, there won't be just the guys and Florian's guys in the street. They ain't going to bide their time until the street's clear.'

'These guys must figure they really need the money,' I say to him. 'I mean they're going to have to spend it awful quick, they realise that don't they?' Pete shrugs. 'They got their plans.'

'And who are these optimists,' I ask him. 'What's their names?'

'Well, that's what I want to tell you – if, you know, it's like always.'

One of Moses's staff drifts nearby on the area below, picking up glasses. Murdock grips him and the man drifts off to get three more drinks.

'Sure,' I say to Pete, 'it's like always, but this time you better get hold of Miller. We don't have the time right now, we've got something else on our minds.'

'Oh?' Pete says.

'Yeah,' I say, and I tell him all about our little mission. When I've finished Pete says, 'You're crazy.'

I don't say anything.

'I mean,' he says, 'you're never going to find who this guy is unless he makes a mistake in how he sets up the deal, on the day or something like that.'

'Well, that's what we're inclined to think, too, Pete,' I tell him. 'But you never know. And if you were to fall over the guy, then it'd be worth more than anything you'd get for the kind of information you've got on you right now.'

'O.K.,' says Pete, 'but in the meantime, I guess I'll give Miller a call.'

Pete gets up.

'You've got a drink coming,' Murdock says.

I take a sip of my drink.

'We go back to the route, check out as many places as we can.' 'We could still be doing that next Thanksgiving.'

'Like Pete says, the only way we're going to find this guy if he exists is with his rifle in his hand.

Just before or just after he's pulled the trigger.'

We finish our drinks and get up and go out of Clark's and leave them all to the smell of their perfume.

The Hillcrest Hotel isn't on a hill and it isn't really a hotel, just a rooming house with a lobby big enough to hold a desk and a desk clerk. Murdock and me are standing at the desk going through the register and the desk clerk is standing behind the desk, going through his nostrils, first one, then the other, devoting equal time to each.

'Who's this?' Murdock says, pointing a finger at a name.

The clerk leans slowly over and turns the book around then turns it back again.

'A bum,' he says.

Murdock and me wait for him to go on.

'A lush,' the clerk says. 'Up there right now. Saw him this morning around ten. Goes out, ten minutes later comes back with a grocery bag. Two bottles of gin, some other stuff. Probably sleeping right now.'

'And this one?' I say, pointing to another name.

The desk clerk shrugs. 'Young guy. I don't know. My guess is he could be a hustler.'

'So he's a hustler. Does he bring them back here, or does he deliver on the street?'

'Couldn't say about that. See, I'm not here all the time.'

'So he brings them back here. How long's he been here?'

'It's down there, in front of you.'

'How long?'

'Couple months. Maybe a little longer.'

'He in now?'

'I guess so.'

Murdock flips over a couple of pages.

'You seem to be pretty well full up,' he says. 'One moves out, another moves in. Hardly time to change the sheets.'

'We do all right.'

'Except this room,' Murdock says. 'This room here, number fourteen. That's been empty a couple of days.' The desk clerk nods.

'How come?' Murdock asks. 'Why not takers for fourteen? It being redecorated or something?'

I grin and light a cigarette. The desk clerk says, 'No. I guess it's just one of those things.

Nobody to use it for a couple of days. It'll be taken soon.' 'Faces front, does it? Like those other two rooms?' 'Yeah.'

Murdock closes the book.

'Let's go and take a look,' he says.

The clerk leaves his nose alone long enough to pick the keys off the rack, comes round to our side of the desk and starts to go up the stairs. The stairs are steep and the naked light bulbs do nothing for the wallpaper or what passes for the stair carpet. Just before he gets to the top he says, 'you going to bust that hustler?'

'Why?' Murdock asks him. 'You get yours on the house?'

The desk clerk doesn't answer but instead turns right at the top of the stairs. We follow after him and we're on the first-floor landing. There are three doors on either side of the passage and some more light bulbs and another passage creating a T-junction at the far end.

'This is Mr Cassidy's room,' the clerk says, stopping by the first door on the right. He looks at us to see what we want him to do and I indicate for him to knock on the door. When he's done that there's silence and some more waiting, then the clerk knocks again and there's a thud from somewhere behind the door, then a voice asking who it is knocking, making the words sound like all one word.

'It's Lewis,' the clerk says. 'I got someone wants to see you.'

The voice thinks about that for a while and then asks who it is wants to see him. At that point I finally get pissed off and tell the clerk to unlock the door. The clerk doesn't bother with an argument, but goes ahead and does what I tell him. The door swings inwards and we're presented with the sight of Mr Cassidy sitting on the edge of his unmade bed, pulling on his pants. On a low table next to the bed are his morning's purchases and on the bed itself there are girlie magazines strewn all over the crumpled sheets. The room stinks of alcohol and stale sweat. The curtains are drawn and at the foot of the bed a portable T.V. is soundlessly giving out a Bowery Boys movie. Cassidy stops pulling on his pants when he sees us standing in the doorway.

'Cops,' the desk clerk says. 'They wanted to see what you looked like.'

Cassidy's mouth falls open and his hand strays out for a glass on the edge of the bedside table. The movement reminds me of a crab trying not to be noticed. I take a step forward and stand in the doorway, looking round the room. Cassidy's hand finally closes on the glass.

'That make this place look good to you?' I ask him, indicating the glass. 'Make the stink go away and the pictures come to life?'

I walk over to the bed and pick up one of the magazines.

'He should meet Harold Schwarz,' I say to Murdock. 'Soon tell him not to waste his money on this crap.' I drop the magazine back on the bed. Cassidy is looking up into my face, the glass poised a couple of inches away from his mouth. Cassidy's probably around forty-five, but he looks ten years older. His hair is thin and dry, the way it is with all lushes, and his skin is the colour of chewing-gum. I pick up one of the unopened bottles and look at it.

'And talking about money,' I say to him. 'This stuff don't come cheap these days. What do you do to make the dough to keep yourself in the manner to which you're accustomed?'

Cassidy keeps on looking at me for a while and then looks at his glass and says, 'I got a pension. I used to be a Navy man.'

Murdock's low laugh comes from the doorway behind me.

'Yeah, I guess he'd float at that,' Murdock says.

'I ain't lying,' Cassidy protests. 'I got a busted knee. Got it off the coast, Korea, that is.'

'You got a busted knee?'

'Yeah,' Cassidy says, finally putting the glass to his

mouth and swallowing half the contents.

'Show me,' I say to him.

'Ask him,' Cassidy says. 'Lewis'll tell you. He sees the way I walk. I got a stick, look over in the corner.'

'That's right …' Lewis begins, but I tell him to shut up.

'Show me,' I tell Cassidy again.

Cassidy takes the other half of his drink and puts the glass down on the table, stretches out his arms behind him and begins to lever himself up off the bed. When he's standing up he almost overbalances and I catch hold of one of his arms and straighten him up. Now he's upright and his pants slip down to his ankles. One of his knees is sort of pushed to one side, as though he was a robot and somebody'd taken a hammer and just tapped him a bit to send the knee a little out of true.

'You want to see how I walk?' Cassidy says.

I tell him to sit down.

'Yeah,' he says, and does that and then pours himself another tumblerful, his trousers still round his ankles. Murdock comes into the room and begins to go through the drawers and the closets.

'But even so,' I say to Cassidy, 'a Navy pension. I mean, you got a bill for what you bought this morning?'

I pick up the empty grocery bag from off the floor and feel inside it.

'I don't know,' Cassidy says. 'Maybe. There may be one in there.'

I shake my head.

'No,' I say to him. 'There doesn't seem to be.'

Cassidy shrugs. I drop the bag back on the floor.

'Maybe you could tell us where you bought the stuff,' I say to him. 'I guess they'd remember you, a regular customer with a gimpy leg.'

'I don't know what it's called,' Cassidy says. 'It's a place just up the street. That's where I go, mostly.' Murdock stops going over the room, looks at me and shakes his head.

'That what you looking for?' Cassidy says. 'A guy that knocked over a liquor store?'

I look at him but I don't say anything.

Cassidy shakes his head and looks at his knee and laughs. 'Man,' he says, 'if it were me, I'd still be only half-way to the door, don't you think?'

'Come on,' I say to Murdock. 'The Navy man's got some drinking to do.'

'I'd ask you to join me,' Cassidy says, 'but I only got one spare glass, and I don't like the taste of toothpaste.'

We walk out of the room and close the door behind us.

'O.K.,' I say to the clerk. 'Down the hall, to your friend's room.' 'He's out,' the clerk says.

'That's O.K. We won't mess anything up.'

The clerk turns away and we follow him down the hall. He unlocks the third door down and we walk into the hustler's room. This time we're presented with a different kind of smell, which, although it's cleaner, turns my stomach almost as much as the last one.

The clerk closes the door behind us.

'Well,' Murdock says, looking round the room, 'maybe

it won't get into *Good Housekeeping*, but it sure is sweet.'

The room is a carbon of the last one except that it's one hundred per cent cleaner and the air is fresher and the bed is made, complete with a couple of embroidered cushions decorating the counterpane that don't come with the fixtures and fittings. There are other personal details, like the poster of Brando on the motorcycle that's tacked up on the wall, and the brand new cassette machine that's within easy reach of the bed, and the stack of well-preserved old movie magazines placed neatly on a stool at the far side of the bed.

I sit down on the bed and Murdock goes through the room the way he did the last one. It doesn't take him long and the result is just the same as before. Murdock shrugs and I shrug and the clerk who is leaning up against the wall and watching us both says, 'I guess I realise now what attracts somebody into joining the police department.'

'Oh?' I say. 'And what have you figured out?'

'I figure out that it gives a guy lots of opportunities for jollies. You know, like reminding a crippled lush he's a crippled lush.'

I smile at the clerk.

'What would you like me to remind you you are?'

The clerk doesn't answer that.

'Sure,' I say to him, 'but you're right. It's easy to figure out. It's like you say, we're just pigs having fun. We do this, we spend our time in crummy rooming houses because that's what we like to do best. It's more fun than bowling. And we'd much rather talk to people like you and Cassidy than, say, going out on a double date with Raquel Welch and Jane Fonda. Isn't that right, George?'

Murdock moves slowly across the room and stands in front of the clerk, no more than a few inches away from him.

'That's right,' Murdock says. 'Like you say, we're just pigs having fun.'

The clerk doesn't say anything and he tries to avoid Murdock's gaze, which is very difficult considering the amount of space Murdock has left between them.

'That's right, isn't it?' Murdock says again.

The clerk tries to get into the wall paper but Murdock closes up a little bit more.

'Isn't it?' Murdock says, but before anything else happens there is the sound of voices on the landing outside, and then the voices stop, and the door opens and we're presented with our first look at the hustler and his new-found friend.

The hustler is dressed in the typical stud outfit, the jeans and the denim jacket and the sweat shirt decorated with the dangling medallion. His hair is black and beautifully combed in the approved mid-fifties style, but it's apparent that the blackness is achieved with a little outside assistance and although I'm not close enough to tell, I'd take bets that there are some well concealed crowsfeet around the corners of his eyes, because this hustler is no longer a young one, he's closer forty than he is twenty but like the rest of them he wants to look the eternal teenager.

His companion is something else again. There's no doubt at all about his age. He's somewhere in his late fifties, wearing a Panama hat, milk white shirt, beautiful grey suit, handmade shoes. Like Cassidy, he's brought some groceries, clutching the bag against his middle, but unlike Cassidy's these groceries are to help things along, not blot things out. The hustler's companion lets the grocery bag slip a little, catches it then hugs it a little tighter to himself.

'Oh Christ,' he says.

The hustler looks at me and then at Murdock and then he sees the clerk round the corner leaning against the wall and he says to him, 'What's happening, Lewis?'

The hustler's voice is deeper than you'd expect, also tougher, hard-edged. 'I don't know,' Lewis says. 'These gentlemen are just doing their job.'

The hustler looks at Murdock and me again.

'You have warrants?' he says.

'Come inside and close the door,' I tell him.

'I said – '

'I heard what you said. Do what I told you.'

The hustler's companion puts the groceries down on the floor and closes the door.

'Now look – 'the hustler begins, but this time it's his companion's turn to interrupt him.

'Cliff, listen, O.K.? Don't rock the boat. I –'

'Sure, I know,' Cliff says. 'You got a family, a wife. You all have.'

'They –'

'Shut up. This isn't a bust, is it fellows?'

'Oh?' I say to him.

He shakes his head. 'No,' he says, 'this isn't a bust.'

'You tell us what it is.'

'I hope you got plenty of dough in that fat little wallet of yours,' Cliff says to his companion. 'You're sure going to need it.'

'What?'

'Sure. You're going to have to buy yourself out of this one. And don't think it makes any difference we've just come in.'

Murdock goes over to the hustler's companion and says to him, 'Could I see your wallet, sir? For identification purposes?'

The companion stares at Murdock as if Murdock's talking in a foreign language.

'You do have identification?' Murdock says.

This time the words get through and the companion fusses out his wallet and hands it over to Murdock who flips it open and takes out the companion's driving licence.

'Joseph H. Nicholson,' Murdock reads. '1157 Belle Vue Drive.'

Nicholson doesn't say anything.

'Nice district,' Murdock observes.

'Nice district,' I say, lighting up a cigarette.

Murdock digs a little deeper into the wallet and eases out some photographs.

'This your wife?'

Nicholson nods.

'Nice,' Murdock says, passing the photograph over to

me. 'Yeah,' I say, looking at the picture.

'Your daughters?' Murdock says, taking out another photograph.

Nicholson nods again.

'Beautiful girls,' Murdock says. 'They in college?'

'Yes.'

Murdock hands the photographs to me.

'Beautiful girls, hey, Roy?' Murdock says, then to Nicholson, 'I expect you're pretty proud of them?'

Nicholson looks at the hustler for some help but the hustler has walked over to the window and is inspecting the traffic flowing by outside.

'They proud of you?' Murdock asks. Nicholson snaps his gaze back at Murdock. 'They proud of their daddy?' Murdock says.

I look at the photograph and I'm struck that the two girls smiling out of the picture could easily be the two girls who were accompanying Harold Schwarz early this morning, the same kind of bright smiles, the brilliant teeth, the fresh complexions.

'They carry pictures of you in their billfolds, too?' Murdock asks. 'Say having your dick sucked by guys like Cliff here?'

'I'm telling you,' Cliff tells Nicholson without turning away from the window. 'They're going to shake you down. Just wear it and pay them all your money. You can afford it.'

'What's the matter, Cliff?' I ask him. 'You're talking yourself out of your hourly rate.'

'I'll get by,' Cliff says.

'You bet your sweet life,' I tell him.

Murdock counts the bills in Nicholson's wallet.

'You made a good score this time, Cliff,' Murdock says. 'You know how much he's carrying in here? He's got almost three hundred bucks.'

'Look,' Nicholson says to Murdock, almost whispering, as if he doesn't want anybody else in the room to hear, 'look, take it. The only thing I care about is getting out of here, and nobody knowing, O.K.? Just take it, will you?'

Murdock slams Nicholson up against the door and slaps him across the mouth with the billfold.

'Listen, filth,' Murdock says. 'Shut up, will you?'

Nicholson's eyes are wide with fear and incomprehension.

Murdock looks at him for a minute or two then he slaps him twice more with the billfold and drops it on the floor.

'Come on, Roy,' Murdock says to me. 'Let's leave these two motherfuckers to fix a price for the job.' Murdock pushes Nicholson out of the way, opens the door and goes out into the corridor. I jerk a thumb at the clerk and he goes out too. When I get to the doorway I turn round to Cliff, who has already turned away from the window, surprised at the way things have worked out.

'Listen, sweetheart,' I say to him. 'Those lips of yours, they're your stock in trade. You're lucky they're still arranged the same way.'

I close the door behind me.

'I never could stand guys like that,' Murdock says. 'They give me the fucking creeps.' 'Well, you know what they always say,' the clerk says.

'No,' Murdock says, looking at him. 'What do they always say?' 'Nothing,' the clerk says, looking away.

'Good.'

'That the empty room?' I ask the clerk, pointing to the remaining door. 'That's right,' he says.

'Let's take a look.'

'What for?' the clerk says. 'I already told you about that.' 'Let's take a look, anyway.'

'It'd be a waste of your time. The room's empty.'

I'm about to tell the clerk again when a small sound stops me saying what I was going to say. The sound comes from behind the door of the room which is supposed to be empty, and the sound is the sound of a man coughing, just once. Murdock and me look at one another and then at the clerk.

'The key,' I tell him. 'Which one's the key?'

The clerk selects a key and pushes the key ring at me. I take it off him and say quietly, 'O.K., who's in there?'

The clerk shakes his head. I get a grip on his collar. 'Who's in there?'

'I don't know. Honest. I don't know who it is.'

'There somebody supposed to be in there?'

The clerk nods his head.

'Then who? '

'Look, I don't know. A guy called Newman. He paid me not to tell anybody about him, that's all. I don't know who he is.'

'O.K.,' I tell him. 'All right, you don't know anything

about him. But you can go on right over there and unlock the door, O.K.?'

'Listen –'

'Just like you did the other times. It's easy. You're good at it.'

'I –'

'Do it,' I tell him. 'Right now. Just unlock the door and push it wide open.'

I give him back his keys and he has no choice but to go over to the door and do as I've told him. Murdock and me are right behind him. The clerk puts the key in the lock, we get either side of the door, the clerk turns the key and then pushes the door wide open, almost falling over himself trying to get out of the way.

Nothing happens. That goes on for a moment or two then I draw my gun and stick my head round the corner of the door to take a look.

There's nothing there but an empty room.

I lean off the wall and stand in the doorway taking another look, but the room's still empty. I walk a couple of steps forward. Now I can see the bed and the bedside table and on the bedside table there is a pair of field glasses.

I cross the room and look down at the field glasses. Murdock comes in after me and says,

'What have you got?'

A voice behind us replies.

'So far he's got the glasses, but up to now he's overlooked me.'

We both whirl round in the direction of the voice,

which has come from behind the open door. At first I can't see who the voice belongs to, or do anything about it if I have to, then Murdock moves and I see, leaning against the wall with his arms folded, a guy in a short-sleeved shirt. He's a young guy, a sneer on his fresh face. We cover him and Murdock says, 'raise your arms, you mother.'

The young guy shakes his head, unfolds his arms and says, 'ain't no need. I mean, if I was who you were looking for, you wouldn't be looking at me right now.'

'Face the wall, just face the wall,' Murdock says.

The guy shrugs and turns round.

'Save a lot of trouble if you feel in my vest pocket.'

'Shut up,' Murdock snaps, and goes over the guy. When he's satisfied, he feels in the guy's vest pocket and pulls out what looks like an I.D. wallet.

'My gun's on that chair over by the window, underneath my coat,' the guy says.

Murdock looks at the wallet while I go over to the chair and lift up the guy's coat. Sure enough, there underneath it is a shoulder holster holding a piece of Government Issue.

Murdock says, 'this says this guy's Secret Service.'
'Let me see.'

I take the card off Murdock.

'Can I turn round now?' the guy says.

'Shut up,' Murdock replies. 'Oh, Jesus,' the guy says.

I look at the card for a minute or two, then hand it back to Murdock.

'Turn round,' I say to the guy.

The guy turns round.

'So,' I say to him, 'the card says Secret Service. What did you do, send carton tops for it?'

The guy sighs. 'You know I'm what it says I am,' he says. 'Deep down, in your heart of hearts you know it. But if you want to check it out, it'll give you an extra few minutes before you have to admit you're wrong.'

'That'd be long enough for me to split your lip for you,' Murdock says. 'Yes, I guess it would,' the guy says.

'Oh, shit,' I say to Murdock. 'Leave it. We'll check it out, but we know the answer.' 'Christ,' Murdock says. 'Why don't we ever get to know anything?'

'You mean you couldn't guess?' the guy says. 'You couldn't figure we'd have men covering a thing like this?'

'Sure, sure,' I say, lighting a cigarette.

The guy moves away from the wall.

'Still,' he says, 'the way you came into the room, I can appreciate how you wouldn't figure something like this.'

'Maybe we ought to remind him we haven't checked him out yet,' Murdock says.

I shake my head, then I ask the guy, 'what do you hope to achieve in a flea pit like this?'

The guy jerks his head at the ceiling.

'The roof,' he says. 'It's the highest in this section. On the day, I liaise with your helicopter. In the meantime, I work from here, checking the street, and by the time the day comes we're legislated for everything but the wild card. And that we've got a good chance of reading.' 'Oh, sure,' I tell him. 'No problem.'

'Well,' he says, 'don't forget we've got you scaring him away.'

Murdock makes a move but I slow him down by standing between them.

'Forget it. Forget about him. He's here, but he's not going to be any use. They never are. After it's all over, and he's played it by the book, he says, well, how can I be blamed? I did it right.' 'Yeah,' the guy says. 'Like you came through the door.'

I put my arm out to stop Murdock going forward.

'Come on,' I say. 'Let's get back on the street. There's no point hanging around here. We don't want to spoil his game.'

The guy grins at us as we go out, closing the door behind us. The desk clerk has vanished from the landing.

'He's right,' Murdock says. 'He could have had us cold, if he'd been the wrong guy.'

'Well, he wasn't, and fifty percent of that performance in there was for his own benefit, because he'd been caught cold too, without his gun.'

'You think so?'

'What would you have done, caught flatfooted like that?' 'I guess maybe you're right,' Murdock says.

I tread my cigarette out on the floor.

'Come on, let's go downstairs.'

On the way out I notice that the clerk is nowhere to be seen but I decide to leave it at that.

We walk down the street to where we've left the car, get in and pull away. After Murdock has been driving for a minute or two, I say, 'oh, Christ, let's face it, the guy was right.'

'Sure he was right.'

'Christ, I mean, the way we went in there.' 'Yeah, like Gangbusters.'

I shake my head.

'Gangbusters would have kicked in the door so hard it would've flattened anybody stood behind it.'

We drive along some more without saying anything, until Murdock asks, 'where we going now?'

'Follow the route. Turn into Weaver Street.'

'Then what?'

I am tired and pissed off and I don't want Murdock asking me what I'm asking myself.

'Just cover the route, George. That's all. I don't figure on stopping off any more, right now.'

We drive along some more without saying anything. Everybody is trying to get to their bar or their home or their wife or their girlfriend just that minute earlier than anybody else. The traffic is heavy and slow, horns are honking and the noise is just what I need to set my feelings to music, so I try and switch myself off. When I do that, though, my brother's face keeps floating into my mind, not as it is now, but as it was when we were kids – when he was seven, and I was twelve.

Then other images flood in, like the time he gave Marty Powell cause to want to rough him up a little. In the end it was me that stepped in and got the bloody nose and the bawling out from our mother, and I remember the way my brother kept quiet through all of it, even when my mother was holding him up as an example of how to behave. I'd got so mad that afterwards, when we were on our own, I'd asked my brother why he'd let me take the blame. He's just laughed and told me he thought the reasons were obvious, considering I was the one who'd got the bloody nose and the bawling out from Mom. I took a few minutes of his self-satisfied amusement, then I hauled him one off and paid him the interest on my bloody nose, which of course only gave me short term satisfaction until Mom came on the scene again. I was kept inside for a fortnight while my brother made a big deal out of going out and playing with his friends.

I light a cigarette and swear at myself for allowing the memory of a small incident like that to affect me the way it did at the time; it even makes me mad that I can still remember it, but then every memory I have of my brother affects me that way, because they're all of the same kind; a patchwork of niggling resentment. I flip the match out of the window.

'Why in Christ's name didn't the bastard carve out a career with General Motors?' I say out loud.

'What?'

'Sorry, George,' I say to him, 'I was just thinking about my fuck of a brother. I was thinking, why, at my time of life, am I still keeping his ass clean for him?'

'Well,' Murdock says, 'it don't matter he's your brother, does it? I mean, we'd be in the same position whoever it was.'

'Yeah, I know. But it's because he's a politician this has happened, and I'm involved with him. Christ, he never had to become a politician. He doesn't give a shit about the niggers or Medicare or Channel Thirteen. All he gives a shit about is himself; that's all he ever gave a shit about. It didn't matter what he did, all he wanted was to get himself to the top of the heap. Politics is just like any corporation to him. He doesn't have any beliefs. They're just paper clips to him.'

'Then why those particular beliefs?' Murdock wonders. 'What'd he do, flip a coin?'

I shake my head.

'He likes them,' I reply. 'He doesn't feel them, but he likes people thinking he's got courage, character. A hero. He's always wanted to be a hero.'

'Like you, you mean,' Murdock says.

I laugh. 'That's right, a big successful hero like me.'

We crawl to the end of Weaver Street and stop at the lights.

'What now?' Murdock says. 'Still follow the route?'

'It's getting late. Why don't we turn it in for an hour or so?'

'Fine by me.'

'Look, drop me off at Gardenias' will you? And you take the car and pick up your stuff from your sister's and I'll phone you at the Chandler in an hour or so.'

'Fine,' Murdock says, and a few minutes later he pulls the car into the kerb outside Gardenias' and lets me out and drives off.

The sidewalk is still warm in the evening sun and I can taste the dust in the air, so I cross the sidewalk and walk into Gardenias' where the coffee is good enough to wash away even the taste of this city.

Gardenias' is a long narrow diner that looks like any other diner except that Gardenias is spotless, not a speck of dirt anywhere – not a mark on the table cloth, not a rim inside of a cup, not a splash on the counter. But it's not only the hygiene that attracts Gardenias' out-of-the-ordinary clientèle; it's the food, which is no different from the kind of food served in any other diner in the country, except that it's the best. There is no coffee better than the coffee served in Gardenias', the doughnuts are like you never tasted, the soup is home-made and makes you think of something you may or may not have had years ago, the sandwiches are works of art. These are some of the reasons why Gardenias has the kind of clientèle it's got, because many of this city's beautiful people and trendsetters or whatever they like to call themselves have discovered the place – they like telling the uninitiated how clever they've been to find the joint, and what a character Gardenias is.

As I go through the door it occurs to me that however much of a character Gardenias might be, he could never compare with the three characters who are taking up the space at the far end of the counter, those characters being Leo Florian and the two guys who always walk behind him, Charlie Bancroft and Earl Connors. Florian himself is an extremely good-looking guy in his late fifties, beautifully barbered hair, silvery and curly; the suit he's wearing was of course tailored by angels, the shoes made by somebody who is probably now a millionaire. Florian is sitting at the counter, a coffee pot in front of him, a napkin stuck in his shirt collar, and he's drinking his coffee very carefully, holding the saucer high. He's looking very serious, as if all his concentration is going into appreciating his coffee and nothing else must interfere with that concentration. The other two,

Bancroft and Connors, are not sitting down, they're standing behind and slightly to the right of Florian, holding cups and saucers. No bookmaker would take bets as to who out of Bancroft and Connors was the ugliest or the meanest.

Bancroft is the younger of the two, going slightly thin on top, but compensating for that with the length it is at the back. One of his eyes is made of glass and the other may as well be for all the loving light that shines out of it. Like the cuffs of his pants, his nostrils are flared wide, and the distance between his nostrils and his top lip gives his face the look of an orang-utan.

Connors is ugly in a different kind of way. His ugliness is in his creepiness, in the physical manifestation of his character; you feel that if you touched him, you'd come away with a grey oily film on the tips of your fingers. He's tall and carries himself well and he always has a faint grin on his mouth. If he was ever to allow it to break into a smile you'd expect to see a couple of fangs at either side of his mouth. Unlike Florian, Bancroft and Connors have their eyes on me the minute I walk through the door; they keep them there while I walk across to the counter and sit down. I wait for Gardenias to appear and Bancroft and Connors keep on looking at me and Florian keeps on drinking his coffee. When Gardenias comes out from the back and sees it's me he shoots a glance at Florian and co., then back at me.

'Hello, Mr Boldt,' he says, edging over to where I am. 'What can I get for you?' 'Coffee,' I tell him. 'And liverwurst on rye.'

'Fine,' he says, pouring me some coffee from a pot on the hob and fetching cream and sugar before he goes to work on his bleached wood board and starts assembly the sandwich.

While he's working, he says to me, 'I seen your partner in here, maybe Tuesday. Eats here a lot these days.'

'Yeah,' I say. 'That's right. His brother-in-law doesn't understand him.'

'Oh?' Gardenias says. 'Well, he never speaks about it.'

Bancroft gives a low laugh. 'That's cops for you,' he says. 'They suffer, and yet they never grouse.'

'You're right,' Connors agrees. 'That's why only a certain kind of man makes it on the force.'

I don't say anything to Bancroft or Connors but instead I sugar my coffee and stir it up. At the same time Florian puts his coffee cup down, wipes his mouth with his napkin and gets off his stool. He moves over to where I'm sitting, motioning his boys to stay where they are.

'I heard about your problem,' Florian says, sitting down alongside me. 'You got any news on that yet?'

Florian's voice is rough and ugly, a direct contrast to his cultivated appearance. 'You're interested in that?' I ask him.

'I'm interested in everything,' he says, 'and besides, I don't like wild cards. I don't like a mess. I get upset.

'Even when it doesn't concern you?'

'Yeah,' Florian says. 'Even then. I get uneasy. Things get out of control, I get frustrated, maybe I make some bad decisions. I don't know.'

'Well,' I tell him, 'even if it happens, it's only going to be messy for a few seconds, because after it happens, that's the easy part, picking up the guy.'

Florian thinks about this for a minute or two, then says, 'the guy receiving, he's your brother.'

'That's right.'

Florian shakes his head. 'I hate to see this kind of thing,' he says. 'A guy can't give a shit about his brother getting whacked or not.'

'That's good,' I tell him, 'because in that case maybe you hate it so much you'll go out and find the guy and bring him to me and save me a lot of trouble.'

Florian shakes his head again.

'Charlie,' he says, 'Earl, come over.'

Bancroft and Connors snap to it and when they get to us Florian says, 'Meet a prince, a man of real family feeling. You know, I'm beginning to think maybe you sent the note to the Police Department yourself.'

'No,' Bancroft says. 'You got to be able to write before you can send notes.'

Connors gives a low laugh and Florian looks at me to

see what I'm going to do and at the same time Gardenias puts the sandwich on the counter beside me.

'You like liverwurst on rye, Charlie?' I say to Bancroft.

Charlie hardens himself up. 'Yeah,' he says, 'I really do.'

'Oh Christ,' Gardenias says, turning away from the counter.

'Out,' Florian says.

For a second I wonder whether he's talking to me or Bancroft, but then Bancroft looks at Florian, Florian jerks his head and Bancroft moves towards the door.

'You too,' Florian says to Connors. Connors does as he's told and the door closes behind them both. Florian and me look at one another.

'What would be the use?' he says. 'You all work for me, anyway.'

After a while I agree, 'yeah, what would be the use?'

I turn to the counter and take a bite of my sandwich.

'About that,' Florian says. 'You could work for me for real, you know that. Half the hours, ten times the dough. Your way the payments you get from us, it don't mean much if some kid knocking over a drive-in whacks you out before he pisses himself.'

'As opposed to being whacked out by a pro while I'm fetching and carrying for you.'

'You heard about that?'

'I was the first in the department.'

'And yet it was Lambert who called me. You don't like me enough to call me, Boldt?'

'He likes you better than I do, yes.' I tell him. 'But

you heard about our little problem and I've got no time for anything else.'

'That's what I meant,' Florian says. 'That's what I'm talking about. A thing like this throws everything. Everything gets screwed up. Already I'm affected.'

'I may cry,' I tell him.

'Yeah,' Florian says. 'Anyway, I told Lambert, anything breaks on this, I want to know.'

'Then you'll get to know, won't you, if Lambert guarantees it,' I reply, getting off my stool and beginning to walk over to the door.

'Boldt,' Florian says.

I pause, and turn back to look at Florian.

'I don't like a thing I can't understand,' he says. 'And I never will understand you.'

'Well, I understand you, Mr Florian,' I tell him, 'and isn't it funny, that understanding you doesn't help me to like you either.'

I close the door behind me and stand on the sidewalk waiting for a cab to cruise by. Florian's car is parked about thirty feet along the kerb with Connors and Bancroft sitting in front. When they see me come out of Gardenias' the car slides along the kerbside and stops opposite the diner, the doors open and Connors and Bancroft get out.

'You better hurry,' I tell them. 'Gardenias is holding a shotgun on him for his stick pin.'

They pause for a moment on their way across the sidewalk and Bancroft says, 'It's a funny thing, we protect Florian and Florian protects you. Is that a fringe benefit that's part of the package he hands you?'

'That's right,' I tell him. 'Because, see, I need Mr Florian's protection, because I'm so scared of people like you. I wouldn't be able to handle any of your kind of trouble, which of course you already know.'

Connors puts a hand on Bancroft's shoulder.

'Charlie,' Connors says, 'Mr Florian doesn't want anything like this, don't forget that. He's in there now and he wouldn't be happy.'

Bancroft looks at me. 'Another time,' he says.

I nod. 'There'll be plenty of other times,' I tell him.

Then there's nothing left for Bancroft to do but turn away and follow Connors into Gardenias'. I turn away too and face the evening traffic and suddenly I feel very tired; tired of the whole day and of people like Moses and the hustler and Florian and Florian's boys and most of all tired of myself, a forty-three-year-old cop with an undistinguished career and a distinguished shit of a brother who's still bringing trouble into my life.

While I'm thinking all this a cab cruises into my line of vision and I almost forget to hail it, I'm so preoccupied with my thoughts. The cab makes a U-turn and pulls up. I tell the driver my address and get in the back, lean back in the seat and close my eyes, the stale atmosphere of sweat and old cigarette ends drifting into my nostrils a perfect counterpoint to the way I'm feeling. After a moment or two, though, the sleep begins to creep into my eyelids and as I begin to drift away the cab driver says, 'You know this city never was an actual pleasure to drive in, but Christ, this year, it's worse than ever. I used to live in Des Moines, and that was always terrible, but that's bigger than this town, and I really believe this town's getting as bad as Des Moines. Christ, maybe it's even getting worse.'

I open my eyes and automatically fish in my top pocket for a cigarette.

'Yeah,' I say, blinking the sleep away.

'But a job's a job, and what can you do?' the cab driver continues. 'We all got to work. But listen, did you ever hear of, say, a postman, on his day off, go out and deliver a couple of hundred letters just for fun, to please his old lady? Or maybe a welder, go home and get out the spare kit he keeps in the garage, then go round looking for things to weld? No, you never did, did you? And you never will. But with me it's different. Last Saturday is when my day off falls. It varies. Sometimes I get days in the week, sometimes I get days at the week-end. It varies. But last Saturday, last week, I get my day off. So what happens? What happens is my wife says, "Look it's a beautiful day, why don't we visit with my sister?" Her sister happens to live only a hundred and thirty, hundred fifty miles away, you know? She says, "We can take the kids and picnic on the way, and as Mrs Sloman next door is crocked up, we can take her kids as well. What do you say?" she says. So I tell her. "This is what I say," I say. "All I want is to have a beer or two, get on the swing seat in the garden and read the paper through three or four times and when I've done that maybe I'll do it again. And," I say to her, "what is more, that is what I'll be doing. So what do you think of that?" I ask her. So she tells me and then she gets on the phone to her sister with whom she's already arranged this little joy ride and tells her all the forty-seven kinds of bastard I am, which in itself is nothing particularly new. So in the end I finish up going down to this bar I sometimes go to, and I spend the day down there, and when I get back you can imagine what the evening's like. A great evening. So great I wish I'm out working.'

'Yeah.'

All the time he's been talking I've been rolling the cigarette round in my fingers, waiting for him to stop because I've no more matches left in my book. So I ask him if he has a light and that's a mistake because he tells me he doesn't smoke.

'I had to cut that out,' he says. 'With one thing and another, I found it better not to. And I was lucky. I never tried before, I guess I figured I wouldn't be able to, but when I did no sweat. I smoked the last of my pack, threw the pack in the trash can and an hour later I'd forgotten I was trying to give them up. After that I never looked back. I mean, some guys give up a week, a fortnight, maybe three months sometimes, but in the end, they take it up again, because, really, they know they're going to; while they're not smoking they're just passing the time until they start up again, only they don't admit it to themselves. Me, I figured that, and that's why I guess I beat it.'

'I guess you're right,' I tell him, hoping to Christ that my agreeing with him will shut him up.

'You're right,' he says. 'And that's one thing I've got

over my old lady. She's never going to give up. And so if she ever figures on getting snotty about some of the things she don't like about me, I get in these little remarks, you know, like about how many packs is that she's got through today already, and, by the way, I don't think we can afford the deposit on the violin Joanne wants to practise with for the school orchestra, that kind of thing.'

I nod my agreement and the cab driver makes a right, and in a couple of merciful moments we will be at where I live.

'Mind you,' the driver says, 'sure I can afford a violin, if the day comes I can't afford something like that for my kid, I'll turn this hack in and shoot myself, but Christ, imagine a ten-year-old kid let loose on a violin, round the house …'

'Just over there,' I interrupt him. 'The apartment block on the left.' 'Sure,' the cab driver says, and swings over.

I get out and pay the fare and the cab driver takes it without a word. It's as though he's never spoken to me, as if the monologues he's been delivering were for his ears only. He drives off and I cross the sidewalk, climb the block stairs to the second floor and walk down the landing. I stop outside my door, put the key in the lock and push. Inside I take off my jacket and drop it on the table in the hall then walk through into the living area, go over to the table in the corner and pour myself a vodka. I cross to the window and look out into the dusty evening air and take a long drink.

The apartment is full of dead air so I put my glass

down on the sill and raise the window, which lets in the dust and the sounds of the traffic and the smells from the restaurant on the ground floor. I drain my glass, go back to the table and make myself another drink, then I lie down on the divan and shake off my shoes, balance my glass on my chest and close my eyes. But though I'm still tired, now I'm able to sleep the sleep won't come, so I give up and get up and go into the kitchen and begin to scramble eggs. While I'm doing that the phone rings. I go back into the living area and lift the hand set.

'Yeah?'

'Listen,' the voice at the other end says. 'It's Pete.'

'Who?'

'Pete.'

'Yeah, I know it's Pete, I can hear. Pete who?'

'Pete Foley, for Christ's sake.'

'Right.'

I wait for him to go on.

'You there?' he says.

'Yeah, I'm here.'

'Well, listen, you asked me to phone you, right?'

'That's right,'

'Well, that's what I'm doing. I may have something for you.'

'Yeah?'

'Listen, I could just as easily put the phone down and go back to my beer, you know that?'

'Get on with it.'

There is a pause, then Pete says:

'Well, look, there's somebody in town maybe you don't know about.'

'Yeah?'

'I'm damned sure you don't know. In fact, except for interested parties I guess I'm the only guy apart from those people that knows, know what I mean?'

I nod my head, but really I feel like shaking it. From the kitchen comes the smell of burning eggs.

'So we got to meet and talk, don't we?' Pete says.

'Pete,' I tell him, 'say what you've got to say now, O.K.?'

'Jesus,' he says. 'Look, you're crazy, you know.'

'O.K., Pete,' I tell him. 'Let's forget it, right?'

'Listen, listen,' Pete says. 'You forget it, you'll regret it. Believe me. This got something or nothing to do with what you said, it don't matter. You'll want to know it anyway. All sorts of people going to want to know this anyhow, and I call you up first, O.K.?'

The smell of burning is getting worse.

'Where are you?' I ask Pete.

'Shit!' Pete says, 'where I am going to be approximately another fifteen seconds, I been here too long already. You say a place, but make it safe will you, not on the steps of City Hall or something.'

'Why not come here?'

'Are you crazy?'

'All right,' I tell him. 'Up at the Point. I'll be there in forty-five minutes. Will you?'

'I'll be there,' Pete says, and rings off.

I put the receiver down and go into the kitchen. When

I've scraped the eggs out of the pan and put the pan in the sink, I open the fridge and take out a grapefruit. I cut it in half, sugar it and leave it while I take off my clothes and shower. When I've showered, I shave and put on fresh clothes and after that I sit down and eat my grapefruit, wondering what in Christ's name Pete Foley can possibly tell me that's going to make my life any easier for me.

I sit in my car, looking at the evening city and listening to its sounds. From where I am, perched on the top of the Point, parked among the sweet clean-smelling bushes, the city looks nice and clean too, like an architect's model does without people and cars and all the different kinds of dirt to fuck up the nice new surfaces.

The sun is low now, distorted and larger than life through the thick hanging haze, its rim dirty in the bottom quarter as though some kid has wiped his sticky fingers over it.

A faint breeze ripples through the leaves of the Point's bushes and I remember when I was a rookie spending most of my night shifts up here shining my flashlight in the backs of the parked cars, and wondering each time I caused some couple to scramble back to a semblance of decency what the fuck I was doing when in most cases I'd have liked to have been the guy in the back feeling up the girl. But at this time of a summer's night there are no cars up here, just mine, so I light a cigarette and throw the match out of the window. As I do that, I hear the sound of a car slowing down and then the sound stops, a door slams and a couple of minutes later the image of Pete Foley appears in my driving mirror, parting the bushes, looking as if he's just scaled Rushmore. He walks over to the car and gets in.

'Hello, Pete,' I say to him.

He takes his cigarettes from his coat pocket.

'Give me a light, will you.'

I give him a light and he inhales, leaning back in the seat.

'So,' he says, 'you don't think I've got anything for you?'

'Pete, I'm here,' I tell him. 'Just give me the message'

'Well,' he says, 'you'll know what I'm talking about when I give you a name, and that name's Styles.

I don't say anything. Pete shifts his position slightly, pleased to have some effect.

Albert Styles. A hit-man, a craftsman, but without one conviction, and he's been responsible for at least a dozen hits I can think of, around the country, and Christ knows how many more there must be that nobody knows about.

'O.K.,' I say to Pete. 'Albert Styles. Now how is that supposed to interest me?'

Pete's mouth falls open and he stares at me. Eventually he says, 'Listen, you know what Styles is. I mean, you do know?'

'Yeah, I do know.'

'Then what are you saying? Styles is a hit-man. Your brother's been sent a letter, a proposition. He's in line for being whacked out. And here's Styles.'

I look out through the windshield. The evening is

getting darker now, and the city's dust haze is mingling with the gathering dusk. Some of the cars on the freeway over in the east already have their lights on.

'And so,' I say to Pete, 'Albert Styles is in town and in his pocket he has a contract on my brother.'

'Well,' Pete says, 'Christ, he's in town, after all.'

'And it's obvious, this great hit-man, this great asset to the organization, he's going to whack out my brother, after, of course, sending the department a note telling us all about it, just so's we'll know who to pick up. The only thing about it all that surprises me, Pete is that in the note Styles didn't tell us how he's going to carry out the contract, and where he's going to be afterwards, so that we don't have to waste time looking for him.' Now it's Pete's turn to be quiet for a while.

'Pete,' I tell him, 'I know you need the dough, and in one way, it's useful for the department to know that Styles is in town, but, seriously, in your heart of hearts, you know that no way could a hit- man like Styles be involved with a thing like this.'

'I guess you're right,' Pete says. 'Looking at it logically, that is. I agree, hit-men and politicians, they don't mix, but that's only so far. There's got to be a first time for everything. Now supposing –'

'Supposing you leave the speculative work to me, Pete, and just give me the details of what you've told me, and then I can go away and you can go away and I can get on with what I'm supposed to be doing.'

'Details?'

'Like if he's here yet, where he is, where he's going to be. Christ, Pete, you know, details.'

'I don't know no details, Mr Boldt,' Pete says. 'Jesus, you know better than to ask me if I know any details.'

'All right, all right,' I tell him. 'Just tell me this: is he here already, or not?'

Pete shakes his head.

'I don't know. My source don't know. All I know is, if he ain't here already, then he's going to be here inside of twenty-four hours.'

I don't say anything.

'Look,' Pete says. 'I can't tell you anything else. I mean, you know what I mean.'

'Yeah,' I say. 'But if he's here, or when he comes, he's going to have to be somewhere. Now can you tell me that, Pete?'

Pete shakes his head. 'I've told you what I know,' he says. 'There's no more I can tell you.'

'O.K.,' I say to him. 'That's fine. You've been a great help, Pete. From this point on, I've got no more worries. Everything's virtually sewn up. I'm going to get a promotion for this one, and believe me, I'll remember the part you played in the whole business, I really will. Now just run along, and when I get my share of the reward, I'll be in touch, O.K.?'

Pete turns to look at me and opens his mouth but before he can speak I say to him, 'that's all, Pete.'

His mouth stays open so I reach across him and open the door on his side of the car.

'That's the way out, Pete.'

Pete's mouth snaps shut then he shuffles along the seat and climbs out. He thinks about slamming the door then decides against it and closes it quietly, but what he does do is stick his head back in through the open window and he says, 'You're a bastard, Boldt, and I want you to know this: if I ever hear there's a contract out on you, then I'll find out who's going to carry it out, and I'll tell them to take the day off, and take the money, and I'll do the job for them, for free.'

I nod my head. Pete stays the way he is for a moment or two more, then jerks his head back through the window and walks off towards the bushes. I take out another cigarette and light it from the butt of the last one, then throw the butt out of the window. There is a faint rustling of leaves behind me and I look in the mirror. Pete Foley has gone.

The bar at the Chandler Hotel is altogether different at this time of the evening. The cocktail hour crowd is spilling into the pre-dinner crowd, which is being augmented by the crowd that don't bother about dinner at all. All the stools at the bar are occupied so I sit down in an empty booth and wait for Murdock to come down. I manage to grab a waiter who's working very hard at trying to avoid catching anybody's eye and I get him to bring me a vodka and while I'm waiting for that important event to happen my attention is focused on the girl I had the brush with earlier, in reception. My memory has done her no service, because she's even greater than the picture I've been carrying in my mind.

She's wearing different clothes, for one thing. Now she's dressed all in cheesecloth, white – a white sleeveless top and a long white skirt. The material is almost thin enough to see her underwear through it, but not quite, and the effect it has is to keep you looking, just in case. Tonight she's wearing her hair up, kind of Roman style, and that doesn't do her any harm either, because it shows off the grace of her long neck and although she's too far away from me to smell her perfume, I know it's going to smell fresh and innocent and at the same time be enough to have guys jumping out ten- storey windows.

While she's looking round for some place to sit, everybody else in the bar is looking at what she sits on and all the other places of her anatomy that provide some kind of equally interesting function. Now that interesting point about the situation is this: that all the stools at the bar are taken, and all the other booths except mine are crowded. Now no doubt she could make her way to the bar and there'd be seven or eight guys who'd not only be willing to give up their stools for her, they'd be prepared to rush out and get the tools and the wood and run up an extra stool if it came to that. Also, although the booths are crowded, there isn't one she couldn't squeeze into with one of the current occupants. But, as I say, mine is the only one with only me in it, and she looks round the bar and takes in all the situations, including mine, and then turns quickly, her body expressing the suddenness of her choice, and she makes for my booth. As she approaches there's no pretence in her face that she doesn't really take in the fact that it's me sitting here; in fact just the opposite, she looks me straight in the eye and resumes the expression she'd been wearing the last time we met. She slides into the booth, opposite me, and her perfume is precisely how I'd imagined it would be. This time the waiter's by the end of the booth almost before the cheesecloth hits the seat and she doesn't fuss, she just orders rum and coke and the waiter sprints off to fulfil the order.

Then the girl takes a pack of foreign cigarettes from her purse and lights one and as she blows out the smoke she says, 'You must have had a long hard day of it.'

I just carry on looking at her and not saying anything.

'I mean,' she goes on, 'it must be tiring, working at it all day, with nothing to show for it.' I still don't say anything.

'Or did you give a chambermaid a few dollars for a hand-job?'

I shake my head. 'No, the ones I approached were already booked. I can come back tomorrow, though, so they tell me.'

'That's good,' she says. 'That's something at least. But how are you going to hold out till then?' 'Oh, I'll manage,' I tell her. 'A few of the gay crowd get in here later in the evening. I should be able to make out with one of them.'

I guess you should,' she says, and leans back in her seat, smoking some more, and looking at me.

'You waiting for someone?' I ask her.

'There you go,' she says.

'Just interested,' I tell her. 'Just passing the time.'

'Sure.'

I shrug.

'Well, I'll tell you,'she says. 'It's none of your fucking business.'

'I agree,' I tell her. 'You're right.'

She nods and leans back in her seat again. The waiter comes back with her rum and coke and the ice cubes clink in the glass as he sets it down in front of her.

'Madam,' the waiter says, almost creaming his jockeys.

'What's this?' she asks.

'Madame?' he says.

She pings the glass with her fingers. 'What's this? In the glass?'

The waiter leans forward and picks up the glass and examines it every which way.

'I'm sorry, Madame,' the waiter replies. 'I can't see anything in the glass.'

'You can see those two white things floating about in there can't you? And that other thing?'

The waiter stares at the glass some more and creases up his brow even tighter, until it dawns on him. 'You mean the ice?'

'Yes,' she says. 'The ice. And the lemon. Did I ask for any of that crap?'

'Well, no, but –'

'Then why give it to me?'

'Well, because, in most cases …'

'I'm not most cases. Take it away and bring back a rum and coke and nothing else, right?'

'Madame,' the waiter says, and makes a big production out of turning on his heel.

'Hey,' I say to the waiter. He turns back again.

'Bring me a refill, will you? And don't worry, it's O.K. to put ice in mine.'

The waiter picks up my glass without a word and goes off again. The girl leans back in her side of the booth and we both look at each other for the time it takes the waiter to bring back the drinks. He sets them down and is away before he can get caught up in any further controversy. Then the girl breaks the staring, reaches for her glass and takes a drink.

'I guess that must be the first today,' I say to her.

She puts her drink down. 'You're funny,' she says. 'I'm surprised that your great sense of humour doesn't compensate for your general repulsiveness when you're trying to score.'

'You'd be surprised.'

'That I would,' she says, taking another drink.

'How come you don't like ice in your drink?' I ask her.

'Who says I don't?'

'O.K.,' I tell her. 'I get it.'

'No, come on,' she says. 'What makes you think I don't like ice in my drink? Somebody tell you that?'

'Oh, shit,' I say. 'Oh, Jesus.'

She leans back again and does some more staring at me.

'I'll tell you why I'm here,' she says.

I look at her, enquiringly.

'And the reason I'm going to tell you,' she says, 'is because this is a laugh, it really is, it'll kill you. Here I am, sharing a booth with you, you being the kind of guy you are, and my guy, the guy who should be here with me, he doesn't give a fuck about me, and he never will. If I'm around, that's fine, and if I'm not around, that's fine too. I mean, he's supposed to meet me here tonight, so he gets me to make all the arrangements, fix everything, and I come here from where I live and get here on time and get everything ready. When I've done that he calls, says maybe he won't be here for a couple of days, not till the day after tomorrow, at least, but I'm to wait. That's great, isn't it? But of course, I'll wait, the way I always do. And sometimes I let them, just to pass the time, and even if he knew it wouldn't worry him, whatever I did with them. And that's what I'm talking about, you understand. I mean you and half the guys in this room would dearly love a piece of my ass, and he, when he gets here, I can guarantee, the first thing he'll do is have a shower and then he'll sleep and after he's slept he'll have something to eat and after that, maybe, and only maybe, he'll notice me for maybe five, ten minutes, and after that it's like for him, as though it's never been, you know?'

'But not for you?'

'No,' she says. 'Not for me.'

I take a drink. 'Well,' I tell her, 'maybe you'll not be interested in any more Mr Wonderfuls after this guy.'

'There won't be any more guys,' she says. 'Only people like you.'

I let that one pass.

'I take it he's married,' I say to her.

'What else?' she says.

'What's his story?'

'I thought I was clear about him,' she answers. 'He doesn't care about me enough to have to invent any stories. And besides, he's separated. His wife and kid live in this town and he's due a week with the kid so he decided he'll spend it here, would you believe?'

'It's a great little town,' I tell her. 'All heart and folks are just folks.'

'And so I get to spend the next five days in the company of his brat, which will help things along fine.'

'How old's the kid?' I ask her. 'About your age?'

She sneers at me but the sneer doesn't quite work because there are two small spots of red on either cheek.

'I'm twenty-two,' she says.

'Sure.'

'Oh, fuck off,' she says. 'Let's have another drink.'

The waiter who served us before is passing by, but he doesn't want any more of the same treatment so he avoids my eye. While I'm looking for another waiter the girl says, 'Oh, for Christ's sake. I'm pissed off with this bar. There's enough booze in my suite to float a convention. Let's go drink up there.'

I stop what I'm doing and turn and look at her. She sneers back at me and says, 'What's wrong, did I put you in shock?'

I don't reply.

'Come on,' she says. 'Christ, all you've been thinking the last ten minutes is what kind of percentage you've got.'

'You think so?'

She laughs. 'Christ,' she says. 'You're really funny, you really are.' I glance at my watch, hoping she won't notice, but she does.

'What's the matter? The old lady got the meat loaf ready?' I don't answer.

She gets up, saying, 'Don't worry about it. It probably won't take long.'

Then she slides out of the booth and begins to walk towards the exit. I get up and follow her and our progress is followed by the eyes of all the guys in the house. She walks across the foyer towards the lift and I follow after her in the slipstream of her perfume, like somebody under hypnosis. She gets into the lift and the jockey presses the button. I follow after her and the jockey says, 'Plaza Suite, Miss?'

The girl leans against the lift wall, closes her eyes and nods and begins to sing to herself, a Dionne Warwick number.

The jockey turns to me, 'Which floor, sir?' 'Plaza Suite,' I tell him.

The jockey keeps his face carefully blank and that's more effective than if he'd winked and given me the double O with his fingers. The lift door slides shut and the ascent begins. For once it has no effect on my stomach, which has been weightless and queasy since I left the booth.

The lift stops, the door slides open and the girl is still leaning against the wall humming her song.

The jockey and me look at each other without expression and then the girl finishes her song, opens her eyes and looks at the pair of us as if she's never seen us before, then detaches herself from the wall and floats out of the lift. I follow behind her again and behind me there is a pause before the lift door closes.

The entrance to the Plaza Suite is directly opposite the lift. The girl opens her purse, finds her key and inserts it in the lock. She flicks her wrist and the door swings open. She goes in and I follow her. My immediate thought is that the guy she's been talking about is worth hanging around for.

Apart from anything else he's got to offer, he's certainly got the bread to keep her in the manner to which she probably thinks she's accustomed if he can afford to hire a layout like the one I've just walked into, and not even be there himself to enjoy it. Everything's the way you'd expect it to be in a layout that calls itself the Plaza Suite. It makes the rest of the hotel look a flophouse in comparison. The carpets are white and the pile comes up to my shoulder holster. Most of the furniture is white too, white leather, and the drapes must have cost as much as the carpet, because they match exactly, made of some shimmery, glowing material that I've never seen anywhere else before. In this first part of the suite, there is a sunken area in the middle of the room, sunk just deep enough to accommodate a built-in white leather divan that goes round all four sides of the sunken area except for two breaks where the steps go. In the centre of this sunken area is a glass cube which passes for a table and on top of this are as big a selection of drinks as you'd find in any particularly well-stocked saloon. The neat thing about the glass cube is that set in the table top there is a rectangular compartment filled with ice and in this compartment there are two or three bottles of good-looking champagne. The girl walks down the steps and over to the glass table. She takes a bottle of champagne from the ice recess and I stand on the edge of the sunken area, watching her as she turns two glasses right side up and then holds the bottle to her in an uncorking position, but before she goes to work on it she looks up at me.

'Come on in,' she says. 'The water's fine.'

'I haven't brought my bathing shorts,' I say to her.

'Then swim in the buff,' she says. 'I always do.'

She pops the cork and the white froth spurts out all over the carpet.

'I'm old-fashioned,' I tell her. 'I never swim in the buff unless I've been introduced.'

'You're old-fashioned, that's for sure,' she says, pouring the champagne. 'But my name's Lesley, just for the record. What's yours: Friday?'

'Depends on what day it is,' I tell her, as I go down the steps. She picks up the two glasses and offers one to me and we look at each other and then we drink, still looking at each other. I take my glass from my lips and it's still three-quarters full but she doesn't stop until her glass is empty, and then she fills it right up to the top again.

'Would you say you were on or off duty?' she says, after she's taken another drink.

'Why does that matter?' I ask her.

'You could be a vice cop.'

'I could,' I agree. 'But I'll make a deal with you: if you start getting close to committing a criminal offence, I'll tell you the way you can keep out of trouble.'

'That's great,' she says, 'because, say for instance, if I was a cocksucker, you could bust me for it, couldn't you? If I was to go to work, you could take me downtown, right? You could be one of those guys who makes like a hustler and then snaps up and takes the poor stud downtown.'

'I could be,' I tell her. 'That could be my job, hanging around here all day, looking out for possible cocksuckers.'

'That's what I figured,' she says. 'It's obvious; they chose you for your good looks and incredible magnetic attraction.'

'Right,' I tell her, and I begin to move in but she makes a neat turn away from me and walks up the steps on the other side of the sunken area, over to the stereo unit that's hiding behind a sliding inlaid door set in one of the walls. She presses the button and a Carpenters record drops onto the turntable.

'Normally that would be your move,' she says. 'But this is different, isn't it?'

'I guess so,' I say, and pour some more champagne into my glass. I'm swearing at myself for not being able to figure out whether this is a put-on or whether she's going to come across, but it's the kind of situation that the longer it goes on the less able you are to make a decision to quit. It's like losing at gambling, or sweating it out in a parked car on your first-time date with a particular girl, not giving up after the twentieth refusal just in case you're twenty-fifth time lucky. And at the same time, it's like one of those dreams where all the events lead up to something happening but the dreamer himself wakes up before the events draw to their expected conclusion.

Now she moves across to the picture window that runs the entire length of one wall and she goes through the part that's already been slid open out on to the broad patio that's complete with a barbecue outfit and small pool and enough nicely arranged creeping plants to dress a Universal jungle movie. I climb the steps of the sunken area, cross the room and walk out on to the flagged patio. She is sitting on the retaining wall, her back to the darkening sky, the lights of the city winking below. It gives me the creeps to see her there, leaning back a little too far, but I know there's no use in mentioning it, in fact probably the only thing I'd achieve is that she'd lean back even farther and put an end to a beautiful friendship. So I walk over to the wall and sit on the edge too and look out over the city. I'm looking at it from exactly the opposite angle to the view I had of it in Draper's office, but that doesn't make any difference, it still looks exactly the same.

'So,' the girl says, 'you're a cop. Why are you a cop?'

'I joined young,' I tell her.

'You could have left young.'

I shrug. 'Not that it's a particularly fascinating subject, but in those days, I liked the work.'

'And these days?'

'These days I like only the fringe benefits.'

'Those you can get,' she says, sliding off the wall and walking alongside it, then stopping to turn and look out over the city.

'You ever kill anybody?'

'Not recently.'

'How many? How many people you kill?'

'Four.'

'Why? They didn't give you any choice? It was them or you? Or did you shoot them when they were running away, the way you read in the paper every day?'

'Two of them were under ten and the other two were seventy-year-old cripples. O.K.?'

She smiles at the view then turns away and crosses the patio back into the suite. I shake my head, because there's nothing for me to do but go in after her and by the time I've done that she's back to work on the champagne. When she's filled her glass she walks up the steps and moves towards me and when she gets to me she puts her arms round my neck, still holding her glass of champagne, and puts her face to mine and kisses me.

When she's done that she pulls back slightly and looks at me, laughing. 'Your face,' she says. 'You should see it, you really should.'

Then we kiss again and the champagne glass falls from her fingers, hitting the carpet with a soft thud. This time the kiss lasts longer and one of her hands slides round on to my chest, moves down and unbuttons my jacket and slips inside. The next thing I know she's jerked my gun from my holster. She pulls back and, holding in both hands, points it straight at my chest. Then she looks into my eyes and smiles at me.

'O.K., copper,' she says. 'Come and get me.'

I take a sip of my champagne, then walk down the steps of the sunken area and wearily begin to sit on the leather divan but the sound of the hammer being pulled back makes me stop in mid- movement.

'You've known me less than an hour,' she says. 'How do you know what I may or may not do?'

I straighten up again.

'O.K.,' I tell her, 'you got a point. Now, what do I do? Reach, grab air, pull down some sky, however you care to phrase it?'

'Just move into the bedroom.'

'O.K.,' I tell her, 'I'll move into the bedroom. Only, how about telling me where it is?'

She indicates some double doors over on the far side of the room.

'Is it O.K. for me to bring my drink along?' I ask.

'Sure,' she replies. 'And bring the bottle as well.'

I pick the bottle out of the ice and with the bottle in one hand and the glass in the other I walk up the steps again and over to the double doors.

'This is great,' she says, 'I really like this game.'

I reach the double doors and put the bottle down while I open them, wondering what the percentages are of taking a cocked revolver off a half-cocked girl. I decided that right now I don't really want to put them to the test because after all, the kid's only fooling, I tell myself. But even if she's only fooling, she just has to trip on the hem of her skirt or stumble against a low table and it's Hello and Goodbye so I say to her, 'The only thing is, like you say, you're enjoying this game, and it'd be a pity, don't you think, if the game was over before it started? Like if that gun went off accidentally, if you stumbled or something like that.' Her face loses its smile and a cold hard look snaps into place.

'If this goes off, it won't be an accident.'

We look at each other for a moment or two and then her expression changes completely and she throws her head back and laughs. When she's done that, she says, 'How was I? Good?'

'You were fair,' I tell her.

'Would you say I was more Barbara Stanwyck, or did I veer towards Joan Crawford?'

I shake my head and go through the doors into the bedroom. Bedroom is a misnomer because although it has a bed in it, the room has just about everything else that the magazines consider necessary for gracious living, and it's all the very best of everything, in a setting that seems even bigger than the layout back beyond the double doors, in fact the bed itself seems about as big as the entire layout of my own apartment.

'Now,' I say to her, 'if I keep moving in the direction I'm going, that means I'll end up by the bed, and I want to know, does that mean the gun's likely to go off if I do that?'

'This is a game,' she says. 'You only find out what happens when it happens. So keep moving.'

So I keep moving until I get to the bed, and it's one of those affairs that has all sorts of nice little labour-saving gadgets built into the head and spreading out on either side. One of the built-on pieces is in the form of a table so I put the champagne bottle down and turn round to face the girl. She's still pointing the gun at me and very carefully, holding the gun very steady, she slides on to the bed and gets herself into a kneeling position bolt upright, the gun still cocked and in her hands, her hands in her lap. The Carpenters tape stops for a moment while the stereo changes tracks and the bedroom is quiet and still, the loudest sounds those of the bubbles in my champagne glass as I raise it to my mouth.

'How are you finding the champagne?' she asks.

'Fine,' I tell her. 'It's good champagne.'

'You'd know, would you?'

I just look at her.

'O.K.,' she says, 'take your pants off.'

I look at her some more and she sighs.

'I know I said it right,' she says. 'And I know you heard. So do it. Take off your pants.'

As she speaks the last sentence she wobbles to one side slightly and has to release one hand from the gun to steady herself on the silk counterpane. The gun slips slightly and I blink involuntarily in case her movement's all it needs to set off the hammer, but she straightens up and takes the gun in both hands again, saying, 'Come on, do it. This is the way this game's played.'

I look at her for a moment or two, then I unbuckle my belt, unzip and step out of my pants.

'Throw them on the bed.' I throw them on the bed. 'Turn around,' she says.

I turn around. From behind me I hear the sound of her pulling my pants to her, and then there's the clink of my handcuffs as, if I'm guessing rightly, she's releasing them from my belt. So it occurs to me, if she's doing that, then she's no longer holding the gun, therefore I turn round and find that I'm right; the gun's lying on the bed next to her, and that being the case the first thing I do is to pick the gun off the counterpane and uncock it and put it back in my holster.

'Oh, Christ,' she says, as if she's about to burst into tears. 'Christ. Now you've spoilt everything. Now everything's going to be ordinary.'

Now what is going on inside me can be divided into separate parts: one part is full of rage, anger at my being her fall-guy for the last half an hour, urging me to smack her around a little just to show her how I feel, and the other part is the way I feel about her, the fact that here is this girl, this fantastic girl, kneeling on the bed in front of me, and the things I want to do to her are pulling me in a direction I want to follow.

'Oh, shit,' she wails. 'That could really have been good, it really could.'

Then it breaks and the next thing I know I've stripped off my coat, fallen next to her on the bed and pushed her down beside me. Her clothes are so flimsy and easy that it takes no time at all for me to pull them off her and then when she's naked I make love to her with an almost clinical fury. When I finally enter her, after this furious preamble, she seems to have given herself entirely, insofar as she is totally wild as a result of my attentions, as wild as I wanted to make her, completely loose, her body describing with its motions the effect I'm having on her, and my entry is sublime, a perfection. Even when I'm fully inside her it's as if she wants to turn herself inside out to make more room for me, and we thrust at each other, our sweat soaking the silken counterpane, slipping and sliding towards our separate orgasms, and when they happen, I feel breathless at the release, the way the final shudder seems to last even longer than what's led up to it. When I'm finally spent it's not like with other women, I don't immediately feel the soft flaccid ache and want to withdraw straight away, separating myself from the flesh I've just used; I want to stay the way I am, remain inside her, bask in her inner heat, smell the salty sweat mixed with the perfume that now has a coarser smell, but I'm not allowed to do this because almost immediately after her final shudder she wriggles herself off me and, grimacing, slides from under me off the bed. Picking her blouse and her pants off the bed she walks across the room to a door and goes through it, then I hear the sound of water filling a bath tub. Then she reappears still naked, still carrying the two wispy items of clothing, and she crosses the room again and disappears out of sight through the double doors.

I sit up and swing my legs over the side of the bed and

begin to get dressed and while I'm doing that I hear the sound of a fresh bottle of champagne being popped out in the other room.

When I'm dressed I walk over to the bathroom and go in. Like the rest of the suite, the bathroom is enormous and like the area in the first room the bath is sunk into the floor with steps leading down into the water, the brilliant turquoise of the tiles shimmering through the water's surface and illuminating the room with different shades of green.

The bath is almost full now so I bend down and turn off the gold-plated taps and there is silence again. I go over to the wash basin and turn on the taps and look at myself in the mirror above, but I don't stare into my eyes for more than a moment. I wash my hands and face, then I comb my hair and button up my coat and walk out of the bathroom, across the bedroom and through the double doorway.

The girl is on the divan in the sunken area, drinking her fresh champagne and looking straight ahead of her. She's now wearing her blouse and her pants and she's half sitting, half sprawling, her legs thrown straight out in front of her and even though I've just made love to her, looking at her like that makes me feel like starting all over again. But that is a thought entertained only by myself.

I walk down the steps, turn a new glass right side up, pour in some champagne and take a drink. There is a long silence and finally she says, 'Like I said earlier, after him, there aren't any other guys.'

I finish the rest of the champagne and put the glass back on the transparent table.

'Well,' I say, 'I guess that takes care of everything.'

'You're damned right it does,' she says. 'You should be able to remember where you came in.'

'I guess so,' I say, and walk up the steps, across the room and out.

Outside I cross the hall and push for the lift. When the doors open it's the same jockey with the same dead-pan expression. I get in and he looks at me and says, 'Going down?' 'The lobby,' I tell him.

'The lobby it is,' he says, pushes the button and the lift begins to drop.

* * *

Murdock is already in the bar when I get in there again. The crowd has thinned out a little now, and Murdock is sitting alone in one of the booths, but I pretend not to notice him and go straight over to the bar and sit on a stool. The bartender is not the same one that was on this morning but even so, when he approaches to take my order he lets it show in his face that he knows I'm a cop and that means a stool being used up that isn't bringing him in commission. When Murdock joins me on the next stool the bartender's expression is doubled in spades. But all the same, he can only take our order, and when he's done that, Murdock says to me, 'You walked in as if you were still asleep. You O.K.?'

'Sure, I'm fine. How's the suite?'

'It's great,' Murdock says. 'You should see it. I'm never going to go back home again.'

'That's fine.'

The bartender returns with our drinks. Murdock asks again, 'You sure you're O.K.?'

'Look, I told you, I'm fine. What's the matter with you, you trying to scare the shit out of me so that maybe I should step up my insurance or something?'

'No,' he says, 'but you look as if you've just been screwing or something.'

'Piss off,' I tell him. 'At this time of the evening?'

'That's what it is,' Murdock says. 'You've been screwing. Since when has the time of day bothered you?'

'Piss off, George.'

'Come on,' he says. 'That's it, you bastard. I should know the signs by now. You've been sticking it up somebody.'

I pour some of my drink into me.

'Christ,' Murdock says, 'you really make out, don't you?'

'Yeah, I really make out.'

'I mean, I don't want to drag up things too much, the past, but Christ, it's not exactly surprising that you and Barbara went your separate ways. I mean, I never knew such a guy, even when you were married.'

I take another drink.

'That's right,' I tell him. 'I'm a great character. Everybody knows it.'

'Even when –'

'Look George,' I tell him, 'The point's been made, O.K.?' It's Murdock's turn to take a drink.

'Sure,' he says, 'anything you say.'

I light a cigarette.

'Look, forget it, George,' I tell him. 'I didn't mean anything. I'm tired, that's all.'

'It's all right,' Murdock says.

There is another silence and Murdock takes out his own cigarettes and lights one. When he's done that I say to him, 'I had a call from Foley earlier.'

'Yeah?'

'Yeah. He had some news for me. He told me Albert Styles is due in town, if he's not here already.'

Murdock thinks about that for a moment or two.

'Who in Christ could he be interested in? I mean, don't tell me Florian's been bucking the Organization.'

'Not a chance.'

'One of Florian's boys, then?'

'Florian would see to that himself. He doesn't have to pay out the kind of money Styles works for.'

Murdock thinks some more.

'It could be Florian. For instance, he doesn't have to be out of line; maybe some uncle has some nephew he wants to promote.'

'Then if Florian was whacked out the uncle and the nephew would be whacked out by the Organization. You know that, and so would they. Plus Styles is a very careful guy; he'd make sure he wasn't into anything he could put himself on a spot for.'

'Yeah, I know,' Murdock says. 'So why?'

'Well, Pete put it to me that maybe he was coming to town to hit my brother.'

Murdock laughs.

'Yeah,' I say.

Murdock shakes his head.

'That guy,' he says, then he signals the bartender and orders two more drinks, and after the bartender's delivered them, Murdock says, 'Still, if Styles is around, there has to be a reason. So what do we do, hand over the information to Draper?'

'I guess so. Only thing is, though, if Styles is here, say, at Florian's invitation, for some reason we can't figure, then Draper very possibly knows about the deal already, right?'

'If Florian wanted Styles free to operate, maybe. But then Styles doesn't need that kind of assistance. He's never needed it so far.'

'I guess so,' I say. 'But, shit, if Draper does know, that's fine, but if he doesn't, Christ, let somebody else tell him. He told us how we were to spend our time over the next week, so fuck him, let his other little helpers find out and pass on the good news.'

Murdock thinks about that for a while.

'I don't know,' he says. 'Maybe we should do like Draper said. I mean, he told us, didn't he, anything at all, anything we came up with, go after. Now naturally there's no way that Albert Styles is coming here to hit your brother, it just ain't right, but he's coming, and Draper's going to be jumping up and down on the ceiling if he finds out and we haven't gone after him. And anyway, suppose Florian doesn't know; then Draper doesn't know. Hell, we've got to pass it on.'

'Maybe he's just passing through. And maybe he's not coming at all and Pete's just trying to put a little by for his old age.'

'Pete didn't say where Styles would be?'

I shake my head.

'Then we ought to ask Pete again,' Murdock says. 'At least we ought to get somebody to talk to him.'

'O.K., O.K.,' I tell him. 'We'll go and talk to Pete. Whatever you say.'

'You know I'm right,' Murdock says. 'If we didn't follow this up and Draper doesn't know about Styles and he finds out then we'd be getting our uniforms out of the attic.'

'That wouldn't worry me any,' I tell him. 'Draper can have my badge any day he wants and he knows it. He knows I don't give a shit and that's what sticks in his throat: there's nothing bad enough he can do to me, he knows I'd stuff my badge right down as far as his shoes.'

'I know,' Murdock says. 'That's one area where I envy you, like where I have to work my time, because of my situation, you've got nothing anchoring you; where I sway with the breeze, you, you could blow your nose on Draper's tie and enjoy the memory of it.'

'Hey, bartender,' I call, 'two more, will you. Yeah, you're damned right, I'm in a good position, I don't have to take any crap from Draper. That's why I don't give a fuck about seeing Pete Foley or running Styles out of town or –'

'Or finding out who's out to get your brother,' Murdock says.

'George,' I say to him, 'I know I got a couple of drinks

inside me, but I still get the general aim of remarks like that one, you understand?'

'O.K.,' Murdock says. 'I didn't mean anything. It just seems, even though you …'

'You know nothing about it, George, and you never will. I'm the only guy who's an expert on that subject, O.K.?'

The bartender brings two more drinks and we sit there in silence for a while. Eventually George says, 'Where's Pete most likely to be tonight?'

I shrug.

'That bastard could be anywhere. What we could do is go to a few places and ask around if he isn't there. What do you say to that, George? How does that plan grab you?'

'That's fine with me,' Murdock says, draining his glass. 'Why don't we do that?'

I smile to myself and reach for my glass and that is how we spend the rest of the night, going round places, looking for Pete Foley. But on this particular night, it transpires that Pete is nowhere to be found, and it takes about a dozen places and four or five hours and various drinks to come to that conclusion, and by that time I also conclude by default that it's time for me to go home. On the way back, it comes over the car radio that a couple of kids have tried holding up a liquor store and get away with around four hundred dollars, having shot and killed the owner's wife in the process, but we keep on heading for my apartment, because that little event is no concern of Murdock and me.

At least, that's where I thought we were heading, back to my apartment, but when I open my eyes to the morning light I find I'm staring at a different ceiling from the one in my own place, a ceiling all bright and fresh painted. As my eyes are taking in this surprising aspect, I become aware that the sounds of the morning are wrong, too, they're different from the ones I usually take for granted. I jerk myself upright and look round at my surroundings and I'm in a very nice, very spacious, very sunny double bedroom and the first thing I realize is that the paintwork is the same colour as the paintwork in the Plaza Suite.

I look across at the other bed and it's been slept in. While I'm taking that in, the headache, that's been waiting in the wings of my temples, swoops into the centre of my forehead and rocks me back, so I swing my legs over the edge of the bed and stand up, working on the assumption that if I move about I might shake the headache back where it came from. This, of course, is sheer optimism on my part because the headache hammers away even harder while I'm standing by the bed. I move away from the side of the bed and as I do that, I notice my suit and shirt, neatly laid out on the back of a chair over by the window so I go over to the chair and pick up my pants and put them on and go over to the bedroom door and open it and I'm presented with the sight of a spacious reception room. In the centre of this George Murdock is sitting on a divan, in front of him a low table, and on the table is a breakfast tray with eggs, bacon, toast, coffee, everything, and George is totally absorbed in working his way through what's on the tray, a napkin tucked neatly in his collar.

I stand in the doorway for a moment or two and if Murdock knows I'm there he doesn't make any sign, he just carries on with his work, so eventually I say to him, 'Nice looking breakfast, George. At least, from what you have on your chin, it looks nice.'

Murdock doesn't look up as he fills his mouth with some more eggs and bacon.

'Right,' he says. 'You'd also have liked the room service that brought it, if you'd been awake.'

'What makes you think I'm awake?' I ask him.

'By the way,' Murdock says, 'I meant to tell you, the booze is over there.'

'You could have let me find it myself,' I tell him. 'You could have left me that.'

Murdock grins and I go over to where the drinks are and pour some vodka into a glass; then I go over to the table where Murdock's eating, pick up a jug of fresh orange juice and fill up my glass. Murdock goes to work on his toast and I go over to the window and look out on the shining morn, thinking of the night before, the way I can't get the images of the girl Lesley out of my mind's eye, the memory of the defeat from my thoughts, and, most of all, how I'd like to go right on back up there and set the record straight. While I'm thinking that Murdock pours himself some coffee, then sits back and wipes his mouth with his napkin.

'Well,' he says, 'like they always say, start the day right, and it stays right.'

'Yeah,' I agree, and take another drink of my vodka.

'We going in to see Draper?' Murdock asks.

'Why should we?' I tell him. 'When we've got something to tell him, we'll go in and see him.'

'So what, then?'

'Like yesterday, we carry on sniffing the way Draper wants us to do. What else can we do?'

'We can't do anything else.'

'Right,' I tell him. 'But first, I'm going to take advantage of this set-up I kindly dropped you into. Where's the bathroom?'

'Right ahead of you.'

'You got a clean shirt I could have, George?'

'In the closet, in the bedroom.'

'Fine.'

In the bathroom I fill the tub and get in and I can't get out of my head the picture of the empty sunken bath up in Lesley's suite, the green water undulating very slightly, waiting. And then after my exit, and the words she spoke before I left.

After I'm dry and half dressed I go back into the room where Murdock is, and he's standing by the door, wearing his hat and coat.

'I'm going to get a paper and a pack of cigarettes. I'll wait in the lobby.'

I nod and Murdock goes out. I carry on back towards the bathroom and as I cross the carpet there's another small table on which there's a telephone. I stop and pick up the receiver and wait until I get the switchboard and then I ask to be put through to the Plaza Suite. When the receiver at the other end is lifted I hear her voice before she puts her mouth close to the phone and she's talking in a happy fashion to somebody who's in the room with her. The way she's talking it can only be the guy she's been telling me about so when she finally says 'Hello' I put the receiver down. I carry on back to the bedroom and find Murdock's shirt and his electric shaver and when I'm shaved and fully dressed I phone room service and order some scrambled eggs and fresh coffee. While I'm waiting for that to arrive I pour another drink and try not to think of the evening before.

When I've breakfasted I go downstairs and find Murdock in the lobby, sitting on one of the divans, smoking, his unopened newspaper beside him, and when I get out of the elevator he watches me walk all the way over to where he's sitting. When I get there I don't bother to sit down. 'O.K.?' I say to him.

'You better sit down,' he tells me.

'Why?'

'Sit down and I'll tell you.'

I sit down.

'Styles is here,' Murdock says.

I look at him.

'In this hotel,' Murdock says. 'He checked in ten minutes ago. A whole flock of suitcases.'

I light a cigarette and when I've done that I say to

Murdock, 'You sure about this?' 'Yeah, I'm sure. But if you don't think I'm sure –'

'O.K., you're sure.'

Neither of us says anything for a minute or two.

'So,' I say eventually, 'Styles is here, in this hotel, but why should we care about that? We knew he was coming to town, and he had to stay somewhere, so he stays here. He's not exactly coming in by the back door, is he? What did he register under?'

'His own name.'

'So he can't be here on business, can he? Styles is protected, sure, but even he doesn't advertise any more than he has to.'

Murdock doesn't answer.

'Well, come on George, what do you think?'

'I don't know what I think,' Murdock says. 'All I think is, Styles being in town, it stinks. He doesn't come to a town like this to see the sights.'

I'm just about to remind him that in any case, it doesn't matter a fuck to us because all we have to do is pass it on when Murdock raises his hand slightly and says, 'The Hitman cometh.'

I hear the elevator doors open but I don't turn my head. Murdock shakes another cigarette from his pack and I wait for Styles to pass by, aware of his approach, but crazily this is not uppermost in my mind. My senses are being disturbed by a different presence that makes itself felt in concert with Styles's passing, and that presence is cloaked in the perfume I've been trying to forget ever since I woke up. As Styles goes past us I look up, and holding on to his arm is Lesley, pressing as close to him as she can and still keep on walking. I watch them all the way over to the glass doors. The guy in the livery steps forward and opens a door for them but only Styles is going out, because the two of them stop and Lesley kisses Styles on the cheek, squeezing the arm she's hanging on to as though there's never going to be a next time, and while that's happening I notice that Styles, with his free hand, is carrying a bunch of gaily wrapped parcels, all strung together. Then Lesley finally lets go of the arm and Styles goes through the door saying something to the liveried guy that makes the liveried guy stick his arm up for a cab. Lesley turns away and begins to walk back towards the elevator, which means passing me again. This time I'm on my feet, but as she approaches me she looks into my face as if she's never seen me before, a frightening blankness in her eyes. She can either stop or go round me and as she starts to go round me I say to her, 'So that's Mr Wonderful.'

She stops and looks at me.

'That's right,' she says. 'Now you can see why there's no comparison.'

Then she carries on towards the elevator. Murdock stands up. 'What the hell is going on?' I don't answer him. I just watch the elevator doors close on Lesley.

'What are you trying to do?' Murdock asks.

'Nothing,' I tell him. 'Come on, let's go and tell Draper, Styles is here, then for Christ's sake maybe we won't have to think about the fuck any more, O.K.?'

Murdock just looks at me and says nothing. I turn away and walk over to the glass doors, Murdock following and the guy in the livery does his work.

On the way over to the building Murdock and me don't say anything, in fact the only words we say before we see Draper is when we're in the lift, when I ask Murdock to give me a cigarette.

Draper, as usual, looks as though he's just about to host a T.V. show; his shirt looks as though it's just been broken out of its cellophane, his suit like he just had it sent over from the tailor's. He's sitting behind the clear expanse of his desk as if the neatness of the desk top and the elegance of his pose are sufficient to justify his existence.

'Well now,' he says when the two of us go through the door, 'could this mean good news or could it mean bad?'

'Depends on your point of view,' I tell him.

'And what's your point of view?' Draper says.

'I haven't got one. The information we have's got nothing to do with our detail.' 'Well?'

'I don't know whether or not you already know, but Albert Styles is paying a visit to our fair city.'

Draper stares at me, his face expressionless. He doesn't speak for a while and then he says,

'When did you find out?'

'A half an hour ago, maybe.'

Draper leans back in his seat.

'And this has got nothing to do with your investigation?' he queries.

'Oh, sure,' I tell him. 'He sends us a note and then he

books a suite in the second biggest hotel in the city.'

Draper gets up out of his seat, comes round to my side of the desk and stands a foot or so in front of me.

'Jesus Christ,' he says. 'I thought you were supposed to be a cop.'

I let that one pass.

'I suppose it occurred to you that maybe the note has got nothing to do with Styles, that maybe he could be contracted to some little group that wants your brother out of politics for good, that the fucking note is from a different source, and that Styles isn't lying low because he doesn't have to, not until after the hit. Chris, nobody's got anything on Styles, and he's the kind of guy that likes rubbing noses in that fact. And he's such a pro that it gives him a great deal of pleasure to walk in and out of a place without anything sticking to him.'

'Yeah, and his speciality is whacking out politicians,' I drawl.

'Listen,' Draper says. 'You got to take this seriously. If Styles is here, we've got to look after him. Christ, if he's here to make a hit, and it's your fuck of a brother, then it'd be really great for all of us, wouldn't it?'

'He's here to see his wife and kid, that's why he's here.'

I feel Murdock take an interest in what I've just said and Draper says, 'What are you talking about?'

'Styles has a wife and kid. Or at least had a wife. He's separated. She lives in this city. Even hit- men get married and get separated, love their kids. It's his time to see his kid. That's why he's here.'

'Florian would be touched, he really would,' Draper says, 'to know that Styles is in town, but it's O.K., Boldt figures it's only a sentimental journey. Just out of interest, where do you get all this information about the private life of Albert Styles?'

'Does it matter?' I ask him.

Draper looks at me for a moment or two then he turns away, walks over to his desk, then turns back again and leans on the desk edge.

'All right,' he says. 'But what does matter is this; I want Styles out of this city before your brother's in. I don't care how. But that's what I want.'

'Maybe Mr Florian could help us on that one,' I say to him. 'I mean, when he finds out he's here.'

Draper steps forward again, even closer this time.

'Don't push it, Boldt,' he says. 'Don't push by going too deep into those things.'

I shrug. 'So now we devote our time to Styles?' I say to him.

'Until he's out, yes. And don't take long. Whoever sent that letter can still write.'

Murdock and I leave Draper's office and while we're going down in the elevator Murdock remarks, 'I may be a lousy cop, but I guess I can figure out your source of information.'

'Yeah, you may be a lousy cop,' I tell him.

When we get downstairs, I check on the cab company and a quarter of an hour later I have the address where Styles was dropped, 1418 Glendale Avenue. So with that little piece of information Murdock and I get back in the car and drive east on Beacon for twenty minutes or so and then we're on Glendale Avenue, looking out for number 1418.

Glendale Avenue is a nice part of town, if you like the kind of dead life the rising young executives and their families like, if you like the neat lawns and the ranch-style houses and the freshly painted mail boxes. On Glendale Avenue even the dust seems neater than in any other part of town.

Number 1418 is on the left-hand side of the avenue, no different to all the rest, just as neat, just as antiseptic looking. Murdock parks the car and we get out, cross the empty street and walk up the path. On the lawn there are some kid's toys, a bike, a baseball bat.

We climb the steps to the front door and Murdock rings the bell; musical chimes echo inside the house and then Glendale Avenue is quiet again. We wait a few moments and then Murdock pushes the bell again. While he's doing that there is a shadow behind the frosted glass and then the door is opened and we're facing the ex-wife of Albert Styles. She's around thirty years old and she looks as if there's been some colour in her family tree at some time or another. The way she looks at us she doesn't need to see our badges to know what we want. We all look at each other for a moment or two and then she says, 'I wondered if you guys'd be around.'

'We'd like to talk to you,' Murdock says.

'We'd like to ask a few questions,' I say to her.

'Sure,' she says, turning away from the door. 'Whatever you say.'

We go through the door, close it behind us and follow her across the hall into a large living room. As she goes through the door she says, 'I told him. I said, "If you come here, they'll be on your neck, bound to be. Why don't you have Pauly come and stay with you?" But he said no, he wanted to come here, it would suit him.'

She goes over to the divan, sits down and takes a cigarette out of a box on the table in front of the divan. Murdock and I sit down in chairs opposite her. When she's lit her cigarette she says, 'But I knew you'd be around.'

'Mrs Styles –'

'The name's Burnett. Mrs Barbara Burnett. I'm a widow; that's how I'm known round here.'

'O.K.,' I tell her. 'Mrs Burnett. How long have you been parted from your husband?'

'You mean did I ever know what he did while I was married to him? Did I know him when there was all that stuff in the papers where nobody could prove he's knocked over some guys but everybody said he did it anyhow?' She shakes her head. 'When I knew him he was a runner. A bagman. That's what he was when I knew him.'

'And now? Do you believe what they all say, even though it couldn't be proved?'

'Well,' she says. 'I'll tell you. I always knew what he was, that he was in the rackets. But now, he's out with my boy, and that boy is my life, so do you think I'd let that be if I thought what everybody said was right?'

I shrug.

'Everything's possible,' I tell her.

'It sure as hell is,' she says.

There is a silence.

'So why did you separate?' Murdock asks.

'That's not really any of your business,' she says, 'but I don't mind telling you. We didn't officially. He just went away. He left me a lot of money and a note and he went away. And since then he sends me money every quarter, plenty of money, more than I really need. So I live here, in this nice house, with my kid. And that's all.'

'Why did he leave?'

'Does it matter?'

I don't say anything.

'Well, it wasn't because of another woman, that's for sure. In a way I wish it had been. But it wasn't. I guess he just got tired of me, that's all. Not even that; you have to feel something for somebody before that feeling wears out.'

'And you didn't re-marry?'

'No,' she says. 'Nobody else came along, at least nobody who could take his place.'

'You make him sound like a fish on a slab and then say nobody could take his place,' Murdock says. 'I mean, which is it?'

The woman shakes her head and begins to answer but I don't want to hear another description of the charms of Albert Styles so I break in. 'We're wasting time. Where's Styles now?'

'What do you want him for?'

'Like you said earlier that's not really any of your business.'

She stubs her cigarette out in a cut-glass ash-tray.

'Jesus,' she says. 'The kid's only been with him an hour.'

Murdock and I don't respond. Styles's ex-wife leans back on the divan.

'The zoo,' she says. 'He's taken him to the zoo. Then they're going to eat at the restaurant there.'

I stand up and so does Murdock.

'What about Pauly?' she says.

'What makes you think we're going to take Styles downtown?' Now it's her turn to say nothing.

Murdock says, 'If we have to talk some place else, your boy'll be looked after.'

'Sure,' she says.

Murdock and I turn to go out of the room but before we can get to the door Styles's ex-wife says, 'Oh, by the way.'

We stop and turn back to look at her. For a moment she does nothing, then very deliberately she leans forward and spits on the carpet in front of us, and when she's done that she settles back into her previous position, looking at us all the time.

She doesn't speak. Murdock and I turn away again and go out of the house into the sunlight. As we walk down the garden path Murdock says to me, 'She must have meant it, because that was a really expensive carpet.'

Murdock and I wander through the warm sunlit smells

of the zoo, me smoking, Murdock occasionally delving into the bag of pop-corn he's carrying.

'This is the first time I ever came here, you know that?' Murdock says. 'I never once got to bring my kids down here.'

'Probably a lucky break,' I tell him. 'Like the rest of the kids today, they'd probably have asked why don't they have pigs at the zoo?'

We walk along a little more and then, as we round the corner of the lion house, I see Styles and his son, hand in hand, about fifty feet ahead.

'There you go', I say to Murdock, and Murdock scans the crowd for a second or two until he fastens on to Styles.

'That's nice,' Murdock says. 'My feet were beginning to ache.'

I look at my watch. It's twelve forty-five. The restaurant is away over on the left, and Styles and his kid seem to be moving in that direction.

'Let's go and get our lunch,' I say to Murdock. 'I guess it's time for the animals to get fed.'

We drift over towards the restaurant and watch Styles and the kid move in the same direction.

Eventually they climb the broad wooden steps towards the restaurant's entrance. 'What do we do about the kid?' Murdock says.

'How do you mean?' I ask him.

'When we talk to Styles,' Murdock says.

'We don't do anything,' I tell him. 'The kid is Styles's responsibility, not ours.'

We climb the steps and go into the restaurant. Styles and his kid are moving down the endless counter, picking stuff out and putting it on their trays. Murdock and I stand by the beginning of the counter, watching until Styles and his kid have filled their trays, moved away from the counter and decided which table they're going to have. When they've sat down Murdock and I thread our way through the tables until we're at Styles's table. When we get there he's in the process of unloading the trays and he carries on doing this, taking no notice whatsoever of our presence, but the kid is different; he tries to attract Styles's attention, tell him about the two guys standing there just looking at them, but Styles just grins and says to his kid, 'I know. I already seen them.'

Then Murdock and I sit down and watch Styles until he's finished and when he's done that he says, 'Pauly, I forgot to pick up any sugar, go get some for me, will you?'

The kid, almost the image of his mother, only a bit darker, looks at Murdock and me and then gets up and moves off from the table.

Styles says, 'You guys want to talk to me, it's when the kid isn't around. If you start talking now all I do is get up and walk away and there won't be nothing you can do about it. Sure you can take me downtown on any number of excuses, but I like to plan ahead, and I figured, supposing cops got in my way while I'm visiting with my boy, it might be a good idea to hire myself a good lawyer, you probably heard of him, a guy called O'Connell. He'll move me out inside of an hour, so if you know that, then you'll wait until you think you have something good enough to keep me down there, and I can guarantee that you're not going to come up with anything good enough, because I'm clean, I'm whiter than white, man.'

'Sure you are, nigger,' I say to him.

Styles grins at me.

'Cool down,' he says. 'Ain't nothing like that going to get under my skin, you must know that.'

He unfolds a napkin, tucks it in the collar of his shirt and says, 'But on the other hand, if you want to talk to me, that'd be nice, but after I've eaten, and without the kid.'

'You're sure you can spare the time?' Murdock asks him.

'Leave it,' I say to Murdock. 'Let him have his moment. Let's eat; I'd rather not talk to him on an empty stomach.'

Styles grins again. 'We'll talk outside, O.K.?' he says. 'We'll sit and talk and my kid can watch the animals.'

Murdock begins to step forward but I put my hand on his arm saying, 'I'm hungry. Let's go and get a tray.'

Styles's kid comes back and I turn away from the table. Murdock follows me and we join the queue at the counter.

'That black bastard,' Murdock mutters. 'We should smash his teeth in.'

'We don't have to do that, at least not yet,' I tell him. 'It's good he should think he can push us around. If he thinks we're hicks, it's in our favour, not his.' We fill our trays and go and sit at a table not too far away from where Styles is.

While we're eating Murdock says, 'I wonder what the kid thinks his old man does for bread?'

'Maybe he thinks he's in Civil Rights,' I tell him.

After that Murdock and I finish our lunch in silence, and occasionally I look over at Styles and his kid. Styles is grinning away and joking, making the kid giggle all the time, and never once does Styles look over in our direction, only at the end of their meal, as if to tell us he's ready, to give us a sign. Then he gets up, takes his kid by the hand and weaves his way through the tables towards the exit, Styles all relaxed and slow-moving, the kid all tense with the occasion of holding his daddy's hand.

Murdock finishes the remains of his coffee and we both get up and follow Styles across the restaurant out into the sunlight. We stand at the top of the restaurant steps and watch as he takes his kid over to the bench opposite the monkey house. Styles takes some money out of his pocket, gives it to the kid and sends him off. After that Styles sits down on the bench and takes out a pack of cigarettes. Murdock and I go down the steps over to the bench, and when we get there Murdock sits down on one side of Styles and I sit down on the other. Styles has left his pack of cigarettes lying on the bench seat next to him so I pick up the pack, take out a cigarette and put the pack down again.

'What about one for your buddy?' Styles says. 'I don't care for that brand,' Murdock says.

'O.K., O.K.,' Styles says. 'So let's talk. I mean, you do want to talk to me?'

'We've been told to,' I tell him. 'There's a difference.'

'Sure,' Styles says.

I light my cigarette.

'You've got us all wrong,' I say to him. 'I mean, you seem to be assuming that we've come down here to bust you, come what may. I mean, you must realise in our little town, a guy like you is one hell of a celebrity. I mean, you've really got some fan club down at the department, the way you still happen to be walking around after all the action you've been responsible for. Jesus, it almost got that we should draw lots as to who should come and talk to you, but we were lucky, the chief gave us the detail. And you've got to admit that your arrival has caused an awful lot of speculation as to why you're in this particular town, because when you pay a visit, there's usually a reason, so they ain't no use, Massuh, in playing it like Stepin Fetchit, is there?'

For the first time Styles lets his grin slip a little, but he fights that, and then he says, 'I guess you're right. Maybe I shouldn't worry too much. They got to give you guys something to do, after all.'

'That's right,' I tell him. 'Hell, if you weren't here, Murdock and me'd probably be out busting niggers, and that gets a bore – you know how they're no fun downtown, they crack too early, they holler much too soon.'

'I guess so,' Styles says.

'So all we wanted to do, was to see you, see what you had to say about why you were here.

But now we don't have to even go that far. It's all clear now. You just came to town to see your brat.

Now we can go back to the department and tell them that and get back to our real work.'

Styles throws his cigarette away.

'But I'll tell you,' he says, 'If, while I'm here, I get anybody wants to throw a little work my way, as you've been regular with me, you give me your number, O.K.? Then I can let you know what I may get into, that way everybody'd be helping everybody else, like members of the Great Society should.'

'You do that,' I tell him.

'There's another thing I should tell you,' he says. 'I'm humping a white whore – she's staying with me at the hotel. Now she ain't much, but she passes the time, and there's one thing about that situation; that's if my ex-old lady gets to know about that, she may try and put the blocks on me spending my time with Pauly. What I'd like to say regarding that, is that legally there isn't nothing I can do, but I got a good friend in this town, and people I've worked for in the past wouldn't like it too much if he let me be pushed around, and he knows that, so in the end it'd be better for you guys if you let me alone in that respect.'

'Thanks for letting us know about that,' I say to him. 'Otherwise we'd never have figured it out.'

'I know,' Styles says. 'I kind of guessed figuring couldn't have been your strong point.'

I stand up. 'Well,' I say to him, 'it's been nice talking to you, Mr Styles. Enjoy your stay while you're here. We have a nice little city and make sure you make use of all the facilities we have. I'm sure they'll enhance your stay.'

Murdock gets up too and without saying anything else I begin to walk away from the bench with Murdock following after me.

Murdock eventually falls in next to me and says, 'If there's anything I can't stand it's an uppity nigger.'

'Yeah,' I say. 'But he's only going to be uppity for so long, because as sure as Christ I'm going to have that bastard, and it's going to be all the sweeter to see him fall from his elevated position.'

'You changed your mind?' Murdock says. 'No,' I tell him. 'I just want him, that's all.'

'Nothing personal, naturally,' Murdock says.

I stop and face Murdock and say to him, 'Listen, I don't want your crap as well. I have enough of that without yours. We work together, but there's nothing in the manual that says I have to take your crap when I don't want to. Is that O.K.?'

'Sure,' Murdock shrugs, and follows me across the warm gravel to the zoo exit.

Florian's place is a half hour's drive out of the city, off the freeway, up in the hills at the end of a three-mile private road.

The guys at the gate phone through to the house and then they open up and Murdock rolls the car up the drive and parks it between the circular fountain and the colonnaded front.

We get out and before our feet hit the gravel two of Florian's helpers are strolling down the steps to welcome us and although they know we're not trouble they go through their routine just to remind us of where we are. As we climb the steps the helpers follow us up. The flunkey is standing there holding the door open for us and we go through but the helpers stay outside, at the top of the steps.

'Where the carpet starts, they stop,' Murdock comments.

In the big hall with the sweeping staircase, Ray Hammett is waiting for us. Hammett is the guy that listens to what Florian has to say and then goes and relays the news to whoever Florian has been talking about. Hammett looks like a P.R. man and wears a P.R. man's smile as he greets us. 'Mr Florian is in the library,' Hammett says, indicating the panelled doors on our right, but instead of stepping aside he passes in front of us, opens the double doors and walks through, then he stands to one side so that Murdock and me can go in.

Florian is standing in the classic pose in front of the fireplace, dressed in lounging pyjamas, wrapped in a silk dressing gown, a martini in the fingers of his classically crooked right arm. But for all the studied composure, Florian doesn't look quite himself; there's just the hint of a crack in the smoothly massaged exterior, and the fact that he opens the batting is equally out of character.

'I know why you're here,' he says. 'Ray, give them a drink and then clear out.'

'Yes Mr Florian,' Hammett says, and walks over to an antique cabinet that holds all the stuff. 'What can I get you gentlemen?' We tell him and he gets it for us, then he goes out. 'Sit down,' Florian says to us, so we sit down.

'I just made some calls,' he says, 'and I'm waiting for a few people to call back, but those calls won't really make any difference, because I've had a conversation with someone who tells me that there is no way Styles is here on official business on behalf of the Organization, that I can tell you.'

'That's why you have two or three extra guys on the gate is it?' I say to him.

'Listen,' Florian says, 'I consider that kind of crack to be in poor taste, you know? In fact …'

'Calm down,' I tell him. 'Your circulation can do without that kind of excitement. So you get the word and the word is that Styles is here as a bonafide citizen of this great country. And did you get another word to tell us what to do about it?'

Florian takes a silver cigar case from the pocket of his dressing gown.

'Well,' he says, taking a cheroot from the case, 'look at it this way; he's a highly valued asset to the Organization, even though he's freelance, and as there's no reason for any hassle, then …'

Florian spreads his arms slightly and then sticks the cheroot in his mouth and lights it.

'I take it you haven't talked to Draper,' I say to Florian.

'Oh sure,' he says. 'I talked to him a couple of minutes before you came up here, and he asked for you to call him after you talked to me.'

Murdock and me look nowhere in particular and it seems the only sound in the room is the smoke as it issues from Florian's lips. Then Murdock takes a sip of his drink and the sound the ice makes in his glass is like a sledgehammer. Then there is some more silence and after a while I say to Florian, 'Well, I guess that more or less wraps the whole thing up.'

'I guess it does,' Florian says. 'I'm glad you dropped by before you got into something that'd do nobody any good.'

'That's right,' I tell him. I put my drink down and stand up and say to Murdock, 'Come on George. Let's get back to looking for the nut.'

Murdock gets up too and Florian says, 'Don't forget what I said, about if I can do anything for you guys in regard to that business.'

'We'll do that,' I tell him.

'Fine,' Florian says.

Then we go out of the library, out of the house and get into the car and drive to the gate.

Florian's guys let us off the estate and then after the gate has closed behind us Murdock says, 'Now ain't that peaches?'

I don't say anything.

'Draper changes his mind, just like that, or has it changed for him,' Murdock goes on.

'It was changed for him,' I say.

'Sure it was,' Murdock says. 'But what the Christ is happening? This morning Draper's shitting his pants. Styles could bring him a whole bag of grief; now he's doing what Florian's told him to do? I mean, that still leaves him with the shit in his pants. Assuming, I mean, anything happens, and Styles makes it happen.'

'Yeah,' I say.

'So what do you think?' Murdock asks me. 'What do you think now?'

I shake my head.

'I mean it's got to be a possibility. You got to see that, now.'

'O.K., you tell me, if you're right, what it'd mean. It'd mean Florian would know that was the case; he'd know the note from the nut was a blind, to get everybody running in all directions; he'd know what Styles walking about in broad daylight would throw up, then he comes back and checks and sets our minds at rest, and we lay off. All very nice, except Draper didn't know, then he's told, then he changes his tune.'

'You remember Mutt and Jeff?' Murdock says.

'Sure,' I tell him.

'So maybe Florian and Draper are playing that one. We're bound to come across Styles; maybe Draper knows all the time, but first he convinces us how tight-assed this town's security is going to be, because of the phony note, and he has Bolan tying up everything in Scotch tape, and he has us crawling on our bellies after a non-existent nut, and while we're doing that we're shown Styles, Pete Foley shows us Styles ...'

'Foley could have been insurance, just in case us dumb cops were likely to miss him.'

'Right, and like I say, Draper gives us his Oscar winning performance about how he ain't going to have the world's greatest hit-man in town until your brother's out of it, and then the switcheroo: we're supposed to believe Florian's talked to him and told him not to be such a farm boy from Georgia and get back to flushing out the nut, and so we leave Styles alone and go back to crawling around after someone who doesn't exist. They know we'll do that, because we always accept what we're told from those sources, and they're chuckling to each other right up until Styles squeezes the trigger.'

'You're great at figuring,' I tell him. 'In fact, it's a great surprise to me you're still working at my lowly level, but there's just one thing that worries me. I mean, I'm sure in your great wisdom, you've figured it out like all the rest, it's just that you overlooked explaining it to me.'

'That being?'

'That being that they go to the trouble of setting this up, the way they've done it, and it happens Styles whacks my brother out. But you and I know, you and I know. We've been told to get off Styles's back. So the minute Styles makes his hit what's to stop us laying it on everybody that Draper and Florian warned us off the whole deal?'

'I don't know,' Murdock says.

'Oh, you don't know?' I say to him.

'Listen maybe they've got all sorts of contingency plans. Christ, it'd be easy for Florian to set us up in some kind of poignant situation where we were whacked out while making an arrest – only it was Florian's guys knocking over the liquor store. He could have that done tomorrow, today even.'

'Sure, so why all the double shuffles?'

Murdock sighs and lights a cigarette, then he sighs again and smoke fills the interior of the car.

'I don't know,' he says. 'I don't know. All I know is it stinks, and it stinks higher than Snow Mountain.'

'Sure it stinks,' I tell him. 'I never said it didn't stink. I mean one of the things that stinks most of all is why go to all the trouble. Sure, Styles is the best, but he didn't have to come and stay wide open at the Chandler with his girlfriend. I know he likes publicity but that kind of publicity connected with a nominee wouldn't help if he got caught.

'Maybe he's sure he won't get caught.' 'He's no crazy nigger full of horse.'

'That he ain't.'

Murdock takes a left and then another and stops outside a bar called Swinging London. Of course it's topless and of course its décor is America's idea of what the British Travel Association want America to think of Britain, but it's the first bar we've hit since we've left Florian's so Murdock stops the car and we go in. A girl with tits like footballs comes to our booth, takes our orders and goes off again. We sit in silence until the drinks come back and after the girl's gone away Murdock says, 'O.K., so I'm talking crap. After all the garbage we've been given today, I'm talking crap. But you don't talk crap. You're a smart-ass. So you tell me what you think.'

'George,' I tell him, 'I don't think a thing. Not one thing. I'm pissed off with the speculation you've been giving me since we left Florian's. But I'll tell you one thing, and it's for sure. Draper's told me what to do for the last time. Florian's told me what to do for the last time. As far as I'm concerned, from now on, they're down the can. Now whether there's a nut in town or there isn't, I don't give a shit. If there is, Bolan will block him off, even if it's at the last minute. But with or without you, there's one thing I'm going to do, and that is run that nigger out of town, and draper and Florian can throw the Green Berets and John Wayne and George Foreman or whoever the hell else at me, but that's what I'm going to do. And after I've done that they can rethink all sorts of things to do with themselves and with me, and then they can drop dead.'

Murdock is silent for a moment or two.

'I guess I'm not surprised. I mean, if you won't bother going after some guy who might be going to take out your brother, you may as well pass the time getting even with a jig who's screwing a piece of ass you want for yourself.'

Now it's my turn to be silent. Murdock lights a cigarette and waves at the waitress we got before and orders two more of the same. While they're being brought I say to Murdock, 'you're full of wise ideas these days, George, only some of them aren't too wise, know what I mean?' George just shrugs.

The fresh drinks come and the girl goes away again. Some more silence passes and then Murdock says, 'a few minutes ago, you said you were going after Styles, with or without me. I mean, it sounded as if maybe you thought there's a chance I might be interested in going with you, knowing what I know of your motives.' I shrug and say nothing. 'I guess you think I won't now.' Murdock says.

Again I say nothing.

'Well,' Murdock says, 'it'll be with me.'

I say nothing again but this time I look at him.

'It'll be with me,' Murdock says, 'because I got this feeling, and I don't have to draw you any more pictures. Styles stinks, Draper stinks, Florian stinks and I want that stink to be blown all over this city, like smog, so's everybody can smell it and know what's going on.'

I smile. 'St George the crusader,' I say to him.

'I just want to be around him when you're around him, because if I'm right, your hassling might make him slip, show me something I can pass on to a different organization than the creeps we work for.'

I shake my head.

'Earlier you said I don't give a shit about my badge,' I say. 'Sounds like you've caught something off me, after all these years.'

'The only thing I've caught off you, being with you, is various pains in the ass, and not all from sitting on the upholstery of that crummy car we drive around in.'

There's another silence.

'Of course,' I finally say to Murdock, 'what would be great, what would be really great, would be to fix Styles the last way he'd ever expect to be fixed.'

'And what way would that be?'

I spread my hands.

'Take him out the way he takes out other citizens.' Murdock grins, but it's only a small grin.

'Yeah, that would be good. But however much I believe in my theory, I don't believe that hard.'

'What's to believe?' I ask him. 'We know what he is. We'd be performing a public service. And Jesus, we could do it, no sweat. We'd be as clean as the air on top of Snow Mountain.'

'Sure we would,' Murdock says. 'But that's not the way I want it. That way you're on your own. Whatever he is, if I'm wrong why he's here, I'm not taking anybody out because you don't care for who he's screwing.'

I shrug and take a sip of my drink.

'So what do you intend doing first?' Murdock asks.

'Oh, I've been figuring lots of ideas, lots of things been flying round my brain.'

George frowns.

'O.K., O.K.,' he says. 'So tell me when you're ready, I got till I retire.'

I give him an innocent look.

'Listen,' I tell him. 'I'm going to tell you right now, George. Just order a couple more drinks, will you. You do it so well.'

All the way over to Garfield's Draper tries to get us on the car radio but we just keep quiet and let the static break the monotony until we get to where we're going, a high rise on the south side.

When we've been in and seen Garfield and got the equipment we need from him and promised his payment by the end of the week, we drive on over to the Chandler Hotel and the first place we go to is the manager's office. Santell is still as rosy as ever, looking like a freshly turned-down bed, but his rosiness turns to ashes when we tell him about the tap we want on Styles's phone. He blusters and ifs and buts but finally Santell has to take us to the switchboard-room and while George fixes up the gear, Santell watches as if somebody's trampling over a wedding cake he's had specially made up.

Then, when George has finished, the three of us leave the switchboard-room and I tell Santell that he never heard about what we just installed. After I've told him that I ask for a spare key to the Plaza Suite and again he starts the blustering routine. This time I don't say anything and neither does George, we just stand there looking at him until he's allowed himself the luxury of facing us out, then he goes and gets us what we've asked for, and after he's done that Murdock and me make for the elevator, me saying, 'And now our little rosebud is going to be straight on the line to Florian and in approximately five minutes flat our nice new piece of equipment is going to be ripped out and thrown in the garbage can.'

Murdock shrugs. 'Maybe,' he replies, 'but I think maybe not. See, that little creep knows the set-up in this town being an employee of Florian himself and it's my guess he won't want to bother Florian with a couple of cops and a tape recorder.'

'Good thinking, Robin,' I tell him. 'But there's still a great chance we're going to finish up with our asses splattered from Cape Cod to California.'

'Sure.'

'And what about your badge?'

'I guess that'll be a little bent too.'

We get to the elevator and press the button and while

we're waiting for the doors to open Murdock says to me, 'I get more and more convinced I'm right, so don't screw it up will you? I mean, we play this right, we could be second run Untouchables.'

I make an O with my mouth and say, 'So that's it. Us and Elliot Ness. Maybe they'll make a T.V. series about us.'

Before Murdock can reply the elevator arrives and we get in. Today it's a different jockey and when I tell him we want to go to the Plaza Suite he takes us there without any of the deadpan stuff the other jockey thought he'd worked to perfection. We get out of the elevator, go over to the Plaza Suite and I put the key in the lock and open the door.

The late afternoon sun doesn't exactly do any harm to the Plaza Suite's general atmosphere. Everything's softened slightly and the sleek textures look even more expensive than before. Just to top off the Playboy-Penthouse atmosphere Lesley is standing against the broad windows, the sun streaming through the cheesecloth of her long skirt but not through the material of her top, because she's not wearing a top: she's naked from the waist up, the only decoration from the waistband of her skirt up to her neck being the almost full glass she's holding in her left hand.

She looks at us and we look at her. That goes on for a minute or two and then it's Lesley who's the first to speak.

'So this time you brought a partner,' she says. 'What's your thinking? The two of you can double the reaction?'

I ignore her as much as it's possible to ignore her and I tell George to go to work on the suite.

That makes her start out on a different tack.

'What is this, for Chrissakes? What –'

'Shut up,' I tell her. 'Shut up and put a blouse on and I'll tell you.'

She gives me a kind of smile. 'Can't take it, hey?' she sneers. 'Bring back too many unhappy memories?'

'Just sit down,' I tell her, and this time she looks at me and gets the tone of my voice, and so she walks down the steps and picks up a flimsy robe on the way and drapes it round her shoulders. She doesn't put her drink down, she just slams herself down on the leather divan so that some of the drink splashes onto her breasts and I try not to remember how they felt when I lay with her the night before.

'So nigger's your taste, is it?' I say to her.

'Well, I guess it's like they used to say about white women after the Indians had made them into squaws,' she replies. 'Never used to be the same back at the old corral.' I walk over to the drinks and make myself one, then go down the steps and sit opposite her.

'So the nigger's here to see his wife and kid, is he?' I ask.

'That's what I told you,' she says, 'but I can't imagine the Christ why.'

I don't answer her. I just look.

'So what is this? Morals? Getting your revenge this way?'

'This nigger Styles,' I say to her. 'What's he do? What line of business is he in?'

'Oh, I get it,' she says. 'That's the way. You want him, so I'll suffer that way.'

I take a sip of my drink. 'What line of business's he in?'

'Ask him.'

'Baby, I know. I want to know what he's told you.'

'He's a Good Humour Man.'

George is through in the bedroom so I get up and grab one of her tits. Holding my cigarette

lighter near her nipple, I push my face close to her and say, 'Listen. Just listen. He don't care for you.

You told me yourself. He'll care even less if you're marked. So just tell me the answers to the questions I'm asking, all right? That way you'll have bought yourself a bit more time to hang on to his back with your fingernails.'

The fear in her makes the drink in her glass slop a little bit more and now she knows she's got to tell me what I want.

'He's an insurance salesman.'

I let go of her and sit down again. For a minute or two my mind is blank of any reaction but eventually the bubble of her bursts in my brain and I begin to laugh, and, Christ, I can't stop, and I'm laughing so hard that Murdock comes through from the bedroom and stares at me as if I'm some kind of nut. Lesley takes a pull of her drink and when I've managed to stop laughing, I say to Murdock, 'I just heard how Mr Styles earns his bread.'

'Oh?' Murdock says. 'And how would that be?'

'He sells insurance,' I tell him. 'He's an insurance salesman.'

Murdock just looks at me for a long time and then he shakes his head a couple of times and turns away, slowly going back into the bedroom.

'I expect you think he only sells to his own kind,'

Lesley says. 'That's what you would think, but –'

'Listen,' I tell her. 'Listen to me. You think I'm something out of Peanuts? You must think I'm really something to hand out crap like that. Come on, baby, I know I'm only a stinking pig, but even us stinking pigs got some pride. If you're going to put me on, do it right, hey?'

She looks at me and then she says:

'What is this?' she says. 'I mean, what in Christ's name is this?'

'Listen, sweetheart, I know what Styles does, you know what Styles does. I only asked you because I wanted to hear what you'd say, and now I've heard it I'm getting mad because at least I expected something a little less insulting.'

This time she looks at me without saying anything and suddenly I realise that in fact she knows nothing. Nothing I'm saying to her makes any sense: crazily, she really does believe Styles is an insurance salesman. So we look at each other for a while and eventually I say to her, 'Just how old are you?'

She doesn't answer. Wearily, I say, 'There's two ways; the easy way, the hard way. Which way's it going to be?'

She thinks about that for a minute or two and then she says, 'I'm nineteen.'

'And you never learnt to read yet?'

She doesn't answer.

'Or is it you never got beyond reading the funny pages?'

Still nothing.

'So you're sitting there and telling me that you don't

know that Albert Styles is the biggest freelance hit-man since Attila the Hun?'

I have to give it to her, she doesn't even blink. Of course she may not believe me, but either way she stays as cool as the drink she's holding. 'Can you hear a funny sound?'

I look at her.

'Oh, I know what it is,' she says. 'Somebody's trying to get you on your two-way wrist radio.'

I spread my hands.

'It's true, baby,' I tell her. 'Mr Styles has made the all-time Hall of Fame. He's got so many firsts it just ain't true. I mean, he's the first nigger millionaire hit-man in the history of the United States of America.'

She goes silent again and I realise she's beginning to believe what I'm saying to her. The silence lasts quite some time because there doesn't seem any point in me saying anything else at the moment. I'm just going to let her sit there and wait and see what she has to say and while I'm waiting for that Murdock comes out of the bedroom and says, 'of course, it's clean. The whole place.'

'Sure it is,' I tell him. 'The drinks are over there.' George makes for the drinks and when he's fixed one he wanders out on to the patio and surveys the city.

'So,' Lesley says eventually.

I look at her.

'So what do you think I'm going to do?' she says. 'Throw myself off the roof? Or maybe pack up and leave? That's what you'd like, isn't it?'

I take a sip of my drink.

'You think that's the only reason I'm interested in your nigger?' She doesn't answer.

'I mean, now you know what he does, you think that's all? You don't think our interest is any more than that?'

'Who cares?'

'Presumably you'd care if we put him away and you never lunched on his black cock again.'

She doesn't even react to that except to say, 'if he's what you say he is, you're not going to put him away, because, A, he's not here on business; and B, if he was, he wouldn't carry it out knowing you were on to him; and C, even if he did, he's smarter than you are and so there'd be no way you could lay your hands on him.'

I smile at her. 'You're sure he's not here on business,' I say to her. 'I mean, five minutes ago you didn't even know what he did.'

She shrugs. 'He's here on business, he's not here on business, who cares?' 'The person he's here to hit, that's who cares.'

She shrugs again.

'Well, I wouldn't know that person, and not knowing them, then it doesn't make any difference to me, does it?'

'And it doesn't make any difference to you what I've told you about Styles?'

'Why should it?'

Murdock comes in off the patio.

'Nice view,' he says. 'Particularly of the Department building.'

Neither Lesley nor I say anything, and while that silence is hanging round in the room the main door into the apartment opens and standing there is Styles, all six foot two of him, his white teeth flashing in a grin that seems as broad as his shoulders. He pauses for a moment, easy and relaxed then he looks at Lesley and says, 'Hi, honey.'

She smiles at him and says, 'Hi.'

'Hello, guys,' he says to us. 'Help yourselves to another drink when you're ready.'

He begins to walk forwards into the room and Lesley gets up and goes to meet him. As she throws her arms round him, the robe slips from her shoulders and her naked breasts press into the sheer cloth of Styles's suit as she kisses him on the mouth, a kiss that lasts as long as it takes for Murdock to down his drink and go over to the cabinet to get a refill. While they're kissing, Styles casually feels the breast I'd squeezed earlier, feels it negligently, like somebody weighing a soft ball, clinically, just to see how it feels in the hand, and then Styles pulls back from the kiss and says, 'slow down, baby, else maybe the guys might forget what they're here for.'

She gives him a quick soft kiss on the cheek and walks away from him, back to her drink which she's left on the floor in front of the leather divan. While she's doing that Styles peels off his jacket and says, 'Hey, honey, fill the tub for me, will you? I got to get the stink of this city off of me.'

'Just the city's stink?' I say to him.

As Lesley straightens up from picking her glass off

the floor it looks as though she's about to smash the glass in my face but Styles says, 'Don't bother about it, honey. They want that kind of action. They'll be sick if you don't do it. Just fix my tub, huh?'

Lesley stays the way she is for a moment, then she unfreezes and pours the remains of her drink into her and then walks out of the room into the bedroom. Styles starts unbuttoning his shirt while he's on his way to where the drinks are, and by the time he gets there his shirt is on the floor, where he lets it lay. He fixes himself a drink and when he's taken a pull on it he unzips himself, steps out of his pants and he's standing there in his jockeys as he takes another drink. When that's done he says, waving his glass at the room, 'Well, fellows, what do you think? Pretty plush for a down home nigger, huh?'

Neither Murdock nor me say anything.

'Yeah, I think so too,' Styles says, moving away from where the drinks are. 'By the way, you guys find what you were looking for, the hardware, the equipment?' Murdock fills his glass up again and I rattle the ice cubes in mine. The sound of running water drifts in through the bathroom door.

'I guess not,' Styles says, moving away from where the drinks are, 'but, hey, I'll give you a clue.

You look under the bed; maybe you overlooked that.'

Lesley comes back into the room.

'It's almost ready, honey,' she says. 'Be just the way you like it in a minute.'

Styles walks over to her and puts his arm round her shoulders, starting on her breasts again and she nuzzles up to him.

Then he says, 'Well, I guess I'll go take my bath. You guys'll excuse me, won't you?'

While he's speaking Lesley slips her hand down the front of his jockeys and starts feeling him.

'You can't get into the tub in these,' she says.

Styles grins at us.

'See, these days, when white trash go overboard, they really go overboard, know what I mean? They'll do every little thing for you, you know?' he says.

Lesley kisses Styles at the cleft of his throat just above the collarbone, then the hand that's been inside his jockeys emerges at the waistband and she takes hold of the waistband between her fingers and her thumb, and very gently she pulls his jockeys down until they're at a point where they can slip down his legs of their own accord. Then she gives his prick a squeeze, just on the roll of his foreskin, rolling it between her thumb and forefinger, and then she lets go and kisses Styles again.

'Hey, baby,' Styles says, 'what you want me to do, crack the porcelain?'

Styles grins at us again, steps out of his jockeys and walks through the bedroom into the bathroom. Lesley looks at me and says, 'see why I'd rather fight than switch?'

Murdock tries to look everywhere except at me and I get up to make myself another drink. When I've done that I begin to walk over to the bedroom door but Lesley stands in front of me, starting to ask where I'm going, but before she can finish I smash her in the mouth with the back of my hand so that she flies out of my way, toppling down into the room's central depression by way of the back of the leather divan, narrowly missing cracking her skull on the glass box table.

'Easy …' Murdock says, but I keep on going until I'm in the bathroom. Styles is already laid out in the sunken bath, his body etched black against the turquoise tiles, flecks of soapsuds stuck to his body like wads of cotton. He gives a grin and says, 'Come on in, daddy, the water's fine.'

There is a low gold-plated towel rail running the length of the bath, so I perch on the edge of the rail and look at Styles while he carries on soaping himself with a sponge. Murdock appears in the doorway and leans against the frame, glass in hand, and I say to Styles, 'Any amount of scrubbing won't get it off.'

'I know,' Styles says. 'I tried everything, from Brillo on up.'

There is a sudden screech of anger from the bedroom and I look through the door beyond Murdock, to where Lesley's looking at her face in the dressing table mirror, clawing at the bruise on her face. Suddenly she rushes into the bathroom, screaming at Styles, 'Look what the bastard did. Look what he did.'

Styles looks at what I did without stopping soaping himself and says, 'Gee baby, that's gonna look awful in the morning. Real awful.'

'You cocksucking mother,' she screams at him. 'You fucking cocksucker.'

'Don't throw the crap at me baby,' Styles says. 'I didn't do it. And don't throw it at him either else he'll only do it again.'

She stands there in still fury, not knowing what to do.

'Piss off, baby,' Styles says, 'unless you want to wash my dick for me.'

Lesley screams something unintelligible, whirls round and charges out of the bathroom slamming the door behind her; Murdock has to move fast otherwise he would have got the sleeve of his coat trapped. Styles just keeps soaping himself and the only sound in the room is the lapping of the water round Styles's body.

'Well,' Styles says eventually, 'you didn't find anything. You waiting for me to pull the plug so you can search the tub?'

Murdock moves over to the rail, puts his glass down, grabs hold of the rail with both hands and leans over the bath slowly, saying, 'No, you're right. You're absolutely right. We found nothing. But the thing is, we know why you're here. And you know that, too. So whatever smart-ass stuff you give us, we can take. Because we know. And we can stop you, and we're going to stop you, and gradually, you're going to know that too.'

Styles grins. 'Whatever it is you're supposed to know,' he says. 'Whatever that might be, well, why don't you just haul me in for it, save all the hassle?'

There is a long narrow trough running alongside the bath, gold-plated like the rest of the place, and in this trough is all the crap that Styles and his girl appear to need to take a bath. Styles now finishes with the sponge and places it in the trough.

'Because you ain't done nothing yet, sugar,' Murdock continues. 'And us folks is gonna see you don't.'

Styles throws his head back so it's leaning on the rear edge and laughs and while he's doing that he deliberately raises one of his legs in the bath and farts, just as deliberately. I put down my drink, pick up the soap-filled sponge and twist round and ram the sponge against Styles's eyes, squeezing the sponge so that his eyes are filled with soapy water. He thrashes wildly about and one of his arms crashes out of the bath onto the tiled floor. Murdock moves quickly and stands on his wrist, while with my free hand I hold his other wrist so he can't tear the sponge away from his eyes. I squeeze and squeeze until there is no soap left in the sponge and then I stuff as much of it as I can into Styles's wide open mouth. At last I let go of his wrist and Murdock steps off his arm and we both stand back and look at him as he tears the sponge from his mouth, sightlessly trying to scrabble a towel off the towel rail so that he can clear his eyes. When he's finally managed that I pick up my glass and finish my drink, saying to Styles, 'here's looking at you.'

Then I toss my glass into the sunken tub and Styles rises up out of the foam like the Creature from the Black Lagoon; this time there is no grin, just blind hate. He begins to move for us but Murdock and me just stand there, our turn to grin, and Murdock says, 'You come for us, baby. You do that. That'd make it easy for us but your contractors wouldn't be happy, and neither would we, because we want you while you're going to work.'

Styles stops his forward motion and over balances slightly, steadying himself on the gold-plated rail. He looks at us the same way he's been looking at us for a minute or two and then the grin comes back again.

'Sure you do,' he says. 'But like I say, this is my vacation, and you just began to screw it up, and that is something you're going to regret.'

'Sure we are,' Murdock says as we turn away from Styles and walk out of the bathroom into the bedroom where Lesley is back at the mirror examining her bruise. As we pass her by I say to her, 'If we gave you a working over you'd get to be the same colour as him, then you'd have less trouble when you walk down the street.'

But her fury's now gone and she just keeps on looking at her reflection.

Going down in the elevator I start to say something to Murdock about recent events but he shakes his head, looking meaningfully at the jockey, and when the elevator hits the ground floor Murdock says, 'Let's go get ourselves a drink.'

So we walk through to the bar and I begin to make for the stools, but Murdock turns sharp right and sits in one of the booths so I sit down with him and after a waiter's taken our orders Murdock says, 'I got something.'

'What do you mean?'

'From upstairs. I got something.'

'Like what?'

'Like a phone number.'

'You got a phone number. Now that really is something. So what do we do, call the number, find it's the bookmaker's or his wife's number or maybe the number of a whorehouse or something like that.'

'Yeah, sure,' Murdock says. 'Except there's this about it. The number was on a piece of paper in one of his shoes in a closet. So I took the number and left the piece of paper where it was. Then when he'd gone into the bathroom and you'd followed him in after taking it out on the girl, I checked the shoe again and the piece of paper had gone, he'd taken it out on the way to the bathroom, so maybe he did that because he didn't want no one to know the number of his whorehouse or his bookmaker.'

The waiter comes back with the drinks and goes away again.

'So do I or don't I have something?' Murdock asks.

'Maybe,' I tell him, 'and maybe you don't. So what do you intend doing about it?'

'Oh, what I intend doing, is this. I'll phone the number and ask whoever answers if they know Mr Albert Styles, and if that's so then I'll ask him if they wouldn't mind telling me what business they have with him.'

I take a sip of my drink.

'You prick, we check out the subscriber, don't we?'

'I guess so,' I tell him.

'Christ,' Murdock says. 'What's the matter with you? You're talking as if you couldn't give a fuck, and only an hour ago you wanted Styles's balls.'

'Maybe I couldn't give a fuck,' I tell him. 'Maybe I changed my mind.'

'You mean maybe you got it out of your system by beating up on the girl and hurting Styles a little bit.'

I'm about to answer when a shadow falls across the

booth table between me and Murdock and I look up to see
Lambert standing there looking down at us.

'Mr Draper sent me,' he says. 'Oh?' Murdock says.

'Yeah,' Lambert says. 'Been looking for you all over.
He really wants to see you a whole lot.' 'Piss off,' I tell him.

Lambert doesn't move.

'Oh, Christ,' Murdock mutters. 'Let's go and see the
fuck. We got to see him sometime.'

Murdock gets up and slides out of the booth. I finish
my drink then get up and follow him. The three of us walk
out of the hotel and outside. Parked near our car is a patrol
car with two uniformed men sitting inside.

'You going to escort us back?' I say to Lambert.

'I figure you know your own way back,' Lambert
replies. 'Although some people in the department may
disagree with me on that one.'

'Yeah,' Murdock says, and we get into our car,
Murdock in the driver's seat. As we move away from the
kerb I notice in my wing mirror that Lambert doesn't get
back into the patrol car. Instead one of the uniformed men
gets out and he and Lambert start back towards the hotel.

'I got a feeling we're just about to lose some expensive
equipment,' I say to Murdock.

'Yeah,' he says. 'And that narrows the field, because
we only got tomorrow before the whole fucking circus
hits town.'

Draper says, 'You were told to call me.'

It's the same old scene; Draper behind his desk,

Murdock and me standing there taking the crap, but on the way over in the car, we've agreed to take it – though not too easy because we want Draper to take our answers as being from the gospel.

'Florian told us to call you,' I tell him. 'I mean, we all know the set-up, we're all in it, but some things, like getting your orders via Florian, they kind of rub you up the wrong way, know what I mean?'

'That's not important,' Draper says. 'In the meantime, you could have done a lot of harm, a lot of damage.'

'How do you mean, sir?'

'Don't give me that bullshit,' Draper says. 'We got clearance on Styles. It's like you were told: he's here because of the reasons we know, and that's all.'

'It didn't take a lot to make you change your mind,' I remark.

'That's right,' Draper says. 'All it took was a few words. The right ones. Styles is clean.'

'Yeah.'

'And I suppose since you saw Florian you've been checking up on that small thing.'

'We saw Mr Styles, yes,' I tell him.

'Yes, I know, and I hope to Christ that for your sakes he's still walking around.'

'He was still walking around when we last saw him, wasn't he, George?'

'Yeah, he seemed to be standing on his own two feet.'

Draper gives us a long, long look.

'I mean,' I say to Draper, 'he must have been fit enough to reach the phone and dial a number.'

Draper jumps up from his chair and walks round the desk, waving his finger under my nose.

'And while we're on the subject of telephones, what about all that crap you put in at the hotel?'

'Well, it won't be in there now, will it?' I tell him.

'You're damn right,' Draper says. 'You're damn right.'

Murdock takes a cigarette out and lights up.

'What did you find in Styles's apartment?' Draper asks, sarcastically. 'An armoury?'

'Yeah,' I tell him, 'he even had a couple of tanks.'

'Christ,' Murdock says. 'You think he'd have his gear there with him.'

'Who cares?' Draper says. 'The fact is, the word is, he's clean, and don't think I'd let it go at that if I didn't believe it, because the consequences for me would not be good for my ass.'

'So now we leave Styles alone,' Murdock says. 'So now you leave Styles alone,' Draper agrees.

'Unlike what you told us to do earlier,' I say to him. There is a pause before Draper says,

'that's right.'

There is a silence which is broken when Murdock says, 'Well, I guess that takes care of everything. I don't know about you Roy, but I think we're due an hour or so off.'

'Yeah,' I say.

'Your hours off are when your brother's been and gone,' Draper snaps.

'Yeah,' I said again, and Murdock and me turn round and walk out of Draper's office.

'And another thing,' Draper calls after us as we walk

down the corridor. 'Murdock, you can drag your ass out of the Chandler Hotel. I'm not signing any bills you send in from there.'

'Don't worry,' Murdock calls back. 'I can afford it myself on the kickbacks I make.'

On the way down Murdock says to me, 'Why don't you go on to Clark's and I'll join you a little later after I've checked out that number.'

'I got a better idea,' I tell Murdock. 'You go ahead and I'll meet you at Moses's later than a little later.'

'What have you got cooking?'

'Nothing much. Just some chewing-gum to stick on Styles's heel. I'll see you later.'

Jack Fleming is sitting behind the desk in his box of an office and on his desk is a bottle with about an inch of Bourbon in the bottom of it. Also on the table are Jack's feet and his shoes neatly placed together next to the Bourbon bottle. The office smells of Bourbon and Jack's feet.

'Hi Boldt,' Jack says when he realises who it is calling on him. 'Boldt. Well, well.'

I sit down on the straight-back chair on my side of the desk and look at Jack. He's quite a lot younger than I am but what was once a baby face is streaked with booze lines. His shirt is dirty and his suit has never been cleaned in all the years since he bought it, which if I remember right was just before he was screwed by the Department and made the scapegoat for a corruption scare blown up by a smart reporter on the Globe. But Jack got off lightly compared to what happened to the smart reporter. Jack served a term and they fixed him up with a kickback and a licence to operate privately. At least the kickback was big enough for Jack to soak himself in Bourbon and soften him up enough so he wouldn't feel up to biting the balls off the people who screwed him.

'Hello, Jack,' I say to him. 'Business must be good.' Jack looks at me.

'The feet,' I say. 'You're resting the feet. Must be doing plenty of legwork.'

Jack shakes a little with laughter but no sound comes out. When he's finished shaking he says, 'Yeah, that's right. You got it in one.'

'So, I guess it's a waste of time me coming to see you?'

'Business?' Jack says.

I nod.

'I may be able to accommodate you,' he says. 'Or at least one of my many operatives may.'

We look at each other.

'Well,' I say, lighting up a cigarette, 'first you got to sober up.'

'You think I've been drinking?'

I throw my match on the floor.

'You ever want to get even with the Department?' I ask him.

He spreads his hands. 'Well, maybe if I'd got an atom bomb, I could have done something,' he says. 'But you know how it was. Somebody had to go. They saw I was O.K. when I went out.'

'You hate the bastards. Particularly Draper.'

Jack doesn't say anything for a moment, then he says, 'so maybe you're right, maybe I do, but why're you raking all that up? What's that to do with why you've come to see me? What's me and the Department got to do with anything?'

I blow smoke across the table and reply, 'what I've come to ask you to do will help to screw Draper.'

Jack looks at me.

'Why should you be interested in that?' he says. 'You do your deals and you make your money. You're one of the lucky ones.'

I don't say anything. Then Jack snaps his fingers.

'I get it,' he says. 'I'm just beginning to get it. They need somebody else to heap the shit on, and now it's your turn, and you want me to help.'

He gives his soundless laugh again.

I shake my head. 'No, it's not that,' I say. 'It's not Draper I want. He's incidental. I just thought if you know he was going to be screwed as well you'd snap to it and be interested.'

'Sure,' he says. 'I do a favour for you; it involves embarrassing Mr Draper; Mr Draper finds out, and I'm just full of laughs at the way things work out.'

I shake my head again.

'Nobody'll know anything about you, Jack,' I tell him. 'And that's because you're good. You always were, you still are, if you leave that stuff alone.'

Jack looks at the bottle.

'O.K.,' he says. 'You may as well tell me what I'm going to turn down. It'll pass the time.'

'You know, of course, who Albert Styles is?' I ask him.

Jack leans farther back in his seat.

'It gets better,' he says.

'He's in town for a couple of days. Seeing his ex-wife and kid. A social visit.'

Jack doesn't say anything.

'And that being so, all I want you to do is follow him around, here and there, wherever he goes, and report those things to me.'

There is silence for a moment or two.

'I know I'm not awfully bright,' he says, 'but why can't you do that? Or somebody else in the department?' I don't answer him.

'You answered it,' he says. 'They don't want to, because Mr Florian wouldn't want them to.' I still don't answer him.

'So,' Jack says, 'all you want me to do is follow number one on the Hit Parade, against the wishes of Draper and Florian.'

'That's right,' I say to him.

He sighs and reaches for the bottle but I lean forward quickly and lift it off the table. Jack shrugs and settles back in his seat again.

'And the thing about it is,' I say to him, 'you're going to do it.'

'I'm going to do it.'

'Yes, because the day after tomorrow I'm going to

get Styles in such a way that Draper and Florian won't be able to do a thing about it, except maybe try and have me taken out in two or three years' time. Apart from that, you don't really care what happens to yourself, because you're beyond that kind of self-respect, and I've got five hundred dollars in my pocket just for you putting your feet in your shoes, and there's another five hundred to come in a couple of days' time. That'll buy you a lot of Bourbon, except during the couple of days you're working for me.'

There is a long silence and eventually Jack says, 'O.K., I'll do it. You got a deal. What do I care?'

I take out the envelope with the money in it that I picked up from my apartment on the way over. Jack looks at the envelope. I put the bottle down next to it.

'Who's Styles coming for?'

I shake my head. 'Don't you worry about that,' I tell him. 'All I want from you is where Styles goes all day.'

Then I go on to tell him where Styles is staying and who he's staying with and the address of Styles's wife. Then I describe Lesley to him and ask him if he's got anybody reliable to put on her at a moment's notice.

'Tony Copeland, he does work for me from time to time.'

'I know him. He's good. But if we have to use him, just tell him about the girl, nothing else.'

'Sure,' he says.

I get up. 'Well there you go,' I tell him. 'You start tonight; we'll be around him some of the time, but don't take any notice of that. Just call me at Sammy's tomorrow at eleven.'

I stretch out my arm, take hold of the doorknob and open the door.

'Well,' Jack says, 'thanks for dropping by. I hadn't made any plans for the rest of my life anyway.'

I go out and close the door behind me.

Clark's is pretty full considering it's early evening, but then Clark's is pretty full most hours of the day. Murdock isn't there when I arrive so I go and sit at a table on the raised part at the far end and it's not long after I've sat down that I'm joined by Agnes and Marcia.

'Hello, Mr Boldt,' Agnes says. 'You going to buy us working girls a drink?'

'I'll buy you a drink,' I tell her. 'But you're hardly working girls. Working girls usually dislike what they do.'

'Yeah, we're just lucky I guess,' Marcia says.

A waiter comes and takes the order.

'Where's Moses?' I ask them.

'He's busy,' Agnes says.

'So early in the evening?'

'It's never too early for Moses,' Marcia replies.

'Yeah,' I say.

'You should try it sometime,' Agnes says. 'You might surprise yourself.'

'The day I get to that I'll shoot it off,' I tell her.

'You never can tell,' Agnes says. 'There'd always be us to ease you into it. Now that couldn't be bad, could it?'

'That part'd be O.K.'

'Then why not try that part now? Whoever you're

waiting for can wait for you. It only need take as long as you want it to.'

I shake my head.

'You never stop trying, do you?' I say. 'You know I go with you then five minutes later you're helping Moses stuff his cock up my ass.'

'Or maybe in your mouth,' Marcia says.

'But seriously,' Agnes says. 'Moses is busy.'

'I've never known Moses to tire himself out.'

'Come on,' Marcia says. 'Moses'd never try it on with you. Not with a cop.'

'Moses'd try it on with anybody, even a cop. Moses isn't scared of anybody.' Agnes is just about to give me an answer to that one too when Murdock walks through the far door.

'In any case, my company's just arrived,' I tell them.

'So we see,' Marcia says. 'Why not ask him what he's doing for the next half hour.' 'On second thoughts, don't bother,' Agnes says.

'Yeah,' I say, 'now piss off. I've got my own business to discuss.'

'Sure,' Agnes says. 'Don't stay away too long. There are too few characters left in the world today.'

The girls get up and move down to the lower level and start mingling with the customers.

Murdock gets a drink at the bar then comes up the steps and joins me at the table.

'I traced the number,' Murdock says.

'And?'

'An apartment on Sternwood Avenue.'

'And?'

'No subscriber listed or unlisted. The last person to hold that number vacated that apartment almost a year ago. A guy called Sherman, used to have a small bar in the block but he gave it up and left town. Which would seem to indicate that apartment is empty.'

'That's what it would indicate,' I say to Murdock. 'And that being the case, let's go take a look.' We get up and Murdock says, 'You in your own car?'

I nod.

'We'd better go in that, then.'

'We'd better,' I say, and we leave the atmosphere of Clark's to its occupants.

The apartment block on Sternwood Avenue is like a thousand others, flat, faceless, the only indication that life exists beyond the brickwork being the lights dotted about the blank-looking walls.

Murdock and me sit in the car and look at the apartment block.

'Apartment 28,' Murdock says.

'So, since you traced it, what do you suggest we do? If your suspicions about Styles are right, we don't go and ask the janitor. He's just as likely to be paid off as anybody else if there's a contact in that apartment.'

'Yeah, well let's establish which apartment it is first,' Murdock says. 'I'll go take a look on my own.'

He gets out of the car, crosses the street and disappears

into the brightly lit lobby of Sternwood Apartments. When he's out of sight I look up into the night sky and watch the stars trying to sparkle through the city's evening haze. When I've done that for a while I just sit there and watch the lobby of Sternwood Apartments, and after five minutes or so a guy walks out into the night. This guy sort of catches my attention because he doesn't look the kind of guy to live in a place like Sternwood Apartments; he's a young guy, dressed the way young studs dress – leather jacket, collar turned up, brown cowboy boots. Maybe he's running a visiting service, but I watch him walk to the end of the block and go into the bar on the corner. That must be the bar the previous occupant of the apartment sold out, and it's not a stud's bar. But, Christ, maybe the guy just wants a drink to wash out his mouth. All the same, I keep my eyes on the bar for the few minutes it takes until I'm aware that Murdock is approaching the car. He gets in and says, 'Well, it's occupied all right. You see a guy just come out, in a leather jacket and stuff?'

'Yeah,'

'That's the occupant.' 'He make you?'

'He never saw me. I was outside the apartment door, moving by slow, and I heard the T.V. When I heard it snap off I legged it down to the other end of the corridor round the corner, then when he'd closed the door I took a peek just as he hit the stairs.'

'That's kind of interesting.' 'Yeah, isn't it just.'

'The thing is, he just went into the bar on the corner and is still in there.'

We think about it for a moment.

'I'll go into the bar while you take a look at the apartment,' I tell him. 'I want to take a look at the guy.'

'Supposing he makes you,' Murdock says, 'or maybe somebody else in the bar does?'

I shake my head.

'I've never been in there in two years,' I tell him. 'And I'd have to be awfully unlucky to bump into somebody we know.'

'The guy could still make you.'

'Look, I'll worry about that,' I tell him. 'Give me the phone number and I'll call you from the bar if he moves out before you're through.'

'Yeah,' Murdock says, 'and it'd be just my luck if some drunk's phoning his girlfriend.'

I begin to get pissed off.

'Look, just go up there, will you, and stop acting like you're about to piss your pants.'

'Listen,' Murdock says, twisting round to face me, 'I just want this done right, you understand?

My reasons aren't your reasons, you know what I mean?' 'Just get up there, will you, and stop bleating.'

'I'll do that thing,' Murdock says, getting out of the car and slamming the door. When he's gone I take my glasses from the top pocket of my coat, then I take my coat off and lay it on the driver's seat. I take off my tie and holster, wrap them in my coat and stuff the coat under the seat. Then I put on the dark glasses and roll up my shirt sleeves, get out of the car and lock it and cross over the street, down the block and into the brightly lit bar.

It isn't exactly bulging with customers. There's a man and a woman, sitting at a corner table quietly arguing about something that's important in their lives, they look up briefly when I come through the door and then they go back to their soft intensity. A couple of guys are sitting at the far end of the bar watching a movie on T.V. The bartender's watching the movie as well, arms folded, leaning against a shelf at the back of the bar, but the young guy is sitting on his own, reading a paper he's got spread out on the counter in front of him, his elbows and his drink resting on the open newspaper.

I walk to the near corner of the bar and the young guy takes no notice of me whatsoever.

Neither does the bartender. He just stays where he is, arms folded, staring up at the T.V. screen as Audie Murphy uses his other expression as he talks to the girl. I stand there for a minute or so and I don't want to cause too much hassle but I've got to say something unless it'll look crazy.

Before I can say anything the young guy speaks without looking up from his paper.

'Arthur,' the young guy says. 'There's a guy.'

The bartender turns his head slightly, then takes one last lingering look up at the screen, hauls his body from against the shelving and ambles over to my end of the bar, looking at me without saying anything. I don't say anything either, so for a minute or two it's a complete stand off, then finally the bartender manages to move his mouth and he says, 'What'll it be?'

It occurs to me that that must have been one of the

lines I'd not caught from the movie that's flickering away above our heads.

'You sell drinks?' I ask him.

'Oh, yeah,' he says. 'We do that, from time to time.'
'Am I in luck tonight?'

'Well, I could maybe arrange something.'

'That's fine,' I say to him. 'In that case, I'll have a vodka and a twist of lemon, but if you don't have the lemon, don't bother sending out for it just on my account.'

The young guy gives a short sharp laugh but he still doesn't look up from his paper or change his position in any way.

'Or maybe you have to import the vodka, yet?' I say to the bartender but by that time the bartender has turned away and has started on his hard work. I sit down on a stool at the bend of the bar a couple of stools away from the young guy and look up at the T.V. screen. Audie is drawing his gun and he shoots one of the heavies. At the sound of the shot the bartender stops work and looks up at the T.V., but of course by that time he's too late, he's missed the action and he swears to himself as he turns back to his work, almost hurling the ice into my glass. Then he turns back and brings the drink over. Instead of throwing it at me he sets it down in front of me and walks back to where his leaning was interrupted.

I take a sip of my drink and there is a sudden burst of energy from the young guy; he lifts up his drink from off the spread-out paper and turns over the page, and when he's done that he puts his drink and his elbows in exactly the same places as before.

The movie drones on and the quiet argument at the corner table continues almost inaudibly and the bartender and the other two guys and myself watch the T.V. Then the young guy straightens up and stretches his arms above his head like someone who's been asleep, and when he's done that he slaps a palm on the newspaper and says, 'Arthur, give me one more will you, then I got to be getting back.'

Arthur picks a glass off the unit he's been leaning against and without taking his eyes off the T.V. screen wanders over to the draught tap and sticks the glass underneath. He pulls on the tap and only when the glass is half full does he look down at what he's doing.

'One of these nights the T.V.'s going to break down, Arthur,' the young guy says, 'and you're going to have to learn to do everything all over again instead of using braille.'

'Yeah,' Arthur says, looking back up at the screen as he puts down the drink in front of the young guy. I look through the night black-plate glass and across the road down to where the car's parked. No flashing lights. Murdock's taking his fucking time. The young guy drinks half of his beer in one long pull, and when he's finished taking his first gulp he doesn't put his glass down, as if he's going to make the second half disappear as quickly as the first, and then maybe tell Arthur good night and slide off his stool back to the apartment, so I say to him, 'I used to be a beer drinker, your age.'

He looks at me.

'Yeah,' I tell him, 'drank it all the time, just like you drank that. Bang. Straight down. Then the next thing I know

I'm getting these pains in my gut so I go see the Doc and he says, "Cut out the beer, otherwise you'll have gut trouble the rest of your life." So I say, 'sure Doc, I'll do that, thanks a lot.'

The guy is still looking at me, his face a mask.

'So you know what I do?'

There's still no response and still no flashing lights from down the street.

'So you know what I did?' I raise my glass with the vodka in it. 'I went on to this stuff. Crazy, I know; I mean if the beer was screwing up my gut, what would this stuff do, know what I mean? But let me tell you something even crazier. After I go on to this stuff, my stomach's fine. Never acts up again. Not once. And I went on to this some time ago, I can tell you.'

'That's very interesting,' the young guy says and stops looking at me while he raises his glass to his lips. Still no headlights.

'Yeah, I can tell you,' I tell him. 'Been plenty of years since I was a young guy like yourself.'

I move a stool closer.

'You ever use this stuff?' I ask him, pointing at my glass.

'Sometimes,' he says, then he downs some more of this beer, trying to get it all down in one but this time he doesn't quite manage it.

'I tell you, you should switch, like I did,' I tell him. 'Here, why not join me in one.'

The movie's just finished and the bartender is passing by, so before the young guy can object I order two more vodkas and this time the bartender actually hears first time and looks at the young guy and says, 'you want one?'

Christ, I got a bartender who discusses business. The young guy shakes his head.

I shrug and say to the bartender, 'in that case make mine a double.' Then I turn to the young guy, 'no, don't get me wrong, I'm new round here and so I drop in the first bar I see and try and drum up a little conversation, no more than that.'

'No more than that,' the young guy says, staring at me.

'Well actually, now you mention it,' I say to him, 'I'm kind of new in town and this is my first night, and you looked like a guy who'd know his way around, know where the action is, know what I mean?'

Still no sign of headlights but Murdock walks into the bar and goes over to the counter midway between the young guy and the two guys watching T.V.

'And what sort of action would that be?'

The bartender puts my drink on the bar but he doesn't go away; he stands there and looks from me to the young guy and back again and listens in on our conversation.

'You looking for broads?' the young guy asks.

Murdock raps on the bar but the bartender takes no notice.

'Well, …' I say.

'No, I didn't figure you were looking for broads,' the young guy says. Then he slips off his stool and grabs me by the shirt, pulling me to him and saying, 'I don't like fags trying to make me, you know that? In fact, I can't stand them being around me.'

The bartender still doesn't move. The two guys continue watching T.V. but the couple at the table stop their arguing and watch the scene, and so does Murdock, as if he's some guy passing through and taking in the local colour.

'Well, look,' I tell the young guy, 'you got me wrong. Listen, I only –'

'Yeah, I got you wrong all right,' the young guy says, pushing me backwards as he walks out of the bar. I straighten up my shirt and get back on my stool.

'Some guys,' I say to the bartender, trying to grin, playing out the end of the scene. I feel in my back pocket and begin to draw out my wallet.

'Leave it,' the bartender says. 'I don't want it. Drink your drink up and clear out. This ain't no fags' bar, and I don't want no one coming in who thinks maybe he's going to change the atmosphere of the place.'

'Listen –' I begin, but the bartender cuts me off. 'Drink up and beat it,' he says.

'You want any help, buddy?'

This is Murdock speaking. The bastard. I'll kill him, the bastard.

'Uh, uh,' the bartender says, shaking his head. 'Not with this customer. He ain't got that kind of trouble in him. They never do.'

I pick up my glass and take a big drink. The bartender drifts down to where Murdock is. I finish my drink and get off my stool and walk towards the door. As I'm going out Murdock says to the bartender, 'fags. This town's getting full of them.'

'You let one in,' the bartender agrees, 'and suddenly it's like with niggers, they're all moving in.'

I close the door behind me and walk down the block a way then cross the street, unlock the

car and get in on the driver's side and slide over and light a cigarette, waiting for Murdock. I have to wait around ten minutes and then the door of the bar opens and Murdock comes out. As he crosses the street I can see he's grinning all over his face.

He gets in behind the wheel and says, 'this town, these days you can't go anywhere without fags whenever you turn around.'

I light another cigarette and I say to him, 'You bastard. What the Christ is your fucking game?

What about the arrangement we had?'

'Yeah, that was a pretty good arrangement,' Murdock says. 'The only thing was, I couldn't get in the car, could I? Some dumb bastard of a cop locked it up, all safe and sound.'

'Sure I locked the car. What was to stop you unlocking the car with your own key?'

'Because that's what you used to lock up the car.' I feel in my coat pocket and of course Murdock is right. I'd taken the keys out of the ignition without thinking about it. My own keys make a small jingling sound in my pocket.

'Yeah,' Murdock says.

I roll down the window and throw my cigarette out.

'O.K.,' I say. 'All right. So I lock you out. But do you have to walk in and make a sandwich out of the guy? I mean, the percentages are if he hadn't made me, he would have made you.'

'Yeah, well he didn't, unless he's a better actor than you are,' Murdock says. Then he laughs. 'You were good, you really were. I even began to wonder myself.'

'Sure you did,' I tell him, 'but what did you do up in the apartment apart from jerking off over his old underwear. I mean, what else could have taken you so long?'

Now I know Murdock's got something to tell me because he settles down in his seat, takes out his cigarettes and lights one. Then he takes his turn in rolling down a window and of course I have to go along with the big build-up after the way I screwed up the car routine.

'Well,' Murdock says. 'You still think I'm out on a limb about this business, or have I read you wrong?' I'm tempted to take hold of Murdock by his lapels and shake him until his teeth fly out of the window but I don't, I just say, 'what did you find?'

But I'm still not going to get it that easy. Murdock says, 'I broke no sweat getting in. That part was a pushover. So I'm in. It's a small apartment. The door opens straight into the lounge. Apart from that there's two bedrooms, kitchen off the main living area.'

I feel like telling Murdock I can picture the whole scene he's so beautifully painted because as Murdock knows it's not exactly unlike my own layout, but I let that pass too and Murdock carries on with his monologue.

'A nice little apartment,' Murdock says. 'That's the first thing occurs to me. A nice little apartment. Or rather it would be if it was furnished right. Because the lounge is bare except for a T.V. set, a straight-back chair and a cot. A couple of clean shirts hanging behind the door. Some beer cans. The rest of the place, nothing. Nothing in the kitchen. No food. The ice box isn't even plugged in. Nothing in the bedrooms. So with all this nothing there's got to be something.' He's waiting for me to ask him what the something is, but, I say to myself, fuck him. He waits a while for the reaction he's not going to get, and then he says, 'and there is. In the most obvious place, but do I find it right away? No. I look everywhere. Closets, everything. I even feel the walls, just in case. But the cot has a mattress.'

Murdock takes a left and pulls in at the kerb outside of Clark's and switches off the ignition. I just sit there and wait.

'It's beautiful,' Murdock says. 'All it doesn't have is eight-track stereo. All clean, untraceable, gift-wrapped all in nice polythene. Even my grandmother couldn't miss with it and she's been dead twenty years. With Styles behind it, your brother's career will be talked about as being very distinguished but also very short. And apart from using an atom bomb, it's a certainty.' I sit there and think about what Murdock's said. Then I say to him, 'O.K. so Styles is it. The thing is big. If Styles is it, it's bigger than him and bigger than Florian and Draper and everybody else put together. And that's a hell of a thought to have to come to terms with.'

There is a long silence then Murdock replies, 'yeah. Styles makes the hit, and then the whole machine is oiled so that he's out of town before your brother's brains hit the sidewalk. It just doesn't matter he's been staying at the Chandler like a visiting movie star. That's Florian's, so he's never been in town. And the department isn't exactly going to give the Chandler the treatment. And the reason he stays there, all wide open, is chances are we would have made him anyhow. So they drum up the wife and the kid and the note from the nut and let us find out about Styles and then give us the nice little explanation. And it's so obvious to us that Styles could never be the hit-man that we go along with all the crap and yawn due to all the trouble we've taken for nothing and go back to looking for some guy there never was.'

More silence. A couple of guys go into Clarks; a couple of guys come out.

'Christ,' Murdock says. 'They must have everything laid out, the spot, everything.'

'Yeah,' I agree, 'but there's something you're forgetting. We know Styles is here, and by your figuring we're supposed to know. But we know. And if the hit's successful, and according to you, it can be nothing else, we still know. So what happens to us afterwards? The same as what happens to my brother?'

Murdock doesn't answer.

'And taking that little idea a stage further,' I say, 'why don't they take us out first, before the main event?' Murdock shakes his head. 'Because if they did that there wouldn't be a main event. If you're taken out your brother doesn't come within a million miles of this place.'

'Then why choose this place?'

'Look, I tell you what I'll do,' Murdock says. 'I'll go

and ask Draper or Florian or Styles who's exactly behind all this and then I'll ask for their phone number and I'll call them up and I'll ask all the answers to all the questions that my being a dumb cop I haven't figured out yet.'

I light another cigarette.

'So, according to the way you've got it figured,' I say, 'if we take Styles out, we're taken out. If we don't, he scores. And we're still taken out.'

'I don't know,' Murdock says. 'All I know is this: the man is Styles and your brother's his hit.' There's another silence.

'And your way of dealing with that small problem?' I say. 'I mean, I know you must have got that figured, too.'

'I've got something figured,' Murdock says. 'I mean, I know you're interested in Styles for deeply personal reasons, nothing to do with family or anything as important as that, and that you'd like to fix him in a nice direct personal kind of way. But I want him another way, and I figure it's the only way, if we want to stay breathing, and that's to take him just as he's about to pull the trigger. That way, we got a dead man, who's holding a rifle, and there isn't a lot they can do about that right away because there's going to be a lot of national coverage and a lot of pictures across the country and Draper's going to have to play along with it, maybe even pin a couple of medals on us.'

'And that makes me feel good, because that'll maybe give us six months or so before we're never heard of again.'

'Nominee's brother foils assassination bid? You got to be joking. The publicity'd be too big.

You'd be a national hero, just like your brother. Imagine. You'd finally have caught him up.' I ignore the last part of Murdock's remarks and shake my head.

'This year, next year, five years' time,' I tell him. 'They'll do it. No way they won't. And you got a family. They won't overlook that little detail.'

'So, we type out a little statement of the story so far and we deposit it with some law firm and we let Draper know all about it, and from there they'll all know right down the line.'

I throw my cigarette out of the window.

'Well, I guess the only way to take Styles is your way,' I say to Murdock. 'There's other ways I'd prefer, but I guess you're right.'

It's Murdock's turn to shake his head.

'Well, they always say there's got to be a first time for everything,' he says. 'What are you talking about?'

'You agreed with me,' Murdock says. 'For the first time in your fucking life you didn't give me an argument.' I don't say anything to that. Then, when Murdock's got over his shock he says to me, 'the girl; you think she'll tell Styles about you?'

'I doubt it. She shoots plenty of shit, but whatever she says, the thought of Styles heaving her out on her ass is enough to keep her quiet. Styles will throw her out anyway, sooner or later. She's just Kleenex to him.' Murdock thinks about that and then he says, 'so what did you do while I was tracing the number?'

'I saw Jack Fleming. I thought that just in case there

was the vague possibility you were right, I'd put him and Tony Copeland on to covering Styles and the girl so that we have time to improvise.'

Then I go on to tell Murdock what I've fixed in detail as far as Fleming and Copeland are concerned.

'Well,' Murdock says. 'That seems fair, as long as you can trust a lush like Fleming.' I heave a long deep sigh. 'You trust me, don't you?'

'Sometimes,' Murdock says, and then looks at the front door of Clark's. 'Are we going in there, or are we not?'

We spend an hour or so at Clark's, and while we're in there, we get the treatment from Agnes and Marcia and Moses but naturally we just sit there and hold on to our drinks and the most

significant thing about the evening as far as I'm concerned is that Pete Foley doesn't appear. Then Murdock goes back to the Chandler and I go back to my apartment after agreeing that with Fleming and Copeland at work there's nothing else we can do.

When I get home, I get undressed, put on my robe and start running a bath. While the tub's filling up I put some coffee on the hob and when the bath has filled up I take in a cup and the coffee pot and put them on the small table by the tub. Then I take off my robe, step in and sink into the hot water. I close my eyes and for once in my life I allow my consciousness to drift into a kind of oblivion where dead unexplored thoughts are caught up in the slow swirling steam of the bathroom. The heat of the water seeps into my body and I'm almost slipping into a half-conscious sleep when out in the living area the phone begins to ring. I screw up the skin round my eyes tight and swear to myself, but the phone carries on ringing and so in the end I level myself up out of the tub and wrap my robe round me and, still swearing, I shuffle through to the living area, pick up the phone and wait for whoever it is to tell me whoever it is.

'Roy?' the voice says at the other end of the phone. I close my eyes for a moment or two before I answer. All I need right now, I think, is my brother, calling me up, after what trouble his mere fucking existence has caused me over the last twenty-four hours.

'This is Mr Boldt's answering service,' I say. 'Mr Boldt is out of town for the next seven years so if you wish to leave a message replace the receiver and go look for a map.'

My brother laughs his pro laugh, the way I knew he would and then he says, 'you must be the only cop in the whole of the U.S.A. who's still got a sense of humour.'

'Or maybe it's the other way round,' I tell him, and then I wait. 'Well,' he says, 'how's everything? How are you?'

'I'm fine,' I tell him. 'I never felt better.'

'That's good,' he says. 'It really is.'

I wait again.

'Well, I guess you heard I'm coming to town on a little visit,' he says, putting the laugh in his voice, making like a regular guy with the gags.

'I had heard,' I tell him.

'Yes,' he says. 'I know. But seriously, there's a couple

of things I just wanted to arrange before I arrived. You know how it is on a trip like this, the machine takes over, and they don't let you do little unimportant things like seeing the folks unless they can make some kind of capital out of it, you know the way it is – especially if your brother's a cop who votes for the other guys.'

'Oh, come on, Roy,' he says, this time a little humorous rebuke in his voice, but I know him well enough to catch the hard impatience he's trying to conceal. 'You know what I'm talking about. No, the thing is, I thought – you know how I'm going to be pushed on this schedule – but I thought maybe we could get together, maybe if only for an hour, you know, spend a little private time together.'

'What for?' I ask him.

'Well, maybe we could take a walk down Oakleigh Street. Look at the old house. Just, you know, re-visit the past.'

I'm beginning to get the picture. A typical P.R. double shuffle. Papers full of me, the right-wing cop, walking through times past with a brother who differs politically from me; yet here I am and here he is. Two opposing poles of the establishment, yet both Americans, kids grown up together on a street like a million other streets, me the law-enforcer, him the law-maker. After the assassination attempt's been foiled just think of the play that could be made on the lines of My Brother's Keeper, and how the people who didn't share his political opinions would be drawn that little bit closer to him, because of the obvious affection he'd be showing for me in the pictures, and if we could disagree, and still get along, then maybe that just showed the best side of America, and maybe even he's not too radical after all.

'With or without the cameramen?' I ask.

'Roy, you bastard,' he says, still working on the humorous tone, 'you always have to take things the way you want to see them. Can't you accept I'd just like to spend one small hour with you, for old times' sake? And besides, Louise'd like it. She really likes you, you know that, in spite of what I tell her about you.'

'Well,' I tell him, 'I don't care either way, but we can take a walk down memory lane if you like, if your taste is Early American freeways, that is.'

'What are you talking about?'

'Last year,' I tell him. 'They tore the place down. The whole street. And most of the other streets around as well.'

There's a short pause, almost non-existent, before he says, 'I'd no idea. None at all.'

No, I think to myself, I bet you hadn't, and I also know that some functionary in my brother's machine is going to have a lot of explaining to do.

'Anyway,' my brother says, 'we can arrange something else. I'll get back to you on that tomorrow.'

'Fine,' I tell him.

There's another short silence, and I wait to see how he's going to pick up the words.

'The other business, this threat thing: have you come to the same conclusions I've reached yet? I mean, frankly, I personally think it's just a scare; these things happen all the time.'

That's why you've got guys staked out in flea-traps, I think, but I say to him, 'You're probably right, but I don't have to tell you that the Department is treating this city like there's a small-pox epidemic and we're trying to find the carrier.'

'Of course,' he says. 'Of course I realise that, and naturally I appreciate it. I'm aware of the pressures bearing down on your resources.'

'In that case, why come? Why not give us all a rest?' I ask him.

'Well,' he says, 'it wouldn't exactly take a great deal of imagination on your part to guess that there's been a lot of pressure put on me not to come, but I felt this way: if I don't come, what kind of guy am I? Who'd be interested in me, the first scare letter I get I pull out of my arrangement? I've got a duty to the people, whether they support me or whether they don't support me, to show them that politicians in this country don't run scared, that decisions aren't made by looking down a gunsight.'

Great stuff, I think. And if he was really bright, he should have written the threat note himself.

When I don't say anything he asks, 'don't you agree with what I've just said?'

'Sure,' I tell him. 'I'll be awake all night, just thinking about it.'

'There's no way, is there?' he says. 'I mean, you're determined to be this way for the rest of our natural lives.'

'Well in your case it might not be all that long,' I tell him, and at that point the next thing I hear is the receiver being replaced at the other end of the line. I put my own receiver down and look at it for a moment or two, then I walk back into the bathroom. The water has cooled down by now and so has the coffee so I turn on the hot tap and I drain the cup of lukewarm coffee and I sit on the toilet seat and watch the steam rise as the water begins to get hot again.

The phone takes me out of my dream. In the dream, I'm just about to make love to my wife, and it's one of those dreams that is so real it seems to have more reality than when you're awake; her face is beneath me, her head back-tilted slightly on the pillow, a serene expression on her face, not expectant, wondering, just a wakeful remembering of what is about to happen to her, a still gratefulness for the satisfaction that is to come. I can smell the sweet smell of her body, and the creases in the pillow and in the sheet below her are knife sharp in my mind's eye. There is a small sound from her mouth as it opens slightly, and then I'm awake, listening to the ringing phone. I'm staring up at the ceiling, not at my wife's face and for a long moment I can't believe that I've been dreaming and now I'm awake. When reality settles round me, I lie there for a few minutes, letting the phone ring, trying to recapture the dream's sharper reality. The phone stops ringing and the images of the dream begin to blur and the more I concentrate on retaining them the more they soften. So in the end I throw back the sheets, jack-knife out of bed and pull on my robe, and go through into the kitchen to put the coffee pot on the stove. Then the phone begins again, so I go through into the living area and pick up the receiver.

'Get over here,' Draper says. 'We got something.'

'Anything I can pick up at the drugstore for it?' I ask him.

'Listen, you bastard,' Draper says, 'Bolan's done your job for you. He brought somebody in.'

'How are Mr Florian's boys?'

'Just get over here,' he says. 'Enjoy your funny jokes while you can.'

He slams his phone down.

'Yeah,' I say into mine, then lay it gently to rest on its cradle and go see to the coffee.

He's around eighteen years old. His hair is dirty and worn at shoulder-blade length. His hands are dirty and his face is dirty and his clothes I would guess are the only ones he ever uses, but I've smelt worse. He's sitting in the chair and he's sitting all nice and symmetrical, hands perfectly placed on the chair's wooden arms, feet apart in perfectly matched positions on the bare floor. His head is tilted back slightly but as you face him it's perfectly in line with the straightness of his body. And he's smiling. But not at me, because he doesn't even know I'm there. Or Murdock, who's been reached first.

The guns are laid out on the table over by the wall. There are seven hand guns, four rifles, a shotgun and a machine gun, and lots and lots of boxes of ammunition. Bolan is leaning against the wall over by the table, arms folded, one leg crossed in front of the other, deliberately not looking at anybody from under his sleepy lids, waiting for me or somebody else to talk to him so he can modestly play down his glorious moment.

But Draper is looking at me. And when he's finished doing that he looks at Murdock. And when he's made the most of all that he says, 'it's pretty, isn't it?'

I take out a cigarette and put it between my lips. Before I can even tear a match out of my book Draper quickly steps in front of me and lights me with his gold lighter, then steps back so as not to block my view any more than he has to.

'It's nice, you have to admit,' he says.

I blow out some smoke and nod my head, looking at the kid.

'So where were you?' Draper says. 'Where were you two brilliant bastards while Bolan was completing your part of the deal for you?'

'Looking for this guy, I guess,' I tell him.

'Oh, sure you were,' Draper says. 'I bet you looked just everywhere, that's how you came to pick him up.'

I don't say anything; instead I walk over to the table and take a closer look at the display.

'Where did you bump into him?' I ask.

'I'll give Jim here the pleasure of telling you that,' Draper says, but Bolan has mistimed his moment because he started talking at the same time Draper did so he has to clear his throat and start all over again.

'We had a little luck, I guess,' Bolan says. 'The guy's only been staying a week at the place we picked him up, so the proprietor of the place, the place being the kind of place it is, he took a look in the guy's room, while the guy's out buying some more horse or something. While he's looking round he sees all this stuff, only he's got to get down on his hands and knees so's he can see it because it's under the bed and it's all wrapped up in a couple of top-coats, and even before he's peeled the top- coat away he's got a pretty good idea of what he's going to find. And this proprietor, he likes to keep well in with a particular guy on the force and so he calls him up and tells him that while he's not especially interested in guns himself he knows we are and if we want any there's some over at his place.'

'His place being?'

'Mackay's Rooming House.'

'Mackay's,' I say, bending over the table and taking a closer look at some of the hardware.

'Not exactly a place you could overlook, considering the kind of place you were supposed to be covering.'

'That's right, I guess,' I say, straightening up and turning round to face Draper. 'Only one thing though, Mackay's isn't exactly close to anywhere on my brother's route.'

'So what are you trying to say?' Draper asks me. 'That this high flyer's got a mind like an I.B.M. computer? Is that what you're trying to say?'

'No,' I tell him. 'But sometimes he comes down. He came down long enough to write the note, he came down long enough to get this little arsenal together and get it to Mackay's.'

'Listen, the guy's what he is. Don't give me any crap about this reason or that. We know and you know, you missed him, and whatever you say now is governed by that particular fact.'

I let him think I'm thinking about that for a moment and then I say, 'So you got a guy, and you got some guns,' I say. 'Now I didn't want to seem overly naïve, because in different circumstances I'd have wanted this guy to be the man, then he'd be the man, but I'd just like to ask, apart from the guns, what actually ties him in with the coming attraction?'

Draper shakes his head and says, 'Jesus.'

Bolan unfolds his arms and then refolds them the other way round.

'Paper like the paper he stuck the message on. The glue he stuck it with. Scissors, a pile of magazines and newspapers, all cut up. We found things like that that could tie in the guy.'

There is a short silence.

'Satisfied?' Draper says.

'Like they say on T.V., it looks open and shut,' I tell him.

'Nothing's shut about this case until your brother's out of this town. This guy changes nothing. There could be a dozen others in town just crazy enough to try what this guy did. So get your asses out of here and get back on the street and do it right this time.'

I look at the guy sitting on the chair.

'When did he start flying?' I ask. 'On the way over in the squad car?' 'What do you mean by that?' Draper says.

I shrug.

'Just seems kind of odd. He goes out to get his groceries and instead of waiting till he gets home he fixes himself someplace like a public toilet, someplace one of our vigilant men from another department could bust him, and his little future arrangement.'

'Now, look –' Bolan begins, unsticking himself from the wall, but Draper cuts him off.

'Forget it, Jim,' Draper says. 'He's just trying to ride you because he's taken a fall himself.'

Bolan leans back against the wall.

'Just get back on the street and leave all the figuring to those of us in the department who can still actually figure things,' Draper says to me.

'Come on, George,' I say to Murdock. 'We better go see if we can find one of these ourselves, otherwise we might never get the kind of respect that Bolan so richly deserves.'

'Yeah,' says Murdock, and walks past me to open the door and go out.

'Nice job, Jimbo,' I say as I go towards the door.

'Yeah, except it should have been yours,' Draper says.

I close the door behind me.

'Beautiful,' Murdock says. 'They really thought they were beautiful in there.'

'They were,' I tell him. 'Two of the Beautiful People.'

Murdock is gripping the steering wheel and glaring at the street and its traffic and its people as if each element in his field of vision has contributed to his own present state of mind.

'Those bastards,' he says, and I don't say anything, because Murdock's remark doesn't require any answering. He takes a left and then he says, 'so that's the way they had it figured. They show us the kid, we ease off all around. A hit's made but we can't prove who by because we've let Styles alone and therefore he can make the hit from wherever he likes, and we don't know where that is because we're just covering the kind of garbage they had in there with them. And he's also nice cover for the department because they at least got something to show the world evidence of vigilance, because they have someone they can prove at least intended to take your brother. Christ, they'll keep him so high he'll never even know they're not busting him for flying.'

'George,' I say, looking at my watch. 'The call from Fleming'll be coming through in ten minutes, so leave the story a bit alone will you and concentrate on us getting to Sammy's in time to take the call.'

'I'll get us there,' Murdock says. 'What I'll do to get us out of this traffic jam is to get out the car and make like King Kong.'

But while he's talking the traffic starts to move again and in a couple of minutes we're at Sammy's and I get out while Murdock cruises off to find a spot to park. Sammy's is a little bar that has a few regulars, not the kind of place you'd walk by and think now there's a nice place to drop in for a drink, but Sammy doesn't miss those people, because he runs the bar more for pleasure than for business because Sammy is a retired man. He used to be an explosives man, working on a freelance basis, but one time he made his one and only mistake that cost him one hand, one arm and an eye. Luckily for him he'd made plenty and he'd had a good lawyer and a wife who thought he was the sun and the moon and Gulf and Western. So while he'd been inside his wife had fixed the little bar up for him and he liked it because people he'd worked with from the old days would drop by and chew the fat and his wife would be there doing most of the work, but from time to time Sammy would like to show off how he could fix a drink with his mechanical limbs. I drop in from time to time and he likes that too, because we always got along, unlike the relationships between myself and some of his other regulars, and that adds a little edge to Sammy's pleasure whenever I drop by.

And this visit, it's no different.

'Mr Boldt,' Sammy says. 'A pleasure, this is a real pleasure.'

He stretches out the arm which still has some of him on it and I take hold of the cold steel that's on the end of it and I say, 'Same goes, Sammy.'

Sammy's wife smiles her pleased smile. She's a hell of a lot younger than Sammy, in her late thirties, and there's been plenty of takers in her time with Sammy, especially while he was away, but she's never availed herself to any of these offers. I should know because I've made her an offer she was able to refuse on more than one occasion.

And here she stands, basking in her husband's pleasure, no feelings of animosity towards me because of what I've tried to pull in the past, and able to rationalise her husband's pleasure at someone who would have fucked him behind his back, if that event had been possible. There are half a dozen people in the place, all minor faces; I know them and they know me but they're content to be around the atmosphere Sammy's generating because they're thinking that maybe if they were somewhere else I'd be there other than for the apparent social reasons.

Sammy goes on for a while about why haven't I been in and while he's doing that Murdock comes in, and although he gets the same kind of welcome I get, Sammy and the rest of them get the picture that there's some business on, so it's made easy for Murdock and me to retreat from the bar and sit at one of the tables that run all down one side of the bar.

'Parking in this fucking town,' Murdock grumbles.

I take a sip of my drink and then the phone rings. Sammy's wife picks up the receiver and then she says something to Sammy and he calls over that the call's for me. He puts the set as far down the bar as the lead will allow and then he goes back to his crowd down the other end. I pick up the receiver and speak my name. 'So far,' says Fleming, 'this is what I have; the guy leaves where he's at and he takes a cab to the address you gave me. He's in there five minutes or so and then he comes out again and gets back in the cab along with the kid. Then after that the cab takes them to the park, where they're still at. The only guy the guy's talked to is a guy selling candy. Nothing. But the other party, she leaves where they're staying an hour or so after the guy. She goes nowhere in particular; by that I mean she also takes a cab and goes downtown and wanders around all the big stores, just looking, except there's this one place, a unisex boutique place and she spends some time in there. While she's in there this young guy goes in, and while a shirt she's buying is being wrapped, the young guy strikes up a conversation with her. She doesn't seem to mind too much, insofar as when they leave the boutique they leave together and make for the nearest coffee shop; when they're in there it looks as if a new romance might be blossoming over the coffee cups because they're getting along just fine, so fine that she takes a pen and some paper out of her purse and it looks as though he's getting her address and phone number.'

'And then what happens?'

'Then they leave the coffee shop and go their separate ways, smiling, but separate. How'm I doing?'

'Fine,' I tell him. 'Tell me what the young guy looked like.'

He tells me.

'And where's the girl now?'

'Back home.'

'Fine. What you've told me I've got to think about. When the guy you're on goes back to his place, you call me here. If I'm not here, my alter ego will be. He'll talk for me.'

'Fine yourself,' Fleming says. 'By the way, how's my percentages?'

'How do you mean?'

'Well, I'm still walking around. Is that bad or is it good? I mean, the more I'm still around, are my chances lessened, or is it a good sign?'

He puts the phone down and before I can go back to Murdock and tell him the news Sammy ambles down to where I am, holding two fresh drinks in his machinery and he puts them down on the counter in front of me.

'Two more,' Sammy says. 'Two more for two Good Guys.'

'Yeah, well the Bad Guys always could afford to buy them,' I say to him.

Sammy laughs and picks up the drinks but before I can turn away from the counter Sammy says, 'You know I don't ever say anything like this before, Mr Boldt, but there's only been two times you did business from here before; once was fine because I never heard nothing about that one time, but the other time, there was plenty of shit hitting fans all over town.'

I just stand there and look at him.

'Only, Joan, that's what I worry about. If anything happened to me, you know how she'd take it. So all I'm saying is, if the shit's about to fly, let me know, will you, so's Joan and me can get to take that couple of days in the mountains I keep promising her.'

'Don't fret, Sammy,' I tell him. 'Nothing'll happen here. That I promise.'

'That's good enough for me,' says Sammy. 'You say

that, that makes it right. I'm only sorry I spoke up.'

'Don't worry about it, Sammy,' I tell him and begin to turn away again but Sammy's still got something to say.

'Only,' he says, 'I chose this time, see, while Joan's in back, so she won't see me talking like this, and she'd maybe get a little mad, the way you took care of one or two things while I was away that time ...'

'We never talked, Sammy.'

'Yeah,' he says, and laughs, and goes back down to the bunch at the other end of the bar.

'What's Sammy got to say?' Murdock asks.

'Forget Sammy,' I tell him. 'If I was a gambling man I'd have put you asking that question second.'

'All right, all right,' Murdock says. 'So let me have it.' I tell Murdock what I've just heard. 'Well,' says Murdock, 'there you go. Styles sends the girl out to do some shopping.'

'And it's got to be her who takes home the groceries to wherever Styles is going to be on the day.'

'Styles isn't going to be wherever that may be for more than approximately thirty seconds.'

'And the handover will be as close as it can be, allowing for delays.'

'Yeah. Before or after; when's he going to be there?' We sit there for a moment or two, looking at our drinks.

'I sure as hell hope it's before,' Murdock says. 'I'd hate to be just one footstep behind him.'

That's another one that doesn't require an answer.

'What about Fleming and Copeland?' Murdock says. 'They can't stay on their feet the next thirty-six hours.'

'They don't need to. Nobody's going to play find the lady with that rifle until they have to. No, it's from the moment my brother hits town we start worrying. Then we can use them. With equipment, so we look as though we're playing out our parts in this charade. I'll talk to Jack later and meet him and fit him out.'

'Well, O.K., but make sure he's sober enough to use the stuff.'

'They're both fine. They're not like us; they deny themselves while they're working.' 'Yeah, but they don't do our work, do they?'

I sit in the car outside the Chandler and wait for Murdock. Today's heat seems hotter than yesterday's and the haze seems hazier and I wish to Christ Murdock'd hurry up. He must have made it clear by now; he's too good to make a meal of it. I just sit there with an unlighted cigarette in my mouth staring at everything and nothing, wishing I was in my tub just soaking away the day's dirt.

Then Murdock finally appears and the two members of staff he's got to deport his stuff heave it into the trunk, except for the couple of suits that Murdock takes the trouble of laying out on the back seat himself; why he bothers doing that, I'll never know. So when he's finally in I say to him, 'Like the old record says, should I book you for over-acting?'

'I did it right,' Murdock says. 'Don't crap all over the interior.'

I pull away from the kerb and drive back to my place.

I give Murdock a hand upstairs with his stuff and once it's in there and the doors closed behind us Murdock being Murdock starts right in unpacking and carving himself out a little segment of my living area, so I think what the hell, and lay the divan out for him and go and get some sheets and blankets and dump them down on the divan.

'Thanks,' Murdock says, turning round from trying to find a place to hang one of his shirts. 'Don't bother making it up. I'll do that myself.'

'You don't say,' I reply, and go into the bathroom to begin running my tub.

When I get back to Sammy's Sammy isn't around, just Joan, and the bar's empty of customers.

She smiles the same smile she always does, as if I had no relation whatsoever to the person who's tried to get her in the sack on several occasions.

'Twice already,' she says when I got to the counter. 'You trying to turn us into an "in" place?' 'Yeah,' I tell her, 'I need the commission.'

'Not from what I heard,' she says. 'One to you,' I say.

She keeps her smile going and gets my drink for me.

'Where's Sammy?' I ask her. 'Lying down,' she says.

I leave that one where it is, except to say, 'Listen, if you've got things to do, I'll be fine. I'm waiting for a call so I can just sit here and read the paper. Don't worry about me.'

'Well,' she says, 'if you don't mind, I guess I might just go and see if Sammy needs anything.

You sure?'

I nod my head and there is a slight flickering of her eyelashes, then she turns away and goes out through the door. I take my drink down the bar a way close to where the phone's kept and take a look at the sports page and while I'm doing that the phone rings. I lean over the bar and lift the set from its cubby hole and when I've put it down I lift the receiver and I hear Joan on the extension asking who's calling. Fleming's voice begins to ask if I'm in the bar but I cut in and tell Joan it's O.K.,

I'm on the line, and I hear the extension click and then I say to Fleming, 'It's O.K., you can go ahead.'

'He's back home,' Fleming says. 'Or should I say, down home?'

'How long?'

'Ten minutes ago.'

'Right, well, you and your helper can take the rest of the day off.' 'You mean we've got that long left?'

'If you play it the way I tell you, yes.'

Then I give him the outline and tell him what to do and how and where to be in town tomorrow, and when I've done that I put the receiver down and put the set back in the cubby hole. After that I look at the door that Joan went through, then I slide off my stool and go back to Murdock.

'Do you mind if I open the window?' Murdock says.

'Help yourself,' I tell him.

'I can't stand a fug.'

Murdock gets up from the armchair opposite me and pushes up the window. On his way back he pauses by the table and freshens up both our drinks, then sits down. I reach out from my own armchair and take a sip of my drink. I think that it needs more ice but I can't be bothered to reach out again and take the lid off the ice container. A minute or so later Murdock sits up and says, 'You want more ice?'

I watch him take the lid off the container.

'Only a couple of cubes left,' he says. 'You want some?'

I shake my head. Murdock drops the cubes into his drink and then gets up, picks up the container, goes through into the kitchen and I can hear him refilling the container. When he comes back he takes out a couple of cubes and drops them in the glass I'm holding as he passes by the chair.

'I hate to see a man make a martyr of himself,' Murdock says, and sits down again. 'I guess the Chandler spoiled you a little bit, George,' I say eventually.

'It didn't exactly do you a whole lot of good,' Murdock says.

I look at him and say nothing. After a while I drain my drink and get up and put on my coat.

'Where're you going?' Murdock says.

'Somewhere where the service doesn't talk back.' Murdock grins. 'Have one for me while you're out.'

'Piss off,' I tell him, and close the door behind me.

Clark's is bursting at the seams. Even Moses' select court on the raised part seems to be crowded, but I guess he won't mind too much. The drinks I've had already don't help the feeling the shoving crowd gives me, and I wish to Christ at least the crowd'd sway the same way I'm swaying. I beat my way to the bar and of course while I'm waiting the seventy-five years it takes for me to get attention I begin to wish I'd stayed at home with Murdock, instead of touring the bars after I'd found Jo-Ann and the spade were engaged all night. While I'm thinking that thought I start getting attention, only it's not from one of the bartenders, it's from a hand that's slipped between my legs from behind. Even if it wasn't accompanied by the 'Hi' I get from Agnes, I'd still be able to guess at who the fingers belonged to – not that I'd ever experienced them before, but handling is what you'd expect from someone like Agnes. The bar is so crowded that Agnes's attentions go unnoticed, not that anybody'd care anyway.

'You feeling good?' Agnes says, as she slides round to lean against me as much as against the bar, and the hand now slips between me and the bar.

'You certainly are,' I tell her.

'I know it,' she says. 'No good being modest about it.'

'This is modest?' I say to her. 'In any case, where's your partner? I thought that you worked as a pair.'

'As a pair, not always. With them, all the time.' I get an extra bit of pressure to accompany that remark, and then she unzips me and her hand slides inside.

'Christ,' I tell her, 'you want Moses complaining about the mahogany getting stained?'

'You're not going to come, sweetheart,' she says. 'When that happens, it'll be the way I want it to happen.'

'In that case, what do I have to do to get a drink round here?'

'Wave the magic wand, baby,' she says and inside of my jockeys she does just that. The sweat on my brow is not entirely due to the alcohol in my system. But, like magic, a bartender gets free and asks for my order. I tell him, and whatever Agnes wants, which is the same and then a voice at my ear on the opposite side of which Agnes is says, 'make that three.'

I turn my head and Marcia's squeezed herself in next to me. I tell the bartender to make it three and then Marcia makes the Agnes routine a double act by slipping her hand through and grabbing a piece of the action herself.

'Like I thought,' Marcia says. 'I thought I'd recognised a familiar handshake.'

Agnes says, 'Well, at least we know now he's got one. All those excuses about Moses weren't just excuses.'

'And balls,' Marcia says. 'They always say, Boldt's got balls, even if they say nothing else.'

I push my own hands down which is a pretty difficult operation considering the kind of crush I'm in but I finally manage it and push their hands away.

'I guess this is what is called a squeeze play,' I say to them, 'but however effective it is, it's not going to be effective enough to get me into one of Moses's dens with you two.'

'You don't have to worry tonight,' Agnes says. 'Moses has a real friend with him. He only has eyes for him.'

'Yeah, but what does he have for me?'

'You're crazy,' Marcia says. 'Tonight we're working for ourselves.'

The drinks arrive.

'Even supposing I could believe that,' I say to them, 'how much would it cost me?'

Agnes shakes her head.

'Only the pleasure of your company,' she says.

'Sure,' I say. 'And then I'm in there, and suddenly it's go down on Moses.'

'Listen, one thing Moses doesn't do,' Marcia says. 'He doesn't fuck pigs.'

'That's about the only thing he don't do,' Agnes begins to say, but before she can say it all I've whirled round on Marcia and grabbed hold of her by her neck, just below the upward angle of her jawbone, close to the tendons of her neck. I do this just as she's put her drink to her mouth and she's swallowing; the drink spews out of her mouth and on to my face and the crowd stops swaying and quietens a little bit, because nobody's ever seen Marcia handled like this, especially together with the fact that it's going on before Moses' eyes.

'Listen,' I say to Marcia. 'Listen, you whore, you're talking to me. If you want to look good enough to turn up for work tomorrow, remember that.'

While I'm saying this a lot of things happen all at the same time. Moses rises from his throne, the heat of his outrage burning a path through the crowd. Moses's boys in the ante-room have had the message passed to them and they come steaming in through the crowd, and Agnes jumps on my back and grabs hold of me by my hair. I push Marcia and the guy she's leaning against away from me and I grab Agnes's arms, leaning forward like somebody heaving a sack of coal, and twist my body to one side, dumping Agnes flat on her back on top of the bar amongst all the glasses. She shrieks and pedals her legs around in the air, trying to get off her back, but I give her a two-handed push and she slides across the alcohol-covered bar and disappears over the opposite edge. By the time that has taken to happen Montgomery and the boys and Moses as well are almost on to me so I have no choice but to draw my gun and wave it around, saying to Moses, 'You really want gunshots in here, Moses?'

Moses and the other fellows stop a couple of feet short of me. Now the crowd is very quiet indeed.

'You got no witnesses,' Moses says. 'I got plenty. And I got you covered, anyhow.'

I hear one of the bartenders take a few steps closer to the spot directly behind me.

'Yeah and there's plenty in here who'd like to make a little bread on telling where I was when I got it.'

'You mean you think somebody actually cares enough?' 'That's for you to decide, Moses,' I tell him.

Moses thinks about that for a moment or two.

'I guess just about anything's possible, even that.' Moses says.

'And the thick ear your guy's thinking of giving me as compensation. However hard he hits, I'll wake up and I'll be coming back.'

209

After I've spoken the dead silence goes on a little bit longer and then Moses says, 'leave the pig alone. He's a pig. He's got to live with being one. That's enough.'

Montgomery and the boys hesitate slightly and then they start to go back to the ante-room. Moses gives me his earthquake look and turns away and the crowd parts like a San Francisco chasm as he makes his way back to his platform. I then turn back to face the bar and the bartender who had me covered has discreetly replaced whatever he was carrying and he's looking at me, standing rigid, while Agnes uses his body to pull herself up off the floor. When she sees me she goes for the nearest broken glass and picks it up but the bartender grabs her by the other wrist so that all she can do is make sweeping movements with the glass that stop a foot or so short of me, and as she makes these movements she shrieks obscenities at me but I turn away and begin to make for the door. As I'm doing so I hear Agnes grind the glass into the counter-top and scream out.

'Next time he'll get it in the balls, Christ help me.'

Murdock's still up when I get back. The bottle's a quarter the way down since last time I was home and he's sitting in the same chair with his feet up watching a movie on T.V.

'Have a good time?' he says, not looking away from the set.

I go over and stand a little behind his chair and I look at the screen. A car chase is taking place, a lot of patrol cars after a car full of hoods.

'I had some fun, yeah,' I tell him. 'That's great.' Murdock says.

'Yeah,' I tell him.

I watch the movie for as long as it takes for the hoods to overturn against the studio street lamp-post and then I tell Murdock I'm going to bed. I go through to my bedroom and while I'm taking my pants off I can hear the movie being wound up, the martial music, the stern voice pronouncing on the futility of crime in the face of our vigilant law enforcement agencies.

'The same deal,' Fleming says. 'Only today they've been to the movies. A couple of Disneys.'

'And the girl?' I ask him.

'Almost the same. She goes out an hour or so after him and takes a cab and wanders round the stores, finishes up at the boutique only this time she buys without bumping into the guy and starting a lifetime's friendship.'

'What does she buy?'

'Some kind of evening dress. They boxed it for her; she took it on approval.'

'What was the box like?'

'The box? Well, it was long enough to take the dress without folding it up. I guess they wrapped it that way so if she takes it back there's less chance of getting it all creased up.'

'Yeah,' I tell him. 'Well, keep up the good work.'

Before he can make his joke I put the receiver down.

'I want you to cover Mercer Street and Grove Street,' Draper says. 'Then when he's passed through those you drive ahead through the back streets and cover him getting out at Campus.

Bolan's got everything tight and you just keep hanging in looking for faces, anything. We got the guy who sent the note, but like I say, this thing might have caught on like streaking, become a national pastime. And since you didn't manage to fall over our own local chapter member, you stay awake this time, will you?'

'We'll sleep only in shifts,' I tell him. When it's Murdock's turn I'll nudge him and he can take over.'

'Joke about it,' Draper says. 'I hope you're still in a joking frame of mind in a couple of days time' '

We will be,' I tell him. 'Good old Jimbo's in there pitching for us.'

The evening call comes through and it's like before. Both back home. I make tomorrow's arrangements and I pass this news to Murdock. Murdock as usual thinks about it for a while and then asks the question I expected he'd have asked before this late date. 'Why,' he asks, 'don't we cover them round the clock, just in case they don't play it the way we think they are?' Wearily I tell him that none of them are going to chance being fallen over by us until the last minute they have to. Murdock puts up a few arguments against what I've told him but in the end he accepts what I've told him because he's not got any better ideas himself. I wish I had, because I hope to Christ I'm right; I'd hate to see Styles walk away from this, after everything that's happened.

'Feel like some poker?' Murdock says.

I look at my watch and shake my head.

'No,' I tell him. 'I'm going to have an early night.'

I walk through into the bathroom and start to run my tub. I get my robe from the bedroom and go back into the bathroom, then in comes Murdock as I'm climbing in the tub.

'You're turning in early?' Murdock says.

'That's right,' I tell him, sinking down into the warm foamy water and closing my eyes. I hear Murdock flip down the lid on the toilet seat and sit down on it and then he says to me, 'Now if I was smart I'd run out and get a photographer. I'd bring him in here and I'd hold a large clock above your head and he'd take your picture and I'd be worth a fortune.'

'You're already worth a fortune,' I tell him. 'You're worth a fortune because you've taken what I've taken. We're about even-stephen on that score.'

'Yeah,' Murdock says. 'If I ever go back to her in about twelve months' time, my old lady's going to get one hell of a surprise.'

'Won't she just.'

I begin soaping myself and after a while I say to Murdock, 'How come you never told her?'

I'm looking at him now and he pulls a face and sort of shrugs. 'Well how is it she never asked you how you got to be able to afford things, on your pay?'

'I was careful,' Murdock says. 'I never went over the top. I stashed it, like you. And that's the funny thing. All this time, Joyce, she's done her best to make things work out on what I get. She's really worked at it, you know what I mean? And she never knew, because I didn't want her to. All these years she's given her best, and I never let her know what I'd got cooked up for us in the future. Just selfishness, really. I just never wanted her to know. So she's given all that, her youth, and all the time we've had the bread. Now, sometimes I think, maybe I can't even tell her. Maybe if I tell her, she'll pick up a meat cleaver and split me down the middle and all she'll be able to collect is a manslaughter rap.'

'You tell her,' I tell him. 'You tell her, and while you're telling her have a big suitcase with the money in it on the kitchen table; open it in front of her and let her see how good it looks. Just do that and you'll have no problems.'

'You really know a lot about women, don't you, Roy?' Murdock says after a while.

'I know all I need to know,' I tell him. 'I know they think from between their legs, and where their brains are supposed to be is just a jumble of dollar signs.'

'And that's all,' Murdock says.

'Like I say,' I tell him. 'That's all I need to know. If there's anything else, it doesn't make any difference. The important things are like I've said. These are the things you're up against, if you want to handle them.'

Murdock gets up off the toilet seat.

'Well,' he says. 'Thanks for the advice. I'll bear in mind what you've told me. I only wish we'd discussed it sooner, then maybe I wouldn't be in the jam I'm in.'

214

I don't say anything to him. I just let him leave the bathroom on the crest of his own great natural sense of humour and carry on with soaping my dick.

I wake up and feel worse than usual. My first thoughts are I can't understand it. No booze last night, nothing, and I feel terrible. I get out of bed and look in the mirror and I look like I feel, that is, worse than usual. So I walk out of the bedroom in the direction of the bathroom, but the bathroom door's shut and beyond it I can hear the running of bath water and Murdock's less than average voice trying to catch the notes on 'For the Good Times.' So I turn to the kitchen and at least there's one thing, the coffee's brewing, so I turn up the light and sit down at the kitchen table and wait for the coffee to heat up. Murdock's out of the bathroom before that happens and he comes into the kitchen like a member of class '74 and takes over with the coffee and takes two cups and sets them out and pours.

'Now,' he says, looking round. 'There's the ice-box. And what do we have in it, I wonder?

Because this baby is just in love with the idea of starting the day out right again.'

Jesus, I think to myself. Murdock is no longer interested in living. Murdock opens the door of the ice-box, bends over and peers inside.

'Eggs, bacon, yeah, that'll just about do it,' Murdock says, taking out what he wants and straightening up. 'Can I fix any for you?'

I look at Murdock and that tells him all he needs to

know, and while he's throwing eggs and bacon into the pan I get up from the table and take my coffee through into the bathroom.

The city's not exactly what you'd describe as being expectant, but it has a different feel to it.

It's a little tighter, not quite so sloppy. The day is clear and knife-edge clouds in the sky add to the general sharpness of the day's atmosphere.

I check out the squawk-box on Fleming. He answers right away.

'Came out five minutes ago,' he tells me. 'And he's taking the same route as always.' 'And the other one?'

'As usual, no sign this early.'

'Call me when the other one shows.' 'Sure.'

The equipment cuts out and Murdock says, 'Business as usual?' 'As usual,' I tell him.

We drive around for a while, taking in all the obvious and supposedly subtle signs of Bolan's security operation and having a few laughs. About an hour or so before my brother's due to arrive at the station we drive my car over to within a street or so of where Draper's told us to be when the motorcade comes through. We sit there and smoke cigarettes, watching the people going by. The sun rises a little higher in the sky and about half an hour before the arrival's due Fleming comes back on the airways.

'Two things. First, he's unloaded the kid. Took him to the park, walked round a while, then went to the south gate and there's a car waiting, driven by another black woman.

The kid gets in the back of the car, the car takes off, the guy starts strolling through the park, but even though he's strolling, he doesn't have to put on a great burst of speed to get to any of those parts of the route.'

'And what's the other thing?'

'The other one's out a little earlier. Obviously the item wasn't suitable.' 'Why?'

'She's taking it back.' 'Like before?'

'All tied with a ribbon.'

'Tell Copeland to make sure and keep with her.'

'He will.'

I put the set down and tell Murdock.

'That's nice,' he says. 'We're covering the first part of the route while the good-looking nigger strolls over to somewhere in the downtown section and makes the hit. By the time we get there we run into the ambulances coming back.'

Murdock switches on the ignition but I put my hand on his arm.

'Just wait a while,' I tell him. 'We got time.'

'How much time exactly do you think we've got?'

'At least until Fleming gets back to us again.'

'And of course you know when that'll be.'

'I've a pretty good idea it'll be inside of the next fifteen minutes.'

'Oh, well that's fine, then. I can relax.'

'You do that,' I tell him, and light up a cigarette. I look towards the end of Maxwell Street, to the intersection across which the motorcade's going to pass. There's a few people wandering around, obviously taking up early positions for their rubber-necking, but there's not exactly anything you could call a thronging crowd. We sit there a little longer with Murdock doing everything with his hands except jerk himself off and as I'm throwing my cigarette butt into the street, Fleming comes back on the set again.

'This is what you want,' Fleming says. 'He's near Weaver Street, the park side, but the other one, she went back to the boutique, and she's in there a few minutes when who should show up, but the boy friend, the denim guy, only this time he's in his car. He parks outside the boutique and out comes the girl, still with the box, and she gets in back, and he begins to drive.'

'Copeland still with them?' 'Yeah.'

'Where are they now?' 'Weaver Street.'

I whistle and repeat the name.

'I'm on my way now. Keep hitting me with their progress.' I don't have to tell Murdock what to do because he's already pulled away from the kerb and begun to make for Weaver Street. I look at my watch. In five minutes my brother's train will be pulling into the station, and it's going to take us just over that time to get to Weaver Street. Murdock must be thinking along the same lines because as he drives he says 'You couldn't let us have an extra five minutes, could you.'

'Sure,' I tell him, 'if I'd known where we were supposed to be.'

Fleming comes back on the equipment.

'The girl's walking. The guy dropped her and took

off. She's on Weaver walking north carrying the box. The other guy's still on the park.'

'What's the exact location of the girl?'

'Hold it.' Jack comes back on again. 'She's just waiting to cross the street, on the opposite corner to where Fitch's Department store is.'

I cut Jack out and tell Murdock to get into Grafton Street, the one that runs behind Fitch's, parallel to Weaver Street. When Murdock's back of Fitch's I get back to Jack.

'Where is she now?'

'Hold on.' A short wait. 'She's crossed over, she's about ten yards in from Fitch's corner.'

'Drop me here,' I tell Murdock, picking up the equipment. 'Drive to the next intersection and get out and wait for her on Weaver but for Christ sakes – '

'You think you got to tell me?' he asks as I slam the door. I hurry along the south side of Fitch's and slowdown when I turn the corner to start going north after the girl, but I'm not slow enough not to make her; there she is in front of me, about thirty yards ahead, still floating in her cheesecloth, holding the dress box, walking behind the single file of rubber-necks on the edge of the pavement. I keep my eyes fixed on her and call up Pete as I walk.

'Where's the other guy now?'

'On Brook Street. If Weaver's where he's going, he'll be there in approximately two minutes.'

Brook Street's the next intersection along from the one where I told Murdock to leave the car, the street a block on from where Styles is at this moment.

I cut Fleming out and close a little on the girl, then I get this crazy feeling and my gut turns over, because a few yards farther on and the girl will be out in front of the Hillcrest, the place we rousted the other day. I close a little more and then it happens, a quick left and she's in the Hillcrest. I run to the point where the building starts and contact Fleming again.

'Where is he now?'

'He crossed Weaver Street and he's still on Brook Street.'

I swear to myself. Styles is going in via the back door, and while I'm thinking about that Murdock steams up and tells me that the girl's just gone into the Hillcrest and I tell him that I am aware of that fact. So we look at each other for a second or two and then there is nothing left but for us to go in because we have to be where the girl is before Styles. We go in and I'm thinking of all the ways we can find the girl without rousting the whole place and spoiling Styles entrance when I realise there's one big thing in our favour and that's the perfume, the one she was wearing before I went up to the Plaza Suite with her. I walk up the stairs in its wake, motioning Murdock not to ask the questions he wants to ask, and we're soundless until we reach the first floor, and it's soundless, everything's quiet, just like last time. I look at my watch. My brother's on his way. I look down the corridor. There's still the same three rooms. The gimp's, the hustler's and the one where the agent was. And then it lands in my mind ten minutes late; the hit isn't going to be made next door to where an agent's got a stake-out. Not even in the same building. So either the agent's in on it or the agent isn't an agent.

I raise my right arm and point a finger at the third door along. Murdock nods, whether he understands or not. I make another movement with my arm and Murdock stands to one side of the door and I put my hand on the doorknob and turn it. It turns. I push, hardly at all. And then, as I'm about to go in, a door on the opposite side of the corridor opens and out steps Charlie Bancroft and Earl Connors and they're carrying all they need to make Murdock and me stop the movements we were making to unload our own heat. Bancroft's glass eye winks bright in the corridor's gloom and Connor's faint smile even in this light seems just a little wider than usual. Their appearance is enough to freeze my mind but however strong the shock, it's not severe enough to stop the torrent of thoughts teeming through my head, the possibilities, the alternatives, but the only incongruity is the fact that I notice they're both wearing gloves. Bancroft says, 'Now all you have to do is what you were about to do. And that is go through that door.'

I'm looking at Bancroft and Murdock's looking at me so hard I can feel it without having to look at him. But the nearest we'll be to getting answers is to do what Charlie Bancroft tells us to do, otherwise we'll never get the answer to anything ever again, except the one that's nice and soft and is poised to whisper its truth out of the end of Charlie's silencer. So I say to Charlie, 'You want us to go through the door?'

'You got it in one,' Charlie says.

There's no point in asking Charlie what we're going to find when we go through the door so I follow through and let the door swing inwards and the first thing I'm aware of is the bed because Lesley is sitting on the bed and beside her, lying lengthways, is the box with the lid off it, nestling nice and neat in the crêpe paper is a polythene-encased rifle. But the thing I notice most of all is the kind of smile Lesley is wearing.

I go through the door and Murdock follows behind me and then Bancroft and Connors are in too and the door clicks to behind them.

'First the heat,' Charlie says, 'on the bed. And you know how to do it right, so that's how I'd like you to do it.'

Murdock and me do it right and Connors slides round in front of us and picks up our guns from off the counterpane.

'It's not exactly the Plaza Suite,' Lesley says, looking at me, 'but this time you're going to score, believe me.' While she's talking the door opens and Styles comes in and closes the door behind him and he's got a very happy smile on his face.

'Hello, fellows,' he says. 'Glad you could make it in time for the main event.'

He takes a pair of gloves from his coat pocket and while he's putting them on he says to Lesley, 'unveil the goods, honey.'

Lesley pulls the polythene from off the rifle but she doesn't empty the rifle out of the box. I also notice that Connors and Bancroft have exchanged the heat they were carrying for Murdock's and mine. Styles takes the rifle out of the box, turns to me and looks at me for a long moment, and then he says to me, 'against the wall. Just back up until you reach it and then don't make another move.'

I do as he tells me. When I've done that Styles moves forward until his face is a couple of inches away from my face and his grin is as broad as ever. Then he shakes his head

'You sucked hard, baby,' he says. 'You gobbled up and swallowed every last drop.'

Murdock is frozen in the middle of the room, between Lesley on the bed and me and Styles, with Connors and Bancroft flanking him.

'But being such a dumb cop, that's what we figured, and we figured right.'

I don't say anything. Styles raises the rifle and pushes the muzzle against my mouth. 'Open wide, baby, and take one last suck.'

Behind him, I hear Lesley giggle.

'Appreciate the last drop,' he says, 'because in a couple of minutes' time you're never going to gobble anything again.'

Connors says, 'you finally made the front page just like your brother. A real shame you won't be around to read about it.'

Styles puts a little more pressure on the rifle and I have no choice but to open my mouth and I feel the cold metal against my teeth.

'Don't worry,' Styles says, 'you still got a couple of minutes to savour the sweet smell of my aftershave and all the other things that make life worth living. You got until the parade comes by but then when this little old piece has been fired out the window it goes back in your mouth and the trigger's pulled again, precisely at the moment Charlie here pumps a few from your own piece into your partner's guts as he tries to foil your assassination bid on your brother's life.'

He keeps looking at me and he keeps on grinning.

'Real nice and real neat, wouldn't you say?' he asks me, but I don't answer him.

Then he takes the squawk-box from my pocket and looks at it.

'I got to admit the guy on the other end was pretty good, but that was to our advantage, you know? I guess you do, by now. It's a pity though, the way life's turned out for the other guy.'

He taps me on the teeth with the barrel again.

'O.K., baby,' he says. 'Just wait there and watch and drink in the fresh air while you can. It'll be your turn in a minute or so.'

Styles backs off from me and Connors covers me while Styles walks over to the window.

There's a small stool just below the sill and Styles sits down on it. He props up the rifle, leans his arm on the sill and leans forward slightly to look out on to the street. Bancroft puts my gun at Murdock's throat and so Murdock has no choice but to back up against the same wall and watch and wait like

I've got to. I look at Lesley and she looks back at me

and smiles the smile and gets up off the bed and comes and stands in front of me and leans forward and very gently kisses me on the lips. When she's done that she leans backwards and says, 'one for the road. And it'll be one of my favourites, knowing it's your last one.'

The girl's between me and Connors, and Bancroft reacts to what she's said by looking in my direction for a brief moment and grinning and Styles for all his concentration on the scene outside has taken in the girl's movement and Bancroft's movement and he snaps at them to do what he wants them to do, his voice rising above the noise of the crowd as the motorcade approaches, but it's too late for the effect of his words to be felt by Bancroft because Murdock has made his move and everything happens at once, like concurrent images in a split-screen movie. Murdock grabs Bancroft's gun hand and pushes it wide, at the same time giving Bancroft the full force of his knee in the crutch. Bancroft begins to go down and Connors can't help his reaction, which is for a split second to focus his attention on what's happening to Bancroft. Which gives me the opportunity to go to work on him the way Murdock did on Bancroft, but I've got to make it even faster because Styles has started to move. I've got to give him credit, he's not panicked into using the rifle; instead he rushes over to Murdock as Murdock's stretching down to get his gun pack out of Connors's fingers. While all that's happening I've put Bancroft down and got my own gun back and thrown myself in the direction of the door. That particular action of mine puts Styles in two minds but his

225

decision is made for him by Lesley throwing herself against Murdock and over-balancing him; when she's achieved that she picks up Murdock's gun and points it at him. Now Murdock, when he over- balances, doesn't fall to the floor, he bounces against the wall and when he sees where his gun is he makes a grab for it and Styles can see what's going to happen, and he starts screaming at the girl not to do it, but he's too late: she pulls the trigger, three times she pulls it, the bullets hitting Murdock on approximately the same small area of his stomach. Simultaneously he begins to scream in pain and the blood begins to gush out of him like an echo of his scream, but he doesn't go down; he just staggers slightly, looking down at the blood that's raining onto Lesley's cheesecloth, and, oddly, she's looking down at the red spots on her clothes too, in a kind of mild disbelief, taking a step or two back like someone who's been splashed by a passing water truck. By now Styles knows the whole thing's blown and all he can do is to take me out in a different way to the way he'd planned. He's holding the rifle at waist height and he swings round to hip-shoot in my direction. I start scrambling at the door but Bancroft's started to rise from his knees and as Styles pulls the trigger the top of Bancroft's head gets between the bullet and me, and suddenly the top of Bancroft's head is flying in pieces to all four corners of the room. Styles fires again but by that time I'm out in the corridor and running faster than I ever ran in my life and as I get to the end of the corridor a scream begins all on its own, coming from me because there is no sound at all from Murdock.

Part Two

There is a shiver of wind outside the ranch house, causing the window above the sink unit to shudder slightly. I get up from the canvas chair and throw some more wood on the fire and stand in front of the fireplace, listening hard to see if I can separate the sound I'm waiting for from the wind, but there's nothing but the sound of the night out there in the canyon, so I go over to the table and press a button on the transistor. Straight away the room is filled with the voice of the six o'clock newscaster, winding up his slot with a round-up of the weather, which is something I don't need to know, so I press the button again and the room is quiet once more.

I go over to the camping stove, put a light under it and begin to heat some coffee and while I'm waiting for it to warm I go back over to the fireplace and pick up the newspaper that's top of the heap. Of course it's the Examiner, and it's still got the same front page I've read a thousand times before. I don't have to read it, it's like a printed circuit in my mind, but even though the words are already there, I look at the newsprint anyway, and again, for the thousandth time, I have to admit they did a beautiful job. The headline couldn't be bigger. The picture of my brother in the empty hotel room, looking round in disbelief, Murdock's blood a pattern on the carpet by his feet. Then there are the insets; the rifle, my gun, the one that killed Murdock, a picture of Murdock dead, curled up like a foetus before the room had been cleared, pictures, portraits, of Murdock and myself, from the newspaper files. A shot of Mrs Murdock, sobbing, being supported by her brother.

A mug-shot of Charlie Bancroft, a small-time hood who must have had something, if not everything, to do with the operation, perhaps inveigled into the deal by missing policeman Roy Boldt, now sought by his colleagues as a possible suspect. Of course, on the front page of that particular edition, no mention of Jack Fleming, a private investigator, getting knocked over by a hit- and-run driver as he crossed Weaver Street, and Tony Copeland, unemployed, falling from his apartment window. Those little items were small, in the inside pages, three liners. But the quotes, they really capped the lot, they were the cream. Draper and his vow not to rest until I'd been found, how the whole reputation of the Department rested on that very fact; my brother's statement that he could hardly bring himself to believe I could have had anything to do with it, but he was only looking forward to the day we would meet face to face and only then, by meeting face to face, would he know, and he'd know instantly, whether I was guilty or not. From Mr Florian, a prominent local businessman; how a thing like this could happen in a town like ours defies belief. And so on and so on. But of course, what the papers didn't say was that Draper and Florian and whoever else was involved were hoping to Christ their own boys would find me before the usual agencies did, just in case I got the chance to get my story across, and maybe if I did that someone just might believe me.

The coffee comes to the boil so I go over to the stove

and fill the tin cup from the jug and wander round the ranch house for something to do until the coffee has cooled enough for me to drink it. While I'm doing that I catch sight of myself in the small mirror tacked up above the sink and so I walk a little closer and take a look at myself, just to pass the time. And it occurs to me, looking at my face, looking at the beard and the length of my hair and the greasy collar of my denim, a lot of time has passed. My friend Boldt, the drop-outs' drop-out. But I have to admit, like the man said; so far so good.

It hadn't been difficult for me to get away from the Hillcrest. In fact it had never been intended for me to get away at all and that was what had made it easy. Only Styles and Lesley and Charlie were going to walk out of there, and after the pop-gun popped and my brother's brains had started slip-streaming down the street every cop in the immediate vicinity would have started out for where they thought the pop had come from, and playing percentages, if the whole thing had been regular, maybe two or even three of them would have got to the Hillcrest, maybe even made it round to the back exit. And that's exactly what Draper and company didn't want to happen. So he must have directed Bolan to put his men as far from the Hillcrest as was decent, just far enough to give the first part of the getaway its head start. Christ alone knows what arrangements had been made beyond the first sixty seconds but they sure as hell would have been out of town before my brother's brains hit the sidewalk. So I'd taken advantage of the ignorance of the guys on the beat and getting away from the Hillcrest had been no problem.

Somewhere to go and getting there could have been a little more difficult, but I'd had a little bit of luck and a little bit of inspiration. The luck stemmed from the situation. Nobody knew what had happened up in that room until Styles had gotten out and passed on the good news. So until then Draper couldn't pull the alarm switch on me in case it short-circuited and blew his balls off. That way I had a little time to wait for my inspiration, the time it took for me to get to Murdock's car and put some blocks between myself and the Hillcrest, and inspiration came because of the direction I happened to be travelling in, the direction of Sammy's. Now first of all the thought of ditching Murdock's car without it being a pointer to where I might be heading for had been bothering me, but when I'd got conscious I was making for Sammy's. I'd remembered his lock-up in the alley behind his bar, a place that had once been used for face-lifting hot cars. Sammy had been part of it, but there's been a split and the other fellows no longer operated from there and so Sammy had since taken it over completely and so it occurred to me that the lock-up would be better than the street.

Immediately I'd thought of that, everything else about my getaway came flooding into my mind. So I'd put the car in the alley and gone in Sammy's the back way and the first person I'd seen was Joan, which had been great for me, because I'd laid everything on her as quickly as I could and there'd been no doubt in her mind which way to break. She'd gone and got Sammy and at first all the reasons he'd used a couple of days earlier had made him try and turn me down but Joan had been adamant, so adamant in fact that while Sammy had been starting all over again from A, Joan had gone out in the alley and put Murdock's car in the lock-up and from that point on I'd been there for six weeks. Not in the bar building but in the little hidey-hole of an apartment above the lock-up. It was a nice little place, all set up with a freezer and a stove and other domestic offices and the light came in through an angled sky-light that wasn't overlooked by any other buildings; all I could see was the way the sky changed from day to day over the six-week period. And while I was doing my cloud watching Joan or Sammy'd come in with provisions and the papers and the booze and during the whole of that period they never got a visit from the Department, because nobody in it knew about my involvement with Sammy. Except of course, Murdock.

I never told Sammy or Joan about Styles, never went into any real details at all. I just asked them to trust me, which Joan did and Sammy, I think, didn't, but what Sammy thought wasn't going to make any difference to anything, because I was there, and in no way was I going to move until the time was right. And that time didn't only depend on the town cooling down. It depended on my arriving at a plan. A plan I needed to work out to perfection so the score could be evened out a little bit, for Murdock. And the time had been well spent, because I'd cracked it, with a little bit of inspiration.

I'd left Sammy's in a pick-up, driven by Joan. The pick-up was a nice little affair Sammy'd used in the days he'd been working. He'd fixed it up himself and what he'd done was to engineer a false compartment between the driver's seat in the back of the cabin and the carrying part of the truck. It was pretty tight but I'd only been in it for an hour or so until Joan'd driven out of town and seventy miles down the highway until the desert turn-off and then a quarter of an hour into that Joan'd stopped and let me out and I'd taken over the driving for the next half an hour until we'd come to the first of the derelict ranches. Beyond this the road ran out. Daytime, Joan could've taken over and driven to where we were going but at night there was no way I was going to risk any accident that left the truck wide open in daylight for the helicopter patrol to home in on it. So I got out of the pick- up with my rucksack and my bedroll and said goodbye to Joan, see you soon, Joan, and sacked down for the night in one of the outbuildings of the run-down ranch. I'd waited outside all next day and looked out at the rocks and the desert and got the bearings I'd been given fixed in my mind and then when it got close to dusk I'd started out for Sammy's place. I'd taken just over two hours to get there and the light was just disappearing, but I'd had the place in view for the last half an hour so even in the hurrying light there was no chance I was going to miss Sammy's ranch.

Sammy's ranch looks just as derelict as the last place from the outside, and when I'd got there I'd been wondering if I'd got the wrong bearing, but once I'd unlocked the front door and swung the flashlight around a little bit I realised I'd got the right place.

Sammy acquired the rights to this place seven or eight years ago, before his accident had put him out of business. He took it for the same kind of reason I'm using it, but he never needed it. So he fixed it up a little bit, built in one or two home comforts, and, what the hell, if any prospectors or hippies busted in on it, then, Christ, he wasn't going to lose too much sleep over that; but maybe when he and Joan gave up the bar they could use it some weekends, one of those places people think about like that but never do anything about.

And so here I've been, three months. Joan's been out here twice since, with provisions. And I have to admit, every cloud has its silver lining. The first time she comes out, she helps me unload the provisions, and it strikes me there's a tension about her. At first I put it down to the general nervousness created by the situation, but then I remember she was pretty cool when she brought me out here. So after we stack everything away, I say to her why don't we celebrate our labours with a cup of coffee and she says, 'no, she'd better not, the light'll be going soon, she'd better be getting back.' But I already have the stove lit and I'm working with the coffee and while I'm doing that I'm telling her the light'll stay for an hour yet, desert light's different to anywhere else; I should know,

I'm getting to be a veteran. So she finally says 'yes' but she doesn't sit down, she wanders around the room looking at the stuff in it as though she's never seen any of it before. The coffee boils up and I fill two mugs and while I'm waiting for it to cool I break open a bottle of scotch and a can of ginger ale; the sound of that activity makes her start as if somebody's just fixed a machine gun so I say to her, 'you've got to join me, I mean, I got all next month and some to drink alone.' She stares at the bottle as I gurgle the scotch into the only two glasses in the place, tumblers, and when I've finished I ask her if she'd like any ginger ale and she shakes her head, but only after she's looked at the tumbler for quite a while.

Once she'd made that movement, I get the feeling that it's no longer going to be like when Sammy was away, and I think, maybe the years between have had a lot to do with it. So I go round the other side of the table to where she is and hand her the tumbler. She takes it and holds it against her breasts, both hands, like with a sacramental cup, and she closes her eyes. I stand there for a minute or two, looking at her, and then I take the tumbler away from her and her hands part slightly away from her breasts, and I begin to unbutton her shirt. She makes no move at all, except to drop her arms to her side so that her shirt can slide off her shoulders and down her arms on to the floor. Then I put my arms round her, unhook her bra, slip the straps and then the bra joins the shirt. Still no movement from her, still the eyes closed. So I unbuckle the belt of her jeans and release the press stud and the zip begins to open of its own accord but I give it a little help and the jeans are tight enough so that when I ease them down her hips the panties go with them. Still no movement, so I pull her to me and I kiss her and suddenly there's movement, her arms go round my neck, and I nearly over balance

234

backwards across the table and after that I have no time to think about movement or non-movement because Joan is making up for the absence of the last seven years, feeling hands on her again, and to me seven years is nothing, it's worth a lifetime to be on the receiving end of that kind of tidal wave.

So that's how it was. Afterwards, she could hardly bring herself to stop rushing out into the desert dusk air and vomiting but she managed, somehow, and to give her a break, I walked out on to the boardwalk porch so that she could get dressed without her feeling my eyes on the way she felt. When she'd done that she came outside too and without a word she walked past me and climbed into the pick-up and fired the ignition and a minute or two later the truck was a dark shimmering nothing against the desert dusk.

The second time she comes to me, it's almost the same. Except she's had a month to think about it and this time when we meet it's like being two kids; that time when nothing is so important as to be with the person who's generating that special kind of electricity. Every minute that builds up to the meeting is an hour of superb hell, and then the meeting, the floodgate, the oneness, the unselfishness, the mingling; Jesus, that's what it's like, this time, sweetening the sex and the body- smell of it, making the whole thing a totally honourable estate. And this time, this feeling is what makes her guillotine herself about Sammy. She's in pain, she's in anguish, she wants to be dead, but this is the great thing, the agony is enormous but the enormity of it is cancelled, terrifying for her, by the need for the continuation of what she's feeling for me. And so this time we talk, and we talk with a sureness, taking full account of the pain, a sureness about what we're going to do, taking full account of all the dangers, all the selfishness, all the misery our actions are going to cause. And the talk is about our future. About us. Together. Christ, I think at one point, is this me, in this situation, talking of things like this? But my question is like a double negative because underneath it, even while I'm rationalising it, there's a repose in the knowledge that there's no answer to the question, because there's no need to ask it in the first place.

So that was the second time. The time we arranged our future. And now, now I wait for the third time. This is the last time, here. She's coming to take me out, this time. She's no knowledge of what I'm going to do. She only knows the place we're to meet after I've done it. She had ideas, she has a fear, but unlike her conquering her guilt over Sammy, there's no way any consideration for Joan is going to stop me doing what I'm going to do. All right, she's had seven years to drive her to her present state of mind, but part of her motivation stems from love, and I'm driven by hate, and in my book that's the stronger of the two emotions. I've had three months to stoke up that hatred, and the hatred's not just been warped and hyped-up by mind pictures; I've had real pictures, the pictures in the papers, pictures of Murdock in different attitudes of death taken from the different vantage points of the photographers, almost adding up to a two dimensional essay on death in the round; the blood-soaked shirt he'd been so careful to hang up when he first moved into my apartment; the fingers stiff in their final grab for the gun, now frozen in the futile pose of grasping for life; the eyes like pebbles; the trouser leg screwed up to his knee, displaying a neat, suspender- fixed sock; and the blood itself, on his mouth, on the hand clutching the shirt where his stomach has opened up, on the floor around him. And the counterpoint of the relaxed legs and easy balance of the cops standing around him, dispassionately placed shoes, the way I would have been, viewing just another death.

The coffee boils over and I turn off the stove, but instead of pouring some coffee into a cup I pick up the scotch and fill a tumbler and drink until the tumbler's only half-full, then I open the door and stand on the porch looking down the dry wash of the low canyon. The wind is cold and the desert scene is as usual clear and clean in its sharp deep focus. But there is nothing else. I look at my watch. Late. She's late. Not much, but enough to set me off, like a con who's on his last day, waiting for the screw to come and conduct him through the ritual with the warden, and then to the opening gates; he knows it's going to happen, he knows he's going out, but it doesn't help. His guts are water, and the panic of expectancy matches the panic of the moment of capture, and no amount of repeating to himself that it's true (as opposed to repeating it's not true when the bust happened), none of that helps. Only the closing door is the final convincer.

I turn to go back inside again and as I get to the doorway I hear the sound I've been waiting for, the lurching, hesitant sound of the pick-up, being carried down the wind towards me. I turn back and the pick-up is just appearing at the top of the gully. Then it dips and starts on its downward path towards the ranch. I finish the rest of my scotch and there is a cracking tension in me and without any conscious thought I hurl the tumbler at the nearest rock and spin round and scream into the evening air.

We put my stuff in the pick-up and look at each other.

'Come on,' I say to her. 'Let's go inside. We have to have a farewell drink.' She doesn't say anything.

'What I mean is, this is where we met. You know what I mean. It deserves the honour of a final drink.'

She nods and we go inside. I fill the remaining tumbler for her and take mine from the bottle and when we've taken our drinks we kiss for a long, long time, then after the kiss she rests her head against my chest and we stay that way for a while, no words, scarcely moving, the only sound the wind outside.

It's a small town, on the edge of the highway. Even the main street's been by-passed by the through road. On the opposite side of the town, the railroad flanks the straggling buildings.

Joan drives the pick-up off the main street and takes a left and then another left until she's almost back to the main street again. Then she stops the pick-up and we sit there in silence for a minute or two. I look at the brightly lit car lot on the corner of main street. Then Joan takes out the envelope with the money in it I'd had stashed at Sammy's and gives it to me. I open it and count out what she's going to need and put the rest in my inside pocket. 'Did Sammy ask why I wanted the whole bundle?' I ask her. She nods and says, 'Yes. I told him what you told me to. I told him you'd had this fear that you might have to move fast and without the money you'd be dead.'

'And he still thinks I'm at the ranch?'

'I told you. I told him everything you said to tell him.'

'And when you go back you tell him I want to move on, and that's why you've got to go back to the ranch so soon.'

She nods.

'Don't worry,' I tell her. 'He'll be so relieved he'll never question anything else again. You'll just go and you'll have eight hours start.'

'It's not that I'm worried about.'

'No,' I tell her. 'I know it's not that. I'm just pretending to help us both.'

She nods, agrees, but nothing's helping her. There's another long silence. Then she gets out of the pick-up and begins to walk towards the car lot and I slide over to the driver's seat.

It takes her around twenty minutes. Then I see her drive across the intersection in a '72 Pontiac. I take a pull from the scotch and during the ten minutes I wait I take a couple more pulls and then I switch on the ignition and making a U-turn I drive back round the block and get on to main street and make it back on to the highway. A quarter of an hour later I turn off left and a mile or so down the road the Pontiac's in the pick-up's headlights. I stop the pick-up and get out and Joan gets out.

'Till the day,' I say to her.

Again she doesn't say anything, just nods. We transfer all the gear I need for what I'm going to do and then she gets into the pick-up and I get into the Pontiac and I sit there watching the pick-up's headlights in the driving mirror as she begins her reverse.

Hoffman, in his town, is like Florian in mine. A member of that particular masonic order that stretches nationwide and can call the tune in the Hit Parade. And unlike Florian, he's single, and unlike Florian, he's stupid with the broads. Sure, he's got guys walking behind him, but when he's into a broad or two, that's all that matters to him, all that's in front of his eyes, and that he's lived this long is some kind of miracle. The boys can go home and file their nails or the numbers of their heat and expect to see him in the morning, maybe. A couple of days' watching him, in his town, it makes me smile, and not only because he's so fucking stupid, because his stupidity is an omen. His charmed life is a lucky charm for me.

So on the third night, I follow him through his usual routine. Around ten he comes out of his house. A nice house, well-appointed, secure as Fort Knox. So having a house as secure as Fort Knox, he leaves it. The limousine slides out of the garage, he gets in, the chauffeur eases the automobile down to the gates, the gates are opened, the automobile slides out. And from then on it's the same route as the night before. On to the Blue Dahlia. Hoffman goes in, the chauffeur waits, and so do I. Then, two hours later, a guy comes out, has words with the chauffeur, the chauffeur says something back and about ten minutes later the guy comes back with a tray with some beer and sandwiches on it. The chauffeur takes the tray, puts it on the passenger seat and sits in the car to have his midnight feast. So we're there for another couple of hours. The only activity in that time is the guy coming back out for the tray and taking it back in again. But eventually Hoffman reappears, and like on the last two nights, he's not alone. He has a blonde on each arm, look-a-likes, same kind of hair-styles, clothes, they could be sisters, but my guess is they're just a team; some way back they decided two could make three times as much as one. Last night and the night before Hoffman left the Blue Dahlia with them, and so I know where they're going to be going. I ease away before Hoffman and party have time to get into their job and I drive across town ahead of them, keeping them in sight of my driving mirror. When I get to the house where the blondes hang out I take a left and park and get out of the Pontiac and wait around the corner until I hear Hoffman's car pull in at the kerb. I hear the chauffeur get out and let out Hoffman and his trade and I hear Hoffman tell his man to go on home and he'll call tomorrow afternoon or sometime, when he needs picking up. Then I hear the chauffeur close his door and the car pulls away and when it's passed the corner I'm hiding round, that's when I come out to play.

Hoffman and the girls are on the house steps; one of the girls is trying to put the key in the lock while Hoffman and the other girl are standing a couple of steps below. The house is on the corner of the block, so Hoffman has no real time to make me as I walk up the steps holding what I'm holding. There's nothing but blank disbelief on Hoffman's face, but the girl standing next to him starts to fix her lips to shriek, but I cut that by talking to them and saying, 'no noise. Otherwise the three of you take it here. No noise, no death. Just inside. Open the door and we all go inside.'

The other girl, the girl with the key, she just stares at me.

'You heard me,' I tell her.

'Do it,' Hoffman says, in a voice that only just makes it through the phlegm in his throat. The girl flicks her head in animal-like assent and now she's able to put the key in the lock. 'Wait,' I tell her. 'I want the right answer to this; there anybody else?'

Hoffman answers for her by shaking his head, over and over.

'Fine,' I say. 'So now we all go in.'

The girl turns the key and the door swings inwards; the three of them walk very carefully through the door and I follow them and close the door behind me, and then I bolt it, both bolts.

We're in a very low-lighted hall, very tastefully decorated, a couple of expensive original rubbish paintings and a pedestal bearing a statuette of some Grecian goddess. There are two doors on either side of the hallway and there is a flight of stairs leading to an even dimmer upstairs. I frisk Hoffman and then I say, 'Upstairs. Girls first. Stop on the landing.'

The girls go upstairs, Hoffman follows them and I follow Hoffman. They all do as they're told, and stop on the landing.

'The bedroom,' I tell them.

The girl who unlocked the front door opens a door on the right of the landing. I look through the door, 'O.K.,' I say. 'In. Go over to the left-hand wall and stand with your noses touching it. One at a time.'

The first girl goes in, then her partner, then Hoffman. They all face the wall, like I said to.

The bedroom is just as dim as the rest of the house. It's lit by a central orb of diffused light set in the ceiling. There is an eight-foot-square bed and the wall in back of the bed is all mirror. On the other walls there are half a dozen framed pornographic drawings, each one showing different aspects of a set-up involving two mature girls and a boy of around seven or eight.

'Nice,' I say. 'You never grew up, hey, Hoffman?'

Hoffman begins to speak but I shut him up. Then the room is full of silence and I let it hang for a minute or two. Then I say, 'O.K., girls, listen carefully. When I say go, the one next to Hoffman, turn away from the wall and walk over to the bed and sit on the end, near where I am. Then, you, the other one, you do the same, only when I say so. You got that?'

They nod. There is a visible sagging relief from Hoffman: he suddenly thinks he's got it all figured.

'Fine,' I say. 'First one, go.'

The first one turns away from the wall and sits on the edge of the bed.

'Now you.'

The other one does the same and sits next to her partner. They look ten years older than when they left the Blue Dahlia. I take the bottle of pills out of my top pocket. I hand the bottle to the first girl. They both stare at the bottle.

'Unscrew the cap and shake out all the tablets on to the bed next to you.' She's frozen.

'Do it,' I tell her.

She doesn't move. I let my silence speak for me. Then she moves. When she's emptied the tablets on the bed I say, 'now divide them equally into two heaps. There'll be a dozen each.'

This time she does like I say first time.

'Now pick up one heap and give them to your friend.' She does it.

'Pick up the others yourself.' She does that too.

'Now I want you both to eat them.' They both look at me.

'Don't worry,' I tell them. 'All you're going to do is sleep. But if you like, there's another alternative.'

They begin to eat the tablets. It takes about five minutes until they've swallowed the last one.

Then I take out the surgical tape and hand it to the first girl.

'Your partner's mouth. And you, when she's done that, you do hers.' Again, they do as they're told. Then I say to the first one, 'Now get on the bed and lie face down and put your hands behind your back.'

She twists round and crawls up the bed and lies face down and puts her hands behind her back.

'You,' I say to the other one, 'take off your friend's tights and tie her hands.'

I get no argument from her, either. She crawls up the bed too and kneels next to her partner and pulls up her partner's long dress to the waist and tugs down her tights, fumbling them off her feet, and ties her partner's hands. She knows how tightly I need it done; she doesn't want to have to be asked to re-tie the knot, and when she's done that she looks dumbly at me for the next instructions.

'Lie down like her,' I tell her.

She turns round and lies down alongside her partner. When she's done that I bend down and take the lengths of slim cord from my hold-all and throw them on the bed; they land at the feet of the girls.

'O.K., Jimmy,' I say to Hoffman, 'now it's your turn to get in on the act. You can turn around now.'

He turns around.

'Listen, Mister,' he says. 'Look, you don't have to go this far. You don't have to worry any, you can have them, any way you like, only, let me go home, huh? You don't need me around and I won't cause you any grief. Christ, how can I? I mean, I don't even know you.'

'You know me,' I tell him. 'Take a closer look. And when you realise who I am, don't say the name, or you're dead.'

Hoffman looks at me. Then it falls on him, and he

almost says my name. But not quite. The fear in him is now too great for him to speak at all.

'Yeah,' I say to him.

He begins to shake his head but I wave the gun at the bed.

'Over there,' I tell him. He manages to make it.

'Now,' I tell him, 'I want you to take the tights off your other lady friend and tie her hands the same way.'

Hoffman kneels on the edge of the bed and tries to push up the other girl's tight long skirt but he begins to crap himself because he's not doing it right. He can't push it up, so he panics and in his panic he resorts to solving his problem by ripping the skirt from hem to waist and when he scrambles her tights off he's in so much of a fucking hurry he pulls her panties off with them; then he panics even more trying to separate them from the tights and in the end he gives up and the panties are still interwoven with the tights when he ties the knot on the girl's wrists. When he's finished I say to him, 'now take a piece of cord and tie it tight round the nearest girl's neck and when you've done that carry it on to the other girl's neck, just the same.'

When Hoffman's done that I speak again.

'Run the rest of the cord under the bed and bring it up the other side, then join it to where it goes round the first girl's neck. And I want it tight. You got that?'

He's got that and he does it. Then I tell him to take another piece of cord and tie it round the ankles of the girl on the left and again pass the cord under the bed and join it to the ankles of the girl on the right. When he's done that I say to him, 'now take me to a room where there's a phone.'

I stand to one side and let him pass and as he's passing by he takes his life in his hands by stopping and turning to face me and launching into an appeal but I say to him, 'all you have to do if you want to stay alive is what I tell you to do.'

The resolve breaks up; the muscles of his face go slack and he seems to lose three inches in height. Then he turns away and I follow him out of the bedroom and back along the landing, down the stairs and when we're in the hallway Hoffman turns to the door on his right but he's very careful not to open it without me telling him to. He stands there and looks at me like a dog asking its master if it can go out and take a leak.

'Go ahead,' I tell him.

He opens the door and goes through and I follow him in. This time we're in a broad room with a low circular hooded fireplace set dead centre and around it, echoing the fireplace's circle is a corduroy kind of divan going almost all the way round, broken only by the gap through which you get in to actually sit down. Again the lighting in this room is like the lighting in the rest of the place, and again there's the thinking man's pornography hanging on the room's dark walls.

The phone is on a long lead so I pick up the set and I tell Hoffman to sit down on the semi- circular divan. When he's done that I go through the gap and sit down next to him and put the set in his lap. His hands fall onto the set and he sits perched on the edge of the divan like a girl who's suddenly realized her skirt is too short for comfort.

'This is going fine so far,' I tell Hoffman. 'Now if it continues to go fine, you stay alive. You understand that?'

Hoffman shakes his head.

'I'm dead,' he says. 'There's no way you walk out of here, otherwise. I stay alive, and you're going to be found, and you know that. So I'm dead.'

It's my turn to shake my head.

'Believe it,' I tell him. 'Your living or dying makes no difference to me. All I need is twelve hours. Now I can get those hours with you like the broads upstairs, or with you dead. Like I say, it makes no difference to me, but I feel it maybe makes a lot of difference to you.' Hoffman tries to believe me for a moment or two, then he says, 'what do you want me to do?'

I tell him, and for a while, his fear is overcome by his disbelief.

'You're crazy,' he says.

I don't answer.

'You've got to be crazy,' Hoffman repeats. Again I don't answer.

'I mean,' Hoffman says, 'just supposing I do that. Just supposing I make that call. And it works out the way you want it to. I'm still dead. I do that and I'm dead. No way. So why should I do it? Why should I do the thing that means my own death?'

I shrug.

'If you don't do it, you're dead in a few minutes,' I tell him. 'If you do, you've time to make arrangements.'

'Yeah,' he says. 'For my funeral.' I don't say anything.

'Listen,' he says. 'You're crazy. O.K., so I make the call. How can you guarantee he won't check it out? How can you even guarantee he can be there when you say? I mean it's crazy.'

'Could he be there?'

Hoffman doesn't say anything.

'And your other point,' I say to him. 'The guarantee he won't check it out. You know he won't.

Because you're making the call. No question.'

Hoffman doesn't say anything to that, either.

'So then we have nothing to talk over,' I say to him. 'And now all you have to do is make the call and say what I've told you to say, and after you've done that we can go upstairs again and you can lie down with your sweethearts.' Hoffman is silent for a minute or two then he picks up the receiver and sticks his finger in the dial. He starts to move it and then he stops, letting the dial spin back, and he turns to me and says, 'you're crazy. I mean, you know that?'

'You could always prove that another way, if that's your taste.'

Hoffman dials and he doesn't have to wait long before the receiver is lifted at the other end. Then he says what I've told him to say and I have to hand it to him, he does it well, he sounds the way he's supposed to sound. It doesn't take long, which makes it even better; that makes it right.

Hoffman puts the receiver back on its cradle and shakes his head and then with one sudden movement he sweeps the whole set into my face and jumps up, hurling himself over the back of the divan. Before I can loose anything off at him he's over to the door and through it. He's not stupid so he doesn't try and unbolt the door to get out of the way, but instead I hear another door open and slam and by the time I'm out in the hall I hear the opposite door being bolted from the inside so I start kicking away at it. It doesn't take long for me to loosen the inside fixings and the door flies inwards and there's a bathroom, not big, all black tiled, even on the ceiling, except for one wall which echoes the wall in the bedroom above, just all one mirror. Hoffman's standing on the toilet seat trying to unlatch the bathroom cabinet door and when he hears the bathroom door crash inwards he screeches like a white owl and turns the gun he's grabbed from the cabinet in my direction. Then he hauls off a couple of wild shots, and jumps down off the toilet seat, rushes towards his own reflection in the mirror wall, clawing at the glass as though he's somehow going to make it through to Wonderland, screaming and gibbering at his own screaming and gibbering reflection. Then I get the gun on me again, and for all his insanity a part of his mind is still capable of taking in my double-handed movement as I home in the silencer on him and then I have to adjust my aim as he slides down the glass and on to his knees, imploring to Christ and his own image for it not to be, waving the gun around, and so I pull the trigger twice, and the bullets follow each other in at the base of his skull and part of his face mingles with his reflection on the glass and both slide slowly down towards the floor.

Somehow, the early morning air around Florian's has an expensive feel about it, as if he's had it specially flown in. From my vantage point slightly farther up the hillside, the still blue oblong of Florian's pool looks flat as plastic and the layout around it, the patio and all that stuff, looks as though it never knew a thing like dust existed. Everything's sweet, everything's still, everything's perfect, just poised for the daily routine, which I guess has already started inside the house, and will very soon be moved out into the clear sharp sunshine.

I don't have to wait long.

The sliding glass slides open and Earl Connors walks out carrying a towel and surveys the morning scene. Then he stands aside and out comes Florian, almost Roman in his white towelling robe. He breathes in some of his air and does a few limbering-up exercises and then he unties his belt and Earl helps the robe off his shoulders and lays it neatly on one of the poolside chairs. Florian makes a nice neat dive and breaks up the surface of the pool. That's Earl's cue to sit down and light up a cigarette and enjoy doing nothing for five minutes or so. It's also my cue to move.

I crouch my way down the hillside, doubled lower than the height of the bushes, until I get to the wall that's parallel to the oblong of Florian's swimming pool. Then I turn west and go in the shadow of the wall until I get to the corner and go down the next piece of wall that runs along the blind side of the house and I go along this until I get to a point where there's a hillock of earth. I stand on it and bend my legs, jumping up to hold a couple of the spiked railings that decorate the top of Florian's wall and I pull myself up and take a little look. There's nobody walking around the grounds since I moved down the hillside and nobody can see me because there's no windows on this side of the building. The only evidence of life is the sound of Florian splashing up and down in his pool. So I heave myself up to the top of the wall and gently let myself down the other side and make it silently through the foliage to the blind side of the house and then to the corner, beyond which is the pool. I wait until the sounds of Florian's aqua show are going away from me and then I turn round the corner and there's Earl, his back to me, and Florian swimming to the far end of his pool. I stick close to the wall until I'm about four feet away from Earl and then I say, 'It's Boldt, Earl. And there's nothing you can do. You know that.'

Earl is suddenly like marble. Nothing moves at all.

'So knowing that, take your gun out and put it down by your chair and when Mr Florian touches the far end you get up and you go and stand at the edge of the pool and tell Mr Florian who's here to see him. And explain how I want Mr Florian to get out of the pool and how I want you both to go back in the house.'

Still nothing. But when Florian does a flip and starts heading his back-stroke this way, Earl gets up and goes and stands by the edge of the pool and does just as I tell him to. Florian stops swimming when he hears the sound of Earl's voice and so as to catch what Earl's saying he floats on his back on the pool's surface. Then when he's taken in

Earl's words he paddles his hands slightly and drifts round so he's in a position to verify what he's just been told. He looks at me and I look at him. Then a moment or two later Florian says, 'O.K., Earl.'

Then he twists over in the water, swims slowly over to the side and climbs out of the pool. He pauses at the edge for a moment and looks at me.

'Is it all right if I put on my robe?' Florian says.

'I'll bring it in for you,' I tell him.

Florian nods and begins to walk towards the glass doors and Earl follows after him. I move very quickly and pick up the robe, which is no heavier than it should be, and then I pick up Earl's gun and go in after them.

They're both standing in the broad low room, three or four feet apart, watching me as I come in out of the sunlight. They're both wise enough not to make any move, at least, just yet.

The room we're in is Florian's gym cum den cum games room. There's a lot of pine and some keep-fit gear and a pool table and a bar and some nice self-consciously masculine furniture and sheepskin scatter rugs all over the floor, and on the pool table is Florian's morning gear, all neatly laid out.

'Where's Hammett?' I ask Florian.

'He gets here at nine,' Florian says.

He's also wise enough not to chance any wrong answers.

'Who else is here?'

'The cook. She'll be fixing my breakfast around now.'

'How many on the gate?'

'Only one.'

'The one that's been there since midnight?'

'Yeah.'

'When's the changeover? Eight?' Florian nods.

'That's fine. That's just about great.' I smile at them both.

'Well, Earl,' I say to him. 'I'd like you to lie down on the floor and face the rug.'

Earl looks at Florian as if he's expecting some kind of answer. The only answer he gets is a nod from Florian and so Earl goes down on his knees, turns round and prostrates himself.

'Now,' I say to Florian, 'you flip a switch on your little box there and you tell your cook you changed your mind, you don't feel like your breakfast. You tell her that the guy on the gate's going to come in a little early for his. And then you flip another switch and tell the guy on the gate that you're expecting Mr Draper and when Mr Draper comes through the gate your guy can come in a little early and take his breakfast where he usually does. And in both cases you emphasize you want no interruptions.'

Florian looks at me and there's no expression at all on his face. Then he says, 'Draper.'

'Oh yeah,' I tell him. 'I almost forgot. I want you to call Draper. Tell him you've got news on me. Tell him he's got to get over fast but tell him nothing else. You understand?'

Florian understands all right but at the same time he doesn't understand. All he knows is that for the moment he has to go along with anything I say, because if he understands anything at all, it's what would happen if he were to do the slightest thing any different. So he does the first two things and when it gets to phoning Draper he pauses for a moment to compose himself. Then he lifts the receiver and dials the number and two minutes pass before there is any response at the other end of the line. Then Florian says, 'it's Florian.' A couple of seconds then he speaks again.

'I got news. I got a fix on Boldt just come through.' Another couple of seconds.

'Yeah. Right away.'

Then Florian puts the phone back on its cradle. Naturally he's trying to work out what I have in mind but he's never going to ask, not Florian. So he stands there and waits to see what I have to say next, but instead of saying anything I go over to the pool table and take a look at Florian's clothes, polo shirt, check sports coat, gaberdine slacks, and on the floor calf-skin slip-ons. I feel the clothes and I say to Florian 'Nice. Quality goods. I was just seeing if they carried your trade mark.'

Florian doesn't answer.

'O.K.,' I tell him. 'Now get dressed.'

Florian takes off his robe and his trunks and puts on his clothes.

'Now sit down behind the desk with your hands on top and when Draper comes in you do nothing at all. He'll see Earl but don't let that be any concern of yours. Just stay behind the desk, and no movement.'

Florian does as he's told and sits behind the desk and I go over to the wall next to the door that Draper's going to be coming through and stuff as much of Earl's gun in the top pocket of my denim jacket as I can and then I lean for a while.

Time passes. I look at my watch. I figure a quarter of an hour at most. Soft ripples, reflections from Florian's pool, illuminate the wooden ceiling and the whole house is very quiet.

After a while Florian says, 'I'd like to smoke a cheroot.'

I look at the desk. His silver case and his lighter are lying on the desk in front of him, clear of anything else.

'Sure,' I tell him. 'Why not?'

Florian very carefully picks up the cigarette case and opens it and takes out a cheroot. He puts it in his mouth and the case snaps shut and it's like the sound of a gun going off. Just as carefully he lights his cheroot and replaces the lighter and after he's blown out some smoke he says, 'it doesn't have to work out this way.'

'What way would that be?'

Florian doesn't answer that but instead he says, 'in my library, I got a safe. In it, there's close on forty grand. You walk out of here and it belongs to you.'

'Sure, and then when my blood is seeping into your gravel drive you walk over and pick up the money and put it back in the safe again.'

Florian shakes his head.

'I guarantee,' he says. 'I guarantee you –'

'Shut up,' I tell him.

Florian doesn't shut up. Instead he starts talking to himself, but it isn't what you'd call a conversation, it's a string of meaningless obscenities because there's nothing for him to say that means anything anymore. Then from the rug comes the muffled sound of Earl Connor's voice and for the first time in his life he answers Florian back by saying, 'for Christ's sake, shut up, for Christ's sake.' But Florian doesn't pay any attention, he's in a world of his own, cursing the impotence of his situation.

Then, drifting round the side of the house and in through the sliding windows comes the sound of a car climbing the hill towards Florian's gates. Florian shuts up and Earl stops telling him to shut up and the room is quiet again, gradually filling up with the sound of the approaching car. Then the sound reaches its height and cuts out and a door slams and there's silence for a full minute, during which silence I ease Earl's gun out of my pocket. Then there's footsteps outside, making for the door, and after that the door opens and in comes Draper, making it across the room towards Florian, but before he can speak or even take in Earl I kick the door closed, very hard, and say, 'Hello, Draper.'

Draper spins round like a whipped top.

The smoothness of his appearance doesn't matter any more because anybody looking at him right now would just naturally be unable to tear their eyes away from Draper's face, which has fallen apart completely, like as if somebody had dynamite-blasted Mount Rushmere. His arms automatically push outward from his body, palms open, as though somehow he could stop what he thinks is about to happen by doing that, and he starts staggering backwards as if that might help too, but all he achieves is to get to Earl and fall backwards, hitting another of the scatter rugs and sliding on it across the polished floor until he reaches Florian's desk. Earl himself doesn't move which is what I would have expected. Neither does Florian. But Draper's still a bundle of action, and now he's scrambling himself up the side of Florian's desk but by the time he gets to his feet Florian says to him, 'you try and run out the window you're dead.'

This brings Draper back to some kind of sanity so he sticks by Florian's desk, gripping on to the edge of it like a security blanket, as though without it he'd fall over, which is probably true. And all the while, ever since he came into the room, whatever position he's been in, he's never broken his gaze, his eyes full of terror have never left my face.

I move forward until I'm close to Earl and then I say to the assembled company, 'what we do now is walk out of this room and across the hall to the door that leads to the garage and then you and Draper and me get in the back of the President and Earl drives us out and down the drive and through the gates. Then Earl turns left instead of right and takes the mountain road until it drops down again to where it joins the highway. Everybody got that?'

There's no answer.

'Everybody got that?'

Earl, unable to see anybody else, nods his head into the sheepskin. Draper's still looking at me as though I'm Banquo's ghost but Florian rises slowly from his seat and begins to walk round the desk, close to where Draper is.

'Not just yet,' I say to Florian. Florian stops moving. I step over Earl and feel inside of Draper's jacket and take his gun away from him and throw it on the pool table. During the time it takes for me to do that Draper doesn't move a muscle, he just stays in the same statue-like position. Then I step over Earl and say to Florian, 'it's your house. You lead the way.'

Florian beings to move again and then suddenly Draper finds his voice, only it's not Draper's normal voice, it's like the sound of a tape running on a machine set a little too fast.

'What are you going to do?' he asks me. 'What do you think you're going to do?' Florian looks at him in disgust.

'He's going to kill us, you prick,' he says to Draper. I smile at them.

'That's not strictly true,' I say. 'That's not quite the way it's going to be.'

When we're half-way down the mountain road, about three miles off where it joins the highway, I take the intercom and tell Earl to stop the car so that I can get out, and push the button that locks the back doors once I've done that. Draper and Florian are sitting motionless on the courtesy seats facing me. I have the broad back seat all to myself. The car rolls to a halt and I get out and watch Earl press the button and when he's done that I try both doors and they're O.K., then I walk round to the driver's side and tell Earl to get out and stand by the car, which Earl does.

'Take your clothes off, Earl.' I tell him. 'Take off your suit and your shirt.'

259

Earl looks at me and doesn't move, but I don't repeat what I've just said so Earl begins to do what he's been told. I stand there in the morning's rising heat until he's down to his vest and shorts, holding his clothes, waiting for me to tell him what to do with them, but I'm never going to tell him that. Instead I say, 'remember the bedroom, Earl?'

He doesn't say anything.

'Remember the hotel?' I ask him. 'Remember Murdock's guts all over the floor, spilling out of his shirt front?'

'It wasn't me,' Earl says, dropping his clothes to the ground. 'I didn't shoot Murdock's guts out.'

'But you helped, Earl,' I tell him. 'And if it'd gone a little differently, you would've. Wouldn't you?' Earl shakes his head and beads of sweat flick off him into the heat of the morning.

'I didn't know the deal,' he says, 'all I knew was –'

'Stop it, Earl,' I tell him. 'It won't help.'

'Christ –' he begins, but I cut in on him again.

'No,' I tell Earl. 'He won't help you either.'

I level at a point where the bullets will enter Earl's navel.

'Don't,' he says. 'Please don't.'

'Just about there,' I say, putting the barrel against his stomach. 'That's just about where Murdock got his.'

I look into Earl's eyes and I can see that even though he knows it won't do him any good he's got to try and run, even though there's nowhere for him to go, and at this point I squeeze the trigger, twice. Earl is thrown backwards by the impact, and lands flat on his back among the roadside stones. But he only holds that position for a

260

second because the pain is so great he twists himself over on to his face, clutching his stomach, jack-knifing himself so that his bottom is raised towards the sun.

'How's it feel, Earl?' I ask him, but I'm not sure he can hear me, he's screaming so loud. So I watch him for a moment and then I put the gun to the back of Earl's head and squeeze again, but this time, only once. Earl shudders, but apart from that, he doesn't move for a while, in fact he doesn't move until I've taken off my own clothes and put on his, and by the time I've done that, Earl's relaxed a little bit, as much as he'll ever relax again.

Then I lean into the car and press the button and the rear doors are unlocked again. I open the door on Draper's side and tell him to get out. Draper doesn't move. I tell him again.

'Please,' he says. 'Please don't.'

'Look,' I say to him. 'You got it all wrong. All I want you to do is drive.'

Florian is sitting in exactly the same position as he was an hour ago. The morning traffic on the highway is getting a little heavier, and the sky is a sharp clear blue. This time I have the window between front and back open, so that Draper knows I have a clear shot at his head if he tries anything.

'About a quarter of a mile farther on, there's a turn-off to the left,' I say to him. 'A desert road. Take it.' I look at Draper's eyes in the driving mirror. They flicker like the eyes of a rabbit in a snare. But when we get to the turn-off, the one that leads to the ranch before Sammy's, he takes it, and he keeps on going. Twenty minutes later I tell him to stop the car. I get out and go to the driving side door again and tell him to get out and get in back, an order he's only too glad to carry out because he was thinking that now it was his turn. I lock the two of them in again and press another button, the one that raises the bonnet, and when that operation's finished I close the window between front and back.

Then I light a cigarette and wait. It's getting really hot now. There's no shade; it's almost too hot to lay your hand on the metal of the car. I look in the back. Draper's talking like a crazy man at Florian, but Florian just sits there, having made his own peace.

I smoke another cigarette and I'm almost finished when I suddenly see what I'm looking for, the dust thrown up by the car I'm expecting. Then I get the sound, way behind the mirage-like appearance, and in a couple of minutes the car will be here, so I walk round the front of the President and look in under the bonnet like the driver of the approaching car expects the driver of this one to be doing.

Then the car arrives and stops, parallel to the President. I keep myself well hidden behind the raised bonnet, so I'm not recognised.

The engine doesn't stop on the other car, but the door opens, doesn't close, then there's footsteps. The front passenger door of the President is opened, a button is pressed and the rear windows slide noiselessly down to let out the unintelligible screaming of Draper, trying to let the new arrival know that it's all wrong, it's a set-up; but that noise doesn't last long because it's cut out by the sound of a single shot, and the desert is quiet again except for the echoing ghost of screams and gunshot. Then almost immediately there's another shot, and that part of the job is over. Then the footsteps being to move towards the front of the car, so that a few words can be said to the chauffeur, who's in on the deal, and while the few words are being said, of course the chauffeur's to be taken out too, while he's not expecting it. But it's not going to work out that way, and Styles is just about to realise that.

I have to fire the minute I appear from behind the raised bonnet, but that's fine, because Styles is strolling towards me, gun dangling at arm's length, a pose intended to reassure the conniving chauffeur. Naturally the swiftness of my appearance makes Styles being to go into action but by then it's too late for him. I've loosed off two shots, one in the shoulder and one in the upper arm, shattering it completely, throwing Styles backwards so that he collides with Draper's body which is hanging half out of the rear window. I walk forward and pick up Styles's gun and Styles keeps wriggling backwards clutching his useless arm, trying to bite back his screams of pain. I look in the back of the car. Florian's body is lying across the courtesy seat. Blood is leaking from his ear. I turn my attention back to Styles. He's still trying to crawl away but the pain is great and he's hardly covered any ground at all. I kneel down next to him and smile into his contorted face.

'Your turn, baby,' I tell him. 'Now this time, you eat it.' I raise his own gun and put the barrel against his lips. He thrashes his head this way and that so I put my own gun down and grab his hair and beat his head on the ground a couple of times until he manages to keep himself still. His mouth is wide open with his agony and I'm just about to push the barrel of his gun down his throat when above the sounds of Styles's pain another sound comes through, the sound of another car approaching. I look up and the car is less than two hundred yards away, and in looking up, I give Styles the only opportunity he's ever going to get. In spite of his pain, he shoots out his good arm and grabs my gun off the ground by my knee, sweeps his arm upwards and fires. The bullet catches me in my right side and lifts me backwards, so that I hit the open door of Styles's car. My body floods with pain but I hang on to the door and squeeze the trigger of Styles's gun and the bullet bounces off the ground a couple of inches from Styles's head. I squeeze again, unable to aim, and the bullet goes for the same spot, only Styles, in his efforts to line me up, has moved his head into my own line of fire, and the bullet enters his head next to the bridge of his nose, just below his right eye. There is a sound like a bag full of water bursting and Styles's good arm shoots skywards, perpendicular, still holding my gun. The arm quivers, shudders, then abruptly crashes to the ground again and after that Styles is completely still. Then I look down at Earl Connor's shirt and the stain is spreading all over the front and I can no longer hold on to the open door, so I have to let go of it, let go of Styles's gun; all I can do is fall to the ground and clasp with both hands to where I'm bleeding, drawing up my knees as if that will make the pain go away.

A car door slams. Running footsteps. And then Lesley comes into view, appearing from behind Styles's car. She stands stock still by Styles's body. Then she screams and throws herself across him and calls his name and screams again and while she's doing that all I can think of is I didn't count on Styles having a back-up, in case of anything going wrong for him. I should have counted on that; after all, I've arranged a back-up for myself. When Lesley's finished her screaming and her sobbing and her calling, and when she's seen the figure lying there who's responsible for Styles's death, she picks up my gun and begins to walk towards me, her face blank, and that's when I hear the sound of my own back-up approaching, the sound of the pick-up lurching along the desert road.

But I'm never going to hear it arrive.